Song of the Ankle Rings, based on *Silapathikaram,* an Indian classic set in Tamilakam—present day Tamil Nadu, Kerala, and Telangana, and parts of Karnataka and Andhra Pradesh—at about 3rd century B.C.E. to the 4th century C.E. traces the destinies of Kannagi (a chaste woman), her husband Kovalan (a merchant prince), and his mistress Madhavi (a courtesan) who lived during the reign of the Cheran, Cholan and Pandyan kingdoms.

This work of fiction is an adaptation of the original story. *Song of the Ankle Rings* introduces new characters and subplots to dramatise the story and render it more acceptable to modern readers.

TESTIMONIALS

Your use of the language borders on the poetic. I loved reading it as it has all the visual attributes to transport one into the scene as a silent and invisible watcher... You know how to give us the full treatment, drama, philosophy and a hint of the Kama Sutra along with very careful research — Ian Grice (Brisbane Australia)

You have very beautifully brought out the communication gap between Kannagi and Kovalan after marriage... and her trying to fit into a "chaste wife" mould are wonderful as well as the depiction of Kovalan's character. The explanation of the ankle rings and the mystery behind them is beautifully explained — Sasi Kandasamy (Sri Lanka-Singapore)

I'm enthralled at the amount of thought you are putting into this narrative. The characters come forth as real people — Jane Stansfeld (Texas, USA)

Amazing, how the author took a simple storyline and made it gripping. Love the dialogue. Authentic. Written in the first person but the characters had distinct voices — Jasey Chua (Singapore)

You have done something important and worthy of praise... you will be remembered for this work — Rasu Ramachandran (Singapore Book Council)

You are such a superb story teller — Onyango Makagutu (Nairobi, Kenya)

Source: Written Words Never Die

Table of Contents

1: Anklets, One of a Kind

My wedding date loomed, and with dozens of matters requiring attention, the well-ordered household had grown chaotic. Heaps of shimmering fabrics, a jumble of brass and silverware, and piles of perfumed wood and eye-catching oil lamps and figurines assembled for the wedding cluttered the courtyard.

Father attended to the prominent officials and Mother to the ladies and their whims. It fell on me, despite constant interference from relatives and well-wishers who kept flaunting age and experience to steer things their way, to arrange for the garments, jewellery, and dowry for Kannagi. My bride.

I smiled. Friend, confidante, and even competitor. But bride? Kannagi and Kovalan. Kovalan and Kannagi. Day and night. Sun and moon. Two earrings to complete the whole. Paired all our lives, it was difficult to mention one name without the other rolling off the tongue. Promised at birth, and the day would soon be upon us.

The principal article for Kannagi's dowry had caused many sleepless nights and several days of counsel as I sifted through a vast selection of treasures fit for my future queen. I exercised great diligence because family, friends, and wider society would be quick to fault any shortcomings, whether real or imagined. As I was my parents' only son, my future wife, the incoming flame of the family altar, would in time hold the keys to our fortunes—the keys to the iron safes. A heavy responsibility that my parents would transfer after a suitable passage of time and when the first grandchild arrived. Until then, the elders deemed the newlyweds as too inexperienced and too preoccupied with one another, and even too frivolous, to shoulder the burden.

With celebrations stretching for days, Mother had declared that her new daughter-in-law would not wear the same set of clothing and jewellery twice. There were plenty of all nine auspicious stones: brilliant white diamonds; fiery red rubies;

flawless green emeralds; perfect milky pearls; flaming orange coral; honey-coloured yellow sapphires; multi-hued blue sapphires; lustrous hessonites; and, lightning streaked cat's eye gemstones. Added to these were the usual gold and silver. I selected the finest silks imported specially from *Seenam*, the mighty nation of the Middle Kingdom in the Orient. The ship survived the perilous journey, several weeks long, and when the captain finally dropped anchor, Father heaved a sigh of relief. And as the days progressed, the symbols of high wealth scattered throughout the house continued to grow.

The entire city had some part to play at the wedding. And when Anandan, my friend of six lives, appeared, with welcomed relief I embraced him. He was second only to Kannagi in my heart. He would provide a respite from the chores and perhaps even a solution to my problem. Anandan did not fail me on both counts.

He fetched Telamonius the Greek, a man of many years and merchant of sorts, who had in his possession an intriguing article.

"The perfect gift to adorn the slender feet of your bride," said the Greek. He spoke Tamil with a heavy accent, but passable enough for us to understand his words. Many years ago, the man had taken a Tamil girl for his mistress and gained an intimate knowledge of our local mores and quirks. He liked all things Tamil, and his inquisitive darting eyes always settled on any young woman in the vicinity.

Having noticed the Greek's roving interest, I shot sharp looks at the servant girls and they vacated the courtyard. The Greek spied my silent dismissal but, feigning ignorance, he said,

"This one-of-a-kind artefact was specially crafted for the fortunate. The blood red rubies within give voice, and the anklets sing divine music."

"How did you come by these precious works of artisanship, Sir Telamonius?"

"Dear Sir Kovalan, hear the full story and the ankle rings will draw you as I was when my eyes first beheld them. I had the good fortune to call on a dear friend, one who lives in a foreign land, who lately returned from his manufactory. He was the portrait of dejection. I enquired after his dull state, and the accomplished craftsman related a sorry tale.

"His wealthy client, who had commissioned the anklets, not only rejected these marvels of craftsmanship but also commanded him to melt the pair; destroy the mould. It broke my dear friend's heart to destroy this divine miracle. It was at this juncture, troubled as he was, that I, having chanced upon his predicament, suggested gaining purchase of the beautiful twins. He expressed reluctance tinged with fear, for he dared not disobey his client, but I relayed my plan to merchant the peerless pair in the pearly cities of Greece. There are many brown-eyed damsels in my sunny country, who will press their kings and lovers to acquire an article as rare as these wonders.

"For truly, Sir Kovalan, this pair created with tender patience and unrivalled skills is for new lovers. These were my thoughts, as your friend and mine, Sir Anandan, here, mentioned your esteemed name and a potential need for some special gift to form part of the dowry for your virginal bride."

"Dear Sir Telamonius," I said, "you offer the pleasure of ornaments, beautiful as they are in all aspects and of high value, but already rejected, even if the rejecter may be of noble birth. Why do you think I wish to adorn the feet of the queen of my heart with these discards? Do you not think my bright new wife deserves better?"

"Truly spoken, Sir Kovalan, but please hear my feeble words," said the Greek. "There are no flaws, seen or unseen, in these marvels. But my friend's client sees no merit in the music made by rubies. Does that diminish their worth or value? There are some who prefer the song of the Malabar, and for others, the Bulbul is more divine. These prejudices are as unique as the judgements of one who sees beauty in one maiden but not in another, even when the second is more pleasing."

The Greek leaned in and I, catching a whiff of his stale, disagreeable breath, bent back but held his fixed smile. He said,

"Can one man's prejudice diminish the beauty of a fair maiden or the song of a gifted bird? You will not find such a pair anywhere in the three worlds, Sir Kovalan. I was on my way to the harbour where even now my galley tugs at her moors, ready to catch the wind, but providence intervened and our thoughtful friend, Sir Anandan, who loves you as a brother, intercepted me. So, here I am thanks to the bidding of friend and fate."

Ordinarily, such rambling would irritate me. But on this occasion, the man's verbosity gave me time to think. Taking my smile as an invitation to continue, he said,

"Your bright new wife-to-be is the only person worthy to wear these anklets. And favoured fate has chosen you, already promised a blissful communion, to relish the whispered melodies of this divine creation. Take the high ground, Sir Kovalan, and recognise the hands of gods at play. They wish to bless your union and had these marvels crafted and, lest these fall into wrong hands, charged me as their instrument of deliverance into your possession.

"Though I have not yet had the pleasure and privilege to set eyes on your dear promised wife, Kannagi, whom I already consider my little sister, I hear said by all who know her, in person and in passing, that she is herself a creation of great purity and the gods broke the mould after breathing life into her. She, and only she, is fit to wear these anklets. Hear the music within, Sir Kovalan, sung by the finest of rubies."

The Greek shook the anklets, and indeed the tones mesmerised with their fine clean tinkling that soughed and sang. The ankle rings spoke to me and I imagined the music accompanying the footsteps of my beloved Kannagi as she moved about our home. And the thought of the mellifluous melody of the many tongued ankle bracelets whispering various enchanting modes filled me with immense joy.

At long last, I had found the important addition to Kannagi's dowry. A peculiar arraying of birth stars had denied my Kannagi the skills of music, a vital attribute for a high-born woman such as herself. The music from these ankle rings, I supposed, would veil and compensate for her lack of artistic skills, and please my parents and dispel the gossip.

The Greek misinterpreted my reticence as reluctance to proceed with the purchase. To bolster his case, he said,

"I am told, Sir Kovalan, in Tamil norms, no blame attaches to one who speaks a thousand lies to facilitate a welcomed marriage. There is no lie required or attached to this gift of love. Simply, do not reveal its pedigree. When a man adorns his lover's neck with a sparkling diamond, does he also regale her with tales of the slaves who work the dark mines? Some things are best left unsaid and when you don't speak, Sir Kovalan, you don't lie.

"Watch your relatives and friends behold these delicate beauties with awe. Let them envy your resourcefulness in locating such rarities. There is no story here; only a clean palm leaf. Write your own epic, Sir Kovalan, as you lovingly slip these over your wife's slender ankles. If these ankle bracelets are beautiful now, imagine them when worn by your peerless queen."

"And what of the price, my dear Greek?" said Anandan. "I remain wary for my friend, Kovalan, for I know well your reputation for hard bargains."

Insulted by Anandan's sudden talk of money, my cheeks flushed red. Though a dear friend, he had spoken as a new-rich which was thanks to his father. He is yet to learn that real wealth does not speak of money.

"You must excuse our dear friend, Anandan," I said. "He exhibits a direct streak which is refreshing, but also promises an occasional shock."

"His intentions are laudable, Sir Kovalan, to keep you as sharp as a sword and to keep me as honest as daylight." Telamonius tapped Anandan on the shoulder and said, "But as you can see, Sir Anandan, your friend and mine, Sir Kovalan, is a cultured man, and his regal bearing and words are in concord. It is not the ways of the learned to let coin come between them, for she owes no man her loyalty."

"Wisely spoken, Sir Telamonius," I said, "for *panam*, gold coin, indeed lacks loyalty and she is a tenuous lover."

Nevertheless, with the subject of money now in play, I felt compelled to commit.

"Hear me, Sir Telamonius," I said, "and let us not dwell on this base topic of money. Whatever your planned profit, I shall double it, for my delicate love, my wife-to-be, deserves a gift that remains in the dreams of all others."

***

And so, it was on the day of the wedding, with hundreds of eyes watching in rapt awe and envy, that I, Kovalan, only son of Sir Masattuvan—he of a long line of renowned merchant princes, patrons of the arts, and philanthropists extraordinaire—bent and touched the trembling skin of my bright new wife and embellished her dainty feet with the tinkling anklets, even as her toes curled in virginal modesty. I drew my dagger and twisted it, releasing the fine gold thread linking the two ankle bracelets.

"Let these be a symbol I have chained you with my love and unchained you also, to come and go as you wish. Remove these not for any man, woman, or god."

"I will remove these beauties only for you," said Kannagi. "I thank you, my dear husband, for this great generosity of freedom. My place is beside you and I freely choose your wishes for my chains."

Over the next days and weeks, all in my household marvelled at the choral music of the rubies singing from my wife's feet, as I had first imagined, when she moved about the house. And many times, Kannagi said,

"Dear *Athan*, these ankle rings are musical; lovely. I am not blessed with the talents of music or song, and my parents did not see fit to have me schooled in these arts, but in my stead let these marvels sing for you and keep you blissful."

###

2: Kannagi's Destiny Foretold

My father, Manayakan, named me Kannagi, but not once did he use that name. Instead, he drew from a chest full of pet names: gold, diamond, ruby, and so forth. I loved the names more than the actual jewellery. To Mother's great consternation, I refused to wear jewellery and resisted until I came of age. Mother also complained that I had a runaway mouth. Perhaps she was right. Perhaps I should have started from the beginning.

I was born in Kaveri-Poom-Pattinam, also known as Poom-Puhar, but referred to by her inhabitants as Puhar, ancient capital of the glorious and upright Cholan Kingdom.

Father delighted when the fortune-tellers declared his new-born daughter, Kannagi, would gain fame. Nevertheless, as the celebrations peaked and well-wishers praised his great fortune, the implications of the news seeped in and his spirit waned.

It was bad enough if the son he did not have were to outshine him—but a daughter?

After all, parents nurtured female children only to marry them off to bring good fortune to another house. Moreover, a good daughter-in-law obeyed and respected her husband and her in-laws. Expectations fulfilled did not receive praise, but unworthy conduct found its way to the doorsteps of her parents.

It was a loser's covenant, and not of the kind any shrewd merchant welcomed. And Father was as shrewd as any in Puhar or, for that matter, in all the three kingdoms of Tamilakam: Cholan, Pandyan, and Cheran.

"Will she excel in music or dance?" he asked the astrologers and fortune tellers.

Father wondered whether the fine arts might serve as a carriage for my foretold fame. Such education for girls was a preserve of the upper classes of society. As patriarch of one of the foremost families of the mercantile class in Poom-Puhar, Father was also renowned in the royal court of the Great Cholan, Maha-Rajah Kari-Kaalan himself.

The astrologers blamed the stars, and the fortune-tellers could not provide specifics.

"Perhaps," said the chief astrologer. "Her fame takes root in the west-country and spreads beyond the shores of Bharatham."

Father turned dark in thought, compelling the men of strange rites and magical words to gather their beads and things mystical, and to slink away in silence.

Aunty Chinnamma, my mother's younger sister, told me of Father's reaction to the fortune tellers' predictions. She related stories of Father's unhappiness that his first-born was a girl, would find fame, and so on. My aunty saw herself as the keeper of family secrets.

"But what good is a secret not revealed?" she said. And when I spent time with Chinnamma, she was generous with snippets of our family history.

She was close to Mother, and they shared many intimate details of their lives. I found their relationship remarkable, but even at my young age, I knew I could never share such privacy with anyone.

When Mother could not conceive again, she grew worried, and sought to assure my father. She said,

"I remain of child-bearing age and the gods might yet bless us with a son."

"You dream, woman, of an age long gone."

A male child was important to conduct the last rites for the father and carry the family line. A wife who did not produce a son risked having to share her husband with a second wife.

Father was a wealthy man, and he had a ready excuse acceptable to society. Mother grew distraught. But my dear father was an honourable man. There was no second wife to dethrone Mother, or step-mother to ill-treat me. Then, on another day, when discussing my future, he said,

"My daughter will not master the *veena*, she will not learn to sing, and she will not dance." Not receiving a response, he turned harsh. "Do you hear me, woman?"

"Why do you treat your swaddling daughter so? She needs talents in music and dance to complete her maturity, to keep her future husband entertained, and to gain approval from those whose home she enters as their family light."

"My mind is set, woman, and I will not be moved."

More silence followed, for Father always went quiet when deep in thought. After a long hush, he said,

"I will betroth her to my friend Masattuvan's son, the boy Kovalan. We will seal the union in the prescribed manner before esteemed witnesses, with the exchange of promissory trays laden with gold, precious stones, flowers, and auspicious things."

"Kovalan is a fine boy," said Mother, "and at two years the elder, a suitable match for our Kannagi."

And so it was; while a wet nurse suckled me, my parents decided my future and fate.

We lived in Maruvur District, the seaport side of Poom-Puhar. The city itself lay on the northern banks of the Kaveri River. To the west of Maruvur was Pattinam, the City District with the sprawling palace, royal courts, and residences of nobility and luminaries. The physicians, astrologers, artists, and courtesans lived in Pattinam. Vast well-manicured gardens dotted with luxuriant trees, flourishing flowering plants, and ponds filled with thriving fish and exotic waterfowl separated the City and Maruvur districts. Our king, Kari Kaalan, held great festivals and spectacular games in these gardens, which also served as venues for the daily markets that stretched into the night.

The merchants maintained their primary residences in Maruvur District in proximity to the jetties and warehouses. The place teemed with *yavanas*—foreigners—from Seenam, the Middle Kingdom in the east, the Araby deserts of the shifting sands, and the Grecian islands dotting the turquoise seas in the west. There was a network of noisy alleys crammed with shops and sheds, where artisans worked on leather, cotton, timber, and various metals. Physicians dabbled in herbs; perfumers concocted perfumes; and behind barred doors, skilled craftsmen bent over tables and cut, polished, and set precious stones.

There were whispers of *houses of ill-repute,* but I was ignorant of what it meant. To my young mind, only people acquired ill-reputations, not houses. When I asked, Chinnamma said something vague regarding dancing girls and alcoholic drinks. These houses of pleasure—this was another term she used—sold palm wine, and entertained guests with music and dance of the baser varieties. And they offered maidens and boys.

"Offered? What do you mean by offered?" I asked.

But Chinnamma suffered her usual affliction, one which took hold whenever she did not wish to answer my questions: she became deaf. I never want to grow old, for I wish not to become deaf.

Puhar also boasted numerous temples along packed streets. All one had to do was to look up and there would be a *gopuram*, the monumental and ornate tower heralding a temple entrance, puncturing the clean blue skies.

Standing apart from this noisy, confusing labyrinth of never-ending alleys, lecherous street vendors, and—I too whispered though I do not know why—houses of ill-repute, was a serene enclave marked out by thick trees. Within these confines resided the tall mansions of the wealthiest merchants of Puhar. Soft sand covered the streets. Elegant statues of divine beauties, holding lamps lit by fragrant oils, stood in every street corner.

This was where we lived—Kovalan and I. But at my age, Father's wealth made no impression on me. And even as an adult, I did not care about such ostentatious living.

***

"Kannagi! Stop hiding behind the window and peeping out at the street. What will people think?"

That was Mother calling from her kitchen. She cared what people thought, lived for people and for their approval.

"I'm waiting for Kovalan."

"You're spending too much time with that boy. Father already had words with me."

Mother was the one spending too much time in the kitchen; not to cook, but to harass the poor servants.

"Are we not promised in marriage?"

"Stop being vulgar, and remember, too much honey will bring forth the sour."

What was she prattling about? I ate honey day and night, and it did not turn sour. But I chose not to pursue the matter. Instead, I ventured into her area of expertise—cooking.

"What's for lunch?"

"All six tastes," said Mother from somewhere in the deep kitchen.

I heard her instructing the harried cooks. Mother enjoyed ruling her kitchen: a vast square where a row of wood-fired stoves lined one wall; shelves stacked with silver pots and pans against another wall; and a dozen earthen-ware barrels of water along a third wall. The cooks and their assistants sat on the floor where they cut and shredded vegetables, and ground spices—thudding pestle in mortars, and grating rolling stones over granite slabs. The smells that wafted out of the kitchen and filled the house alternated from fragrant to sharp, depending on the spice and sting of the chilli.

"Whose birthday, is it?" I called out.

"Birthday? Don't remind me of birthdays, silly."

Mother was the silly one in the family. Chinnamma said by ignoring her birthdays, Mother hoped to remain young.

"I'll tell Father you called me silly."

"Go ahead, I am unafraid," shouted back Mother. "And come and help me."

"Yes, you are afraid of Father. What's more, you've more servants than the king has soldiers. What do you need with me?"

"Stop being an impudent gabby and come here and taste the dessert."

"What's for dessert?" I called back, my eyes remaining on the street.

"*Payasam,*" she said, "and tell me whether the sweetness and texture is right."

Mother thought she was clever; poor woman, trying to bribe me with the sweet porridge dessert.

"Your payasam is the best in all of Puhar, Mother, always."

"Really, you think so?"

That was Mother, easy to bait. She also spent hours preening before the mirror—poor mirror. And when she prayed, she made sure people saw. Her prayers were complete only with an audience.

"Do you really think my payasam is the best?" And she always required affirmation.

Mother did not know I had seen Kovalan approaching the house. And I was already tip-toeing to the door. I heard her calling.

"Kannagi! Kannagi! You think so?"

Poor Mother. I left her seeking affirmation from an empty living room.

I dashed out the door and raced down the carriage track to the impressive iron-gate where Old Watchman, in frayed uniform—he had saved his good set of clothes for auspicious days—gave me a toothless grin. He was sweet and quite useless, but I adored him—and he never told on me.

When Father wanted to retire Old Watchman, who was already a hundred years old, I melted into one of my temper tantrums and broke into tears. Father remained unmoved. He was sure it was all a ruse.

When my tears ran dry, I smeared chilli in my eyes. This time I bawled so hard and heaved for breath, even Father panicked and gave in. Poor father. Poorer me, because my crying did not let up. I did not know chilli smarted so badly.

Father blanched with anxiety and sent for the physician.

While my parents hovered in the background, looking over the couch where I lay prone, Grandfather Physician—he too was a hundred years old and toothless, and convinced me never to grow old because I did not wish to be toothless—checked my pulse and eyes. He gave a secret wink and, fussing more than usual, dabbed my eyes with water.

Satisfied from working his magic of medicine, Grandfather Physician declared I had experienced a mild shock but was on the road to full recovery. With a wag of his finger, he cautioned my father not to cause me further distress. After which, Grandfather Physician gave me another wink and departed, leaving poor Father admonished.

Whatever disappointment Father harboured about not having a son had disappeared many years ago, and his love for me was as fierce as only fathers can love their daughters.

Father continued to fuss over me, and Mother tried hard to control her mirth. It was only in my later years I realised mothers have a knack for seeing through all their children's antics—all the more antics from daughters. Mother loved me in her own way, but she had her limitations, and not all of her own doing. Poor Mother was an adult, and age can be an affliction too. The only good thing about growing old: no one will tell you when to go to bed, and when to rise.

Regarding Old Watchman, I got my wish. He kept his job for another hundred years, and I stayed away from chillies—in particular the small red ones.

And so it was; I ran out to meet Kovalan, and Mother continued to call.

"Kannagi! Where are you? Kannagi!"

I grabbed Kovalan's hand and broke into uncontrollable fits of giggles as we ran off. After placing sufficient distance between Mother and us, we stopped and, with hands on knees, panted and laughed through gasps.

"Let's climb trees," I said and raced off. Kovalan, being taller and swifter, relinquished a head start so he could enjoy overtaking me. He liked to win.

Running past, his voice triumphant, Kovalan called over his shoulder.

"Tortoise! Tortoise! Tortoise!"

And I stuck out my tongue. I did these naughty things when there were no adults; and they all complimented my parents for my good manners. It was so easy to trick adults. When I grow up, I will be a smart adult and catch all the naughty children.

When we first plucked up the courage to climb trees, I beat Kovalan to the top and that irked him. His only complaint—*you're a girl*—was more of an accusation. As I scaled another tree, I called down.

"Then better me, and climb faster and higher. Come on!"

Thus challenged, Kovalan scrambled up, lost his grip, and slipped. He earned ghastly cuts and gashes on his knees and legs. He grew dark and, for days thereafter, refused to visit. Wracked with pain, I pined for him. Every time I beat him in a challenge, he sulked and stayed away.

After one such wrenching week, when Kovalan called, I let him clamber up the easier branches while I took a more difficult path. He hurried past and reached the top, then sat on a branch and dangled his feet. He turned smugly and urged me. Upon reaching him, I threw a challenge and said,

"Another one, that tree!"

Again, I took a circuitous route, and he won. He quite enjoyed himself and it made me happy. He had that effect on me. His happiness was mine.

We had another friend, Anandan. He was a year older and bigger than Kovalan. In truth, he was Kovalan's friend, and therefore became my friend too. We played together, fought bullies, pulled pranks, and screamed and ran down streets. We had such great fun. Some adults thought us naughty and complained about our poor upbringing. These remarks came from adults who had forgotten their childhoods, an affliction which most grown-ups suffered.

I was wary of Anandan. Unlike Kovalan, who was soft and kind, Anandan had a mean streak. I wondered what Kovalan saw in him, but I did not ask. Whatever Kovalan decided, I accepted. I trusted him.

Over time, I learned that Anandan's father was once a poor man who had found his fortune in Araby. He exhibited a daring which my father and Kovalan's father, both descended from ancient merchant families, lacked. Anandan, who had inherited his father's hunger, worked hard for luxuries and recognition—trophies that Kovalan and I accorded scant regard.

Though Anandan's lack of wealth did not bother me, his lack of decorum did. For that reason, I did not quite like him.

***

When I returned home, Mother was waiting. "Here you are," she said. "I've told you often enough not to go gallivanting with the boys."

"They're my friends," I said.

"They are young men and you are coming of age, and should start behaving as a proper maiden."

"I'm a child. You've said it many times."

"Not anymore. Go to your father now as he has things, he wishes to say to you."

I heard a throat clearing and saw my father's figure fill the doorway. With a wide smile, I ran and hugged him around the waist.

"Father!"

"How are you, my diamond?"

He led me by the hand to his swing. I waited with eager anticipation and, as expected, Father scooped me up and settled me beside him. My happy legs hung loose, and I kicked my feet as if playing in water.

"What is this, my gold, wet clothes?" Father looked surprised. He pretended.

"She was by the river, with the boys again," said Mother. I made a face at her and she said, "See her naughtiness. It is all your fault."

I twisted my face even more and, with a huff, crossed my arms high on my chest. Father laughed and said,

"Come, come, my emerald, be polite."

"Okay, Father." I unfolded my arms and, with a fake smile, said, "Sorry, Mother."

"See how she dramas. Look at her!" Mother sighed. "You and your father, do as you wish, I don't care." Mother disappeared into her vast kitchen and left me feeling sorry for the poor servants.

"Did you see any crocodiles by the river?"

"No, Father, but the boat sailed well."

"You mean the boat I purchased for your birthday and hid in my secret place?"

"Oops!" I covered my mouth.

Father laughed and, in a gentle voice, he said, "I'm aware, my little ruby, that you've discovered all my hiding places." Then, leaning in, he whispered. "But your mother does not know, so let it be our secret." I rewarded him with several conspiratorial bops of my head.

"Where is the boat?" asked Father.

"Oh, the boys teased, so I rose to their challenge and sailed the boat in the river. Perhaps that was why the crocodiles kept away. You know, it was a wooden boat and crocodiles don't like to eat wood."

"Ah, yes, of course, my blue sapphire, crocodiles detest wood."

"Oh, you know too? You're a clever Father." Seeing my father's pleased look, I brought my courage to full play and puckered to look pitiful.

"But the rocks had no such qualms," I said, "and they smashed my boat and it broke."

"Oh dear, my emerald, some rocks can be so inconsiderate."

I paused and wondered whether Father was teasing me. I had to put him to the test, and so I whined.

"But it was not my fault, and Anandan forced me to sail it."

I tried to force out tears, but it did not work. And I had forgotten to bring along my chilli—the green one. Not the red, because I was not silly anymore. After the *Old Watchman incident*, I resorted to the milder green ones.

"And Kovalan, did he force you too?" asked Father.

I did not wish to blame Kovalan, but also could not bring myself to lie, and so, I nodded and tried harder to cry. I made all the right noises, but no tears flowed.

"There, there, don't cry, my hessonite, but do you think Kovalan might want to sail your boat again?" Father stroked my hair and planted a light kiss on my head.

"I told you, it's broken!"

"And yet he encouraged you."

"But I did not want to, Father."

"Of course, my pearl, I know." Looking me in the eye, he said, "Young men behave so. Once your precious breaks, they will not want it anymore."

"But Kovalan said he will make good the repairs, Father."

"Some things cannot be repaired, my cat's eye."

"What things, Father?"

He called Mother: his voice tinged with irritation. "Where is her lunch?"

"What's the hurry, it's not as if your precious duckling is starving."

Mother brought rice cooked with nuts and raisins, and fruits and milk. Placing it on a low table, she shrugged a shoulder at me and walked away, and I made a face at her.

I drank the milk with relish and chose my favourite fruit— sliced mango. As usual, Father watched as I put on a show for him. I ate and wiped the juice on my chin with the back of my hand, and my antics gave Father much pleasure.

"You remember Uncle and Chinnamma; how would you like to visit them in Madurai?"

"Are we all going to visit Chinnamma?" I could not hide my excitement.

"Yes, as a family."

I threw up my hands and shouted with joy.

"You can stay there until a year."

"And we can all picnic and enjoy ourselves." Again, I threw up my hands with glee.

"Yes, but Father has much work to attend to here and Mother too, and we will visit until a month before returning. But you can stay and enjoy yourself." He leaned close and said, "Without Mother picking on you."

I nodded and gave him a mischievous smile. Then the joy bled off, leaving me empty. I looked forward to the adventure of a new place, but not without Father and Mother. More puckering, and my lips pushed out, seeking sympathy.

"I'll miss you," I said.

"I've told you stories about Uncle and Chinnamma's farm, their cows and goats, and deer and rabbits."

"Horses and bullock carts?" I asked.

"Yes, bullock carts, my red coral, and you can learn to drive them."

"Can I ride the horses?"

"No, maidens don't ride horses, but you can learn to drive horse carts."

"But why can I not ride horses?"

"Chaste maidens don't ride horses. Moreover, horse riding is dangerous and you have the more comfortable and safer horse carts."

"Why-why-why?" In playful tantrum I hit my thighs.

"I've just now told you, my yellow sapphire, and Chinnamma will answer all your questions and teach you many wonderful things."

"But you answer all my questions and already taught me everything there is to know. Is Chinnamma smarter than you?"

Father threw his head back and laughed. He said, "There are some things best left to Chinnamma."

"What things, Father?"

"Things a young maiden, one such as yourself, might wish to know, ought to know."

I was getting bored with talk regarding my forthcoming maidenhood. And I did not want to grow up and lose my teeth or turn bald. So, having finished the first mango, I went for my next favourite—the second mango.

"You'll also study the Vedas and Puranas, my platinum, and learn prayers expected of and befitting a future mistress of a household."

"But Mother is mistress of the household and quite enjoys haranguing the servants."

Father laughed again, and I joined in his laughter. I loved him very much and gave him a great big hug. After finishing my second mango, I reached for my next favourite fruit—the third mango.

Overwhelmed with joy by the prospect of a long journey to Madurai, the first in my life, I shared my excitement with Kovalan. But he grew sullen. I detected a tinge of envy. By going away on new adventures, I was in some strange manner doing better than him. His behaviour was disappointing, for I thought he would be happy for me.

His joy was mine, but he did not share my joy. That made me sad. Now I did not want to go. I wanted to remain in Puhar to keep Kovalan happy.

But Anandan was excited for me and told stories of new adventures that beckoned.

I trudged home, angry and confused, and cried myself to sleep. But by morning, I had resolved myself to Kovalan's apathetic reception of the news. He was right, and I would not abandon him again. This journey would be the first and the last without him. In the future, I would place him before all else, for I believe there was no greater joy than to make him happy.

What I did not know was that, instead of a year, my parents had conspired to keep me away from the boys for several years—until I lost my boyish antics and reached marriageable age.

I lost my rough edges during that time but also acquired a new skill, one that my parents had not wished—I learned to ride horses. But it was a poor trade for all those years without Kovalan.

###

3: A Child leaves and a Maiden will return

The days leading to our departure were busy, harried, and filled with confused urgency. A steady queue of tradesmen and suppliers called on Father. He arranged provisions, bullock carts, and a dozen other items. Father also settled many matters regarding his business affairs and our house. There was much excitement among the servants selected to join us on the journey, and all of them received impressive new uniforms.

Mother was in a constant hair-pulling frenzy—and drove our servants to distraction—as she tried and retried garments for every festival and conceivable ceremony she planned to attend.

"The villagers will expect no less from us," said Mother.

After several days and having decided that nothing in her wardrobe met her needs, a foregone conclusion whenever she prepared for a journey, Mother sent for the fabric merchants and tailors. The poor men presented dozens of samples. Soon, heaps of bright-coloured saris and shimmering silks dotted the central courtyard. After several days, she decided the new wardrobe was too grand for her sister's farm and better reserved for occasions involving royalty and important people. She settled for the saris and fabrics from her many bureaus—material she had selected on the first day. After all, she reasoned, the people in the villages would not recognise her old garments and everything would be new to them. Thus, Mother resolved the most challenging of her preparations and the servants sighed with relief.

The morning of departure arrived and people in the neighbourhood turned out in force to wish us farewell. Stewards were busy with final preparations, there were hurried voices, and the mood was urgent and celebratory.

But I remained depressed. I longed to see Kovalan. I kept looking up whenever someone entered the house, confident he would appear. He could not let the moment slip. Surely, he would surprise me. And so, I consoled myself. But as the time ripened, I hoped. Then, in the last hours, I prayed.

Anandan appeared with a gift, a wooden boat similar to the one destroyed in the river—Kovalan had forgotten the repair. On the day the boat smashed on the rocks, Anandan had laughed and clapped with glee. But on this day, he looked remorseful and without his usual spirit. Earlier in the day, he had met Kovalan, but before I asked, he said,

"His father sent him on an errand to Pattinam."

There was a lie in Anandan's eyes, but I was grateful for his feeble attempt to make me feel better. I had always disliked Anandan. He was a bully, plain-speaking even when he knew it would be hurtful, and quite vulgar in his interests. But he was also an enigma.

"You leave a child and will return a maiden," he said. "Be safe, little sister. I am your brother and will always love you. I promise."

Upon hearing Anandan's words, I rushed to my room and cried. I had not expected such maturity from this irreverent boy. Perhaps I had been quick with my harsh judgments.

But I also cried for Kovalan. After some time, my tears emptied. Mother called and, burying my pain in my chest, I re-joined the preparations and farewells.

Our servants secreted much coin in their hands in return for carrying letters and news. Unlike the wealthy who wrote on velvety cloth, the common folk wrote letters on palm leaves. Our servants, worthy of working for Father, an accomplished merchant, charged more money for messages carrying commercial import.

There were half-a-dozen bullock carts, each drawn by a pair of sturdy well-nourished buffalo. Father, his man-servant, and the caravan master rode the first cart. Mother and I, and our hand-maidens, followed in the second. The third cart carried our luggage, and presents for Uncle, Chinnamma, and people of the village governing council, the *panchayat*. The servants, provisions, utensils, and tent and bedding material filled the rearmost carriages, which were larger and built for load rather than elegance.

Father also hired an armed escort of ten impressive young men, led by a stern captain. These men, *Maravars*, carried iron-tipped spears and swords in scabbards slung across their backs, and wore leather body armour and brightly coloured turbans. Their horses were nervous and energetic and bobbed their heads and stomped the earth with eager anticipation. The escort also roped along several mules which carried their bedrolls, tents, and gear. It was quite an impressive company befitting the wealth and esteem Father enjoyed in Puhar.

In our wake was a long stretch of camp-followers—families, itinerant traders, and lesser merchants—who were also going our way but lacked the resources to hire an armed escort of their own. Travelling in caravan gave the camp-followers camaraderie and security. Unlike other caravan owners, Father did not collect payment from the hangers-on. It was beneath his station to do so. But this did not stop our servants from exacting taxes from these people. Father, well apprised of our servants' activities, chose not to know, provided they did not impose exorbitant levies.

During our journey, I became acquainted with the soldiers of the escort: wonderful and hardy warriors from the *paalai*, the semi-arid regions. These scarred men were bachelors—though many had lovers back in their desert homes. Lovers, and not wives. I found their family arrangement extraordinary but, for now, no one explained these matters. The soldiers yearned for meals cooked by a woman's hands. They missed their lovers and mothers; and relished the food offered by the women of the caravan. I shared leftover meals with them. And these men, who risked their lives every day and some only a few years older than Kovalan, took to the food with such gusto it put me to secret shame. After the first day, I apportioned the food before eating my share. It was a good habit I adopted, and for the rest of my life, I always set aside food for the less fortunate. Father approved.

I wondered why we required an armed escort, for did not our Cholan king's reputation send even snakes slithering into their holes? Mother admonished my careless talk regarding the king, but I persisted with a litany of *why-why-why*.

She said deep forests and hills covered the commons between the Cholan and Pandyan realms, and a wild race of demonic people—*Arakans*—inhabited the lands. I had heard the name mentioned in whispered awe. The Arakans were cannibals and would attack unwary city-dwellers who commuted between the towns.

"And they are especially fond of carrying away young damsels such as you."

"Does that mean you are safe, Mother?" I asked.

She pinched my arm and I let out a sharp cry. But Father's cart was several paces ahead; and the clattering of hooves, the tinkling bells festooned to carriages, and the ever-present noise, that accompanied people on the move, drowned my cries. Not wishing to risk more pinches, I wiped my tears and asked,

"Will we encounter these Arakans?"

"I hope not and, as I said, these thick ugly men are especially fond of young maidens."

And Mother gave me a look of silent challenge. I was young but not stupid, and no naughty words ensued from my runaway mouth.

Mother also recounted stories of debauchery, human sacrifice, and drinking of blood. When I asked about the Arakan women, Mother paused. Having made up a story, she said they were even worse than their men: they went about with exposed breasts, and smeared their faces with the blood of young boys. I saw through Mother's ruse and did not believe all she said—except for the part that Arakan women were worse than their men. In that aspect at least, these wild women shared the traits of their more civilised sisters.

I yearned to meet an Arakan, perhaps a young girl or boy who would not alarm Mother. Once, during the journey, the soldiers tensed and the bullock carts tightened into a knot, sending a sizzling fear rippling through the petrified people. Unfortunately, the gods answered Mother's prayers and there were no Arakan sightings. Another night we heard the faint sound of drums in the high hills, but again, nothing more.

Everyone kept saying *Madurai*, which was about a hundred leagues and several days away. But Uncle's farm was on the outskirts of the famed city of culture and worship.

I also looked forward to seeing Chinnamma, who was much younger than Mother, and remembered her as having a wild streak about her. Chinnamma was direct, shocking, and mischievous. She had naughty humour and spoke of matters that made me blush. I last saw her when she and her family visited us during the previous harvest festival, *Pongal*. She taught me many things, including the strange behaviour of adults.

I recalled one late afternoon when Father returned in a foul mood. Chinnamma and I remained cloistered in my room while the drama unfolded in the house.

Father, in his anger, found fault with Mother, and words and voices escalated. I heard a crash, a brass tumbler sent flying across the vast kitchen; then jingling footsteps, and Mother running into her room. Even at home, Mother geared herself for battle and went about dripping in an assortment of jewellery. I welcomed the ornaments because, when I was up to my usual mischief, the tinkling of her bangles and anklets forewarned her arrival. And I always looked innocent by the time she appeared.

After her dramatic but well-choreographed run to her room, Mother remained locked behind the doors. Chinnamma wore an intriguing smile. The servants, intent on not drawing attention to themselves, went quiet, scurried in silence, and spoke in whispers. The household sank into deep gloom. Meanwhile, Father withdrew upstairs to his work room.

Chinnamma and I were having dinner when Father came downstairs and called Mother. We stopped and listened hard. There was no reply. Father called again. He was standing outside Mother's locked doors. Not receiving a response, he persisted.

"Is Father angry?" I asked.

"Not anymore."

"Is Mother angry?"

"Wait and watch the drama," said Chinnamma.

"If Mother does not eat, she will starve, shrivel into a dried pea pod, and perish," I said, with genuine concern.

"Your mother is so layered that she perspires even when bathing in cold water, and it'll take two full moons of starvation before she withers to my weight."

That horrified me. Poor Mother starving and reducing into a stick insect. But recalling that day later, I chuckled. Chinnamma was much fatter than Mother and I wondered how Mother would ever *wither* to Chinnamma's weight.

After a pronounced series of sharp raps and calls, by which time all the servants, their features twisted in anxiety, had gathered to peep from the kitchen, Mother relented and opened the door. Father slipped in, closed the door, and drove home the bolt. Hearing the unmistakable snap of metal on metal, the servants sighed with relief and returned to their chores.

"Will Mother eat dinner?"

As I was not yet clever enough—I became clever only later in the day—I remained worried that Mother might wither and get mistaken for a stick insect.

"Yes, but not until an hour or more," said Chinnamma.

"Why?"

Chinnamma called it a couple's game. I remembered making a face, for I did not know adults played games. According to her, there were several scripts. In this play, the woman took the role of a victim, and often welcomed it because of the rewards promised when the man, feeling remorseful, made amends.

"These little dramas add spice to life," said Chinnamma, "and result in babies, especially drama-children."

"Mother always says I drama, so does that make me a drama-child?"

"You are a drama-child because you were born ten years into your parents' marriage."

"What do you mean, Chinnamma?"

"Well, if you were born in the first year of marriage, you would be a love-child."

"I don't understand!" I stamped my foot and cried.

"No tantrums now. I'm Chinnamma, not your father."

"Sorry, Chinnamma."

"Okay, listen. In the first year of marriage, the honeymoon year, couples seldom quarrel because they're blind with love, or rather with the newness of married life. The man is poetic and the woman never has a headache. But by the tenth year, the man's snoring is not music but an irritant, and the woman's unwashed hair is, well, unwashed hair. Familiarity loses the fragrance of discovery and the stink of life needs perfume and spice."

"And they make a drama-child!" I interrupted and clapped with glee.

Now, as I lay in the tent, the caravan having stopped for the night and Mother's snores keeping me awake, I wondered whether Kovalan and I would have a love-child or a drama-child.

I was sure I would never quarrel with Kovalan. All our children will be love-children.

Chinnamma did not say how couples made love-children. The neighbourhood girls taught me that secret.

It started with an incident that turned my face red. It was an afternoon, and the adults were enjoying their naps. Taking the opportunity, Kovalan and I went to the river and frolicked.

His garment came loose. I gasped and pointed, and jumped up and down with fear. Some strange water creature had latched onto my poor Kovalan. In a flash, he covered himself with his hands and sank back into the water. He told me to go home. When I hesitated, he grew annoyed and railed. His behaviour shocked me, and I ran home in tears.

For many days after that, Kovalan did not visit and his absence broke my heart. It was also about this time he found a new friend, Anandan. Kovalan fetched him to meet me and we resumed our friendship. And we never spoke of the *river incident*.

When I shared my fears with the neighbourhood girls, they giggled and I grew up. No one at home associated the *lingam*, the stone image of Lord Shiva, with such crass matters. For me, the lingam was God. I also learned new words. Distasteful words. And I stayed away from the girls. But the thought of Kovalan's lingam—it was safer to use this innocent word—evoked novel sensations. Embarrassing heart-racing sensations. I learned more adult things because of the boys.

Kovalan and Anandan scratched themselves below their navel and, wanting to fit in, I scratched myself there, too. When Mother caught me touching, as she referred to it, she shrieked so loud that I feared a demon had possessed her. She ran into the kitchen and there was a ruckus.

Within moments, Old Ayah, who had been with us for a hundred years, ran out. The old coot dragged me by my hand—I did not know she could run so fast—to the well in the backyard. Scooping water, she washed my hands and poured several bucketsful over me. The well water was frigid and, as a brisk breeze blew, I shivered in fits. Old Ayah said in a stern voice that I should never touch myself. I did not know what the old coot was on about and my hand, on its own accord, reached to scratch. Without warning, Old Ayah let out a shriek similar to Mother's and gave my hand a sharp slap. That stung. It hurt fiery red. I did not know the coot was strong too.

"Don't touch yourself, especially there, there, and there."

She pointed to my chest and to the spot below my navel. I asked *why-why-why*, and her reply was emphatic.

"Don't! Only bad girls touch themselves."

And she wagged a furious finger near my nose. The poor old woman shook with outrage, and spittle flew from her lips, making me blink and squint. It seemed the demon that possessed Mother had leapt into Old Ayah. Now I had another reason for not wanting to grow old: demonic possession.

"Okay, Ayah," I replied.

"Bad, bad, bad." More spittle from her and more blinking on my part.

"Okay Ayah, okay Ayah, okay Ayah."

I wiped away the imaginary spittle and smiled. The caravan had camped for the night. I was with Mother in the tent and she was snoring beside me. She rolled, faced away, and broke wind. Mother! I stifled a chuckle. Another reason not to grow old.

Then a slight pain seared my heart. I missed Kovalan. Tears slipped out of the corners of my eyes and I sniffed.

But Mother Nature had her ways, and she embraced and carried me into a dream-filled sleep. She was kind.; rewarded me with several short, happy dreams. But one dream discomforted.

Kovalan, riding hard on his horse, caught up with a thick Arakan who was hurrying away with me slung over his sweaty shoulder. Kovalan leaned to his side and grabbed me. With one arm, he scooped up my lithe body and sat me in front of his saddle. The horse veered and carried us away from my abductor, as more howling Arakans appeared from the thickets and gave chase. The Arakans, though fleet footed, were no match for us. Kovalan urged his horse and our hips moved in rhythm with the gallop. Kovalan had one hand on his reins and the other wrapped around my waist. His hand slipped over my smooth silks, and I tensed.

"What are you doing?" I said; must have spoken in my dream; the next moment, I felt a sharp pain.

"Wake up! The sun is up."

Mother delivered another slap to my buttocks and disappeared into the blinding sunlight outside. All around the tent, I heard people going about with breakfast and other chores.

I tried to recollect my dreams, but only the risqué dream filled my mind's eyes. I wondered if I should share this *dream incident*, as I came to refer to it, with Chinnamma. But I discarded the idea. She was an approachable woman, but I suspected she would not entertain such matters. During my time on the farm, she proved me right. Below her jovial veneer, she was quite similar to Mother, but I took several months to recognise this side of her.

###

4: Pleasure Houses and Sensual Maidens

With Kannagi visiting her uncle and aunty, I spent all my free time with Anandan. He had experiences so vast; I held him in awe. He was tall and carried himself with a swaggering confidence while I was retiring and shy.

One afternoon, when his parents were away, we climbed to the loft of his family storehouse. There were tools, articles, and dusty discards of various sorts stashed up there, including what he referred to as his chest of secrets. With unbridled pride, he displayed his hoard of blades and military medallions. Then, with a flourish, he pulled out a velvety scroll filled with shocking illustrations, painted in ochre, indigo, and other colours, of couples in various acts of copulation. He whispered in conspiratorial tones of having secured the racy article from some yavana by the waterfront.

"Wait here," said Anandan.

He scrambled down the stepladder and hurried away. I remained wide eyed, for his eclectic collection included wood carvings of phalluses and flat cracked plates which he referred to as the female thing. In my ignorance, I turned the plate front and back but could not make sense of it. It looked similar to those disgusting clams which fishermen pried open and swallowed raw.

Not long after, he dragged a young servant-girl by her hand into the storehouse. Without hesitation, he pushed her onto the pile of grain-filled sacks and let his spidery hands run all over the girl. He snatched her shawl, prompting a shriek, and she covered her naked chest. He pried the girl's stiff hands apart and fondled and slathered her in a rather rough and repulsive manner. She did not protest, but wore a resigned look. He pulled off the girl's garments and splayed her over the sacks. He did this, I suppose, to accord me an unobstructed view of her nakedness.

In a snatch, he turned the girl on her stomach and, his lingam, very much alive, entered her. Though growing hot with pulsing excitement, his actions altogether outraged me. Overcome with desperate excitement, he thrashed her and, before long, went limp. The girl, tears and eye-liners streaking down her cheeks, grabbed her clothes to her chest. Anandan held out a coin. She hesitated before taking the money and hurrying away.

Anandan lay on his back and looked up with a triumphant grin. I wanted to hurt him, make him suffer a little. But he was bigger and stronger and, for all my bluster about dharma, when confronted with adharma, self-preservation took precedence. My inaction proved my long-held suspicion true. I was a secret coward.

On a second occasion, Anandan violated another servant girl. After satisfying himself, he invited me to enjoy her but, not wanting to be a party to his distasteful activities, I spurned his offer outright. He dismissed the pathetic girl and asked me to choose from the servants. When I again rebuffed him, he shot back.

"You fool, these girls are for our enjoyment."

He boasted and recounted with glee his conquests of the servant-girls in his father's household. And whenever we met, he was relentless in pressing me to have fun with them.

"Pick anyone you want," said Anandan, "anyone."

Over the weeks, my repugnance mellowed, and I offered feeble protests.

"I don't have silver to pay them," I said.

"Don't you worry yourself about money. I'll take care of that. You pay me later, with interest, of course," he said. He proved persistent and annoying. Anandan even hinted that when his mother was away, his father took liberties with the servant-girls himself. I found these revelations abhorrent.

Though I deflected his harassment to *take* a girl, on several occasions I almost succumbed, if not for the thought of Kannagi, which gave me renewed resolve. I also suspected that Anandan wanted an accomplice, for my complicity would justify his actions. And if scandal broke, my father's influence would prove useful.

On one occasion, when we found ourselves in argument, he maintained that the girls welcomed his attentions. And as if to press home his point, Anandan appeared with a much older servant-girl. Unlike the others who lay passive, this servant-girl was the initiator. She proved an expert with her fingers and lips, and watching her rendered me hot and abashed. I would never have dreamt any woman could be so bold in such delicate matters. Some temple statues featured females as the initiators. And Anandan declared that in the days of antiquity, people—and especially the hill tribes and nomads in the arid lands—celebrated open coitus during pagan rituals.

I had felt indignation when Anandan pressed himself on the servant-girls, but here was one who pleasured without prompting. And throughout the act, Anandan kept looking at me with a big grin.

"See, this is how it's supposed to be between man and woman." He then offered the girl, but again, and with great effort, I extricated myself from the situation.

After that incident, I refused to visit his house and thereafter when he suggested a trip to the waterfront instead, I agreed without hesitation. I enjoyed his company, but not when it involved abusing servant-girls.

"Come on, then." Anandan gave me a quick smack and hurried off.

I soon found myself in a labyrinth of tight streets which I, having always kept to the larger and ordered roads, never knew existed in Maruvur. The place was a confused web of shoulder-width alleys and houses packed tight; terraces that leaned on one another. Leathers and fabrics stretched and sagged overhead and connected the opposing terraces, giving cover to the walkway. Groups of men milled outside gaudy coloured doors. Many of the men were *yavanas*, foreigners, but there were also several Tamils. Some of them looked familiar. I wanted to greet them, but they hurried away.

"Not here. Don't stare at the men; keep moving," said Anandan.

"Why not?"

Anandan did not reply; poked my temple with a finger and moved into the crowd. I did not protest; followed him. Excited voices and music and songs filled the air.

We could not see over the tall shoulders of the men. Therefore, we crawled between legs and pushed ourselves to the front of a door. The heavy smell of sweet joss sticks and watered-down perfume greeted us. As my eyes accustomed to the dim within the chamber, my jaws went slack.

A group of girls danced to the music, and men, seated in a circle around them, clapped, cheered, and tossed coins. The more daring dancers, having collected the coins, sat on the men's laps and gyrated their hips.

"Look! Look!" Anandan pointed. A man grabbed a girl and disappeared behind one of several curtained vestibules.

"They're going to enjoy," he whispered. When I looked puzzled, with a show of exasperation, he said, "Coitus, silly, the women sell their bodies for money."

There were others in the room, including an effeminate man, and a matron with a large pink dot on her forehead and lips rendered red from chewing areca nut.

"A woman?" I said, aghast, for here was a mother figure who stewarded the sexual enslavement of young women.

The girls looked radiant enough and wore ready smiles, but I discerned a deep sorrow in the eyes of the younger ones. The older girls looked more resigned to their fate, it seemed.

I felt a shocking pain and lurched forward and landed flat on my stomach. A rough voice bellowed, followed by a second sharp kick to my buttocks. A bearded man stared down and growled.

"Does your father know, boy?"

Anandan had already gone, leaving me with no choice but to attempt my escape. Another blow landed on my back, followed by laughter. A hand grabbed my shoulder, the fingers digging into my flesh. I twisted and sank my teeth in the man's hand and tasted his disgusting salty sweat. The man shouted, but I bit down harder and, cursing, he released his hold. More laughter erupted all around. I picked myself up and dashed off, spitting out the foul taste and wiping my lips with the back of my sweaty hands.

I broke free of the knotted crowds; ran, and after several confused turns, recognised the main street. Guided by landmarks, I took a circuitous route back to the waterfront and our private spot. Anandan was already there, eating a sweet, sticky snack.

"What kept you?" He was nonchalant.

"You left me behind," I said, shaking from anger and exertion.

"You're here and alive." He shrugged his shoulders and laughed. "If you think it's wrong with the servant-girls, pleasure houses are right for the righteous. And if Kannagi refuses to do certain things, seek the devadasis. They will oblige. This is the secret, dear promised-to-be-married friend, for keeping marriages blissful."

I hated him when he mentioned Kannagi in the same breath as *devadasis*, women of lost morals; I hated him when he ill-treated his servant-girls; but I hated myself more because, in secret, I believed him and looked up to him. I lacked his fatal courage; admired his recklessness.

***

The years slipped by, and though Anandan continued to enjoy the pleasures promised by damsels, he also had a distinct interest in commerce. He purchased land and built a palatial mansion in Pattinam. He had also, by the timed interventions of his father's influence, made profitable inroads into various royal and mercantile circles.

Then, as was his nature, he plagued me to join him in Pattinam. When I visited his sprawling new manor, Anandan again pressed me.

"One thing about these courtiers, they never say what they mean and never mean what they say, and it makes you want to pull off your earrings and throw at them."

"Why do you even bother with these people?"

"You ask why, because you hail from a long line of princely merchants, and people readily call on your father. They wait in queues under the unforgiving sun for the pleasure of meeting him, so they can boast to have met Sir Masattuvan and to have drunk his water. But my father has no exalted lineage. Every grain of gold and sliver of silver resulted from his own resourcefulness. It lends a special taste of accomplishment, my gilded friend, and I am emulating my hero, my father. Join me and seek your own fortune."

"My father's fortune is mine for inheritance and enough for an eternity," I said.

"Eternity lasts but for a mere lifetime, if at all. Why, even the peerless Ravana of Lanka considered his lineage everlasting but the Cholan, Cheran, and Pandyan succeeded him. Now, the royal trinity harbours delusions of eternity. And so, history reaches and retreats. Eternity is eternal only if you keep tilling and sowing her seeds, not by suckling from the same breast, no matter how gorged it might be for now."

"Say what you wish, but I don't have a need for more money," I said.

"Treat it as a hobby then."

"I already have a hobby; one I am passionate about."

"Yes, I know. Singing," said Anandan, and he smirked. "Go on then; perform on street corners. That will please your father."

"You think poorly of the arts, my friend," I said. "I compose verses, and I sing songs. Why, even you once praised my abilities."

"True, I did and you have a rich voice, I agree even now," said Anandan. "But keep it a pastime to entice maidens."

"I hone my skills in songs to entertain my future wife and your little sister, Kannagi."

"Kovalan, listen and listen well. We are on the cusp of our journey. Young men have two avenues to attain fulfilment in life. As a warrior or a wealthy man. The former takes one down a harsh path and a warrior's death before time is ready. The latter validates one's worth and along the way helps one to dip into many honeypots." He nudged me and laughed.

"I know where this talk leads and wish not to pursue its end. I also know you well, and your persistence. Out with your scheme so I can decline and move on to other matters."

"You pass sentence impetuously, my friend. Well then. My suggestion is for you to come to Pattinam and seek your own fortune and add to your father's hoard."

"Here I am, already in Pattinam," I said, with a smirk.

"Dear Kovalan, leave the jesting to entertainers. Consider your promised marriage to Kannagi, establish your own household here, in proximity to the centre of power."

"That would mean leaving my father's house."

"That would mean setting up your own house, as I have, and I'm not even married." He spent the rest of my visit repeating the same arguments, but each time clothed in different shades, confident of wearing me down.

As usual, I resisted his blandishments. But over the months, his words became a sculptor's chisel; chipped away at my resistance, and a dream took form.

It was about this time Father discussed my wedding and living arrangements in some earnest. Kannagi would return to Puhar in about a year. And Father had already drawn up grand plans to add a new wing to the house, one that would accord me and my new wife privacy while keeping us under his roof and overview. Father opined he was more experienced in such matters and was being helpful. But as the days progressed, I chafed and wondered if my fate was to hide in his shadow. And Anandan, as was his nature, proved relentless and worked on the part of me that envied his freedom and wanted to spread my wings.

I decided to establish my household, but also expected Father's disappointment to spill into anger. True enough, our probing discussions degenerated and led to many harsh words. Those were tense and terrible weeks in our house, and something I was not proud of as a son to a remarkable and good man.

After one terse exchange, Father curled his fingers and dropped into his seat. He looked small. I felt a sharp prick of pain, for I had knocked him down with my foolish words where many had failed, even with weapons wielded from positions of wealth and power.

"Your words break my heart, my dear son. Better you thrust a blade so I die quickly."

"Father, please trust me," I said, and knelt and placed my hands on his knees. "You have done well in nurturing me, and I will not disappoint you."

He remained silent and tears wet his eyes. That shocked me to my soul, because Father had always been a stoic man; never betrayed weakness.

"Trust you?" His voice was soft.

"Yes, Father, trust me. Please."

"Who else can I trust if not you, my son?" He placed his hand on my head and said, "I fear this path you take, no doubt fed by words of ill counsel, will lead to ruin."

He gave me a light pat and rose and shuffled towards the staircase. Then he stopped at the foot of the expansive steps and turned.

"Do as you wish, my son. You will always have my blessings and fervent prayers for good things to shower upon you. And may our patron gods guide and protect you always."

I won my wish, but felt no joy. I pushed my guilty feelings to the depths of my soul and plunged into the many demands that came with building my new mansion.

Of course, Mother being Mother did not shed tears, but fed the gossip that it was her idea for me to move out. And Kannagi was the reason. As her daughter-in-law-to-be was a chaste and exemplary maiden, it was befitting for Kannagi to have her own household, proclaimed Mother. Kannagi could then receive and entertain family and friends, renowned luminaries and unknown wanderers, the wealthy and the destitute, the learned and the seekers. By so doing, my virginal wife would gain much merit from her boundless generosity and impeccable hospitality. And my dear mother wished for all the merit to collect at her future daughter-in-law's feet. Shrewd Mother, because if matters soured, she had already attached a name to the blame. Such was my mother's philanthropic genius. If my Kannagi served cool, clean water to one dying of thirst, Mother was the water herself.

And the news so let loose took a life of its own and grew into the only plausible explanation for such a remarkable and inventive living arrangement. I steered away from the fray and smiled whenever a meddling acquaintance sidled up to enquire after my moving out of my father's house. Instead, my focus turned to the day I would escort my vivid wife Kannagi over the threshold of her new home to begin our promised life.

###

5: Kannagi and Kovalan's Wedding

When the time came for me to return to Puhar, Father sent to us a band of mounted guards and pack animals bearing lavish gifts for Chinnamma, Uncle, and the village elders. The riders also brought a chest of fine clothes, with instructions from Mother that I change into these for my grand entrance into Puhar.

Uncle harnessed together a caravan of bullock carts and our procession set off for Puhar. Several families who had timed their departure joined our caravan.

We retraced the route taken years earlier. Years! How time had slipped. I had grown rounder, fleshed out over my sharp bones, and blunted my quick tongue. But much more was the change within.

The first few weeks on the farm had been wrenching as I pined for Kovalan, but as the months rolled away, new habits took hold and life became bearable. Chinnamma filled my mornings with prayers and the study of holy texts, and taught many rites and rituals to make me a proper maiden ready for married life, and that included preparing and serving meals.

"Remember," whispered Chinnamma, "delicious food served by your bangled hands is the main course. You are the dessert."

She placed her finger under my chin and raised my face. I bit my lower lip and cast down my eyes.

"Good," said Chinnamma, for that was the prescribed behaviour. It was silly, I protested, but I was no dog's tail and in time she straightened me.

Afternoons were more relaxed, and I got to bathe the lazy cows, feed the skinny goats, and rub down the horses.

"Remember, no horse riding. It is so unedifying for a maiden to straddle a horse," said Chinnamma.

But she and Father underestimated my resourcefulness. The farm was quite sizable and there was a willing stable boy and his grandfather, the stable master. I bribed the old man with my cute smiles, and the boy with sweet rice and honeyed savouries. And they taught me horse-riding. It was our secret.

I harboured many little secrets, such as spying on a young village couple. In the mornings, the man drove his flock of goats, their little tails forever flicking non-stop, to pasture. In the afternoons, his wife brought lunch in an earthenware pot, perched on a cloth bun wrapped on her head. I too tried the balancing act but, after breaking several pots, gave up. The couple shared their meals under the shade of a tree, fed one another, and embraced. On most days, the man, throwing furtive glances, grabbed his wife's hand and disappeared behind some shrubs. I suspected their motives and, embarrassed, covered my face.

"Remember, a chaste woman never leads in bed," said Chinnamma. "Your husband is lord, lover, and leader. You are a book. Let him in, let him explore and relish the leaves of your pages. A fruit which drops at his feet will never hold the allure and sweetness of one which he reaches and plucks. You must be a book and a fruit. Feed his imagination and fill his hunger."

Whenever Chinnamma used the word *remember*, she turned grave, and I committed those words to memory. Except for the horse-riding part.

How the years had passed. I sighed again. Now the time to return had arrived, and I was on my way to join my dear Kovalan.

Throughout the journey, the guards kept a sharp lookout for Arakans but detected no evidence of the wild men's presence. But I felt a strange comfort knowing the beast-men were there, in the hills and trees.

After several days of sleeping in tents, and wearied but with excitement rippling throughout the caravan, we entered Poom-Puhar and made steady progress through Pattinam, the City District. There was already a small crowd along the streets and these swelled in numbers as we made our way east towards my home in Maruvur District.

My marriage to Kovalan was a few days away and Father had launched preparations about a week earlier to coincide with my return. Buntings of glorious flowers of loud colours and subtle fragrances adorned the streets in Maruvur, prayer flags waved in the cool breeze descending from the north, tall sugarcane cuttings heralded the promise of sweetness for the couple-to-be, and lately transplanted banana stems bent heavy with flower and fruit.

As we made our slow way, a party of musicians joined our procession as a vanguard. Drums and trumpets announced our arrival. Street criers ran ahead, shouting our names and a calendar of promised events to follow. Closer to home, several dance troupes and their musicians and criers added to the gaiety. Priests appeared and merged with the motley procession and lent their repetitive chants, adding a touch of mystical spirituality to the celebratory mood.

For a person who had been quite mischievous, I had now grown self-conscious and remained well under the canopy of the carriage, not daring to show myself. And Chinnamma placed an elegant shawl around me and covered my face with a veil.

"Remember," she said above the din, "you're no more a child. Bury your foolishness, be the maiden you are now. Make me proud. Make your parents proud. Make your husband happy."

In keeping with her manner, I nodded with gravity.

"Remember, no more horse-riding," she said.

"What?"

I wanted to protest but, in an instance, realised she and Uncle knew of my clandestine afternoon activity. Chinnamma looked straight ahead. Her faint smile was fleeting, but revealing. The stable master must have secured Uncle's blessings before allowing me on the saddle. My little secret must have made for an interesting topic during the farm workers' meal times.

Another thought planted, an embarrassing one: did they also know about the shepherd couple? I studied Chinnamma's face. After several long moments, she smiled and said,

"Yes, I know, but not Uncle."

I swallowed dry air. With a finger under my chin, she raised my face and whispered in a conspiratorial tone.

"When I was your age, I spied on my neighbours too." And she grinned. I looked away and bit my finger as expected of a shy maiden.

"Here we are, your father's house. And remember, no more mischief."

The grounds of my father's house were ablaze with dozens of strangers moving about and attending to various tasks: putting up buntings and pennants, erecting tents, arranging garlands and flower pots. There were two outdoor kitchens—one vegetarian and the other non-vegetarian—under vast canopies where cooks were churning out meals for the army of helpers and early well-wishers.

Father and Mother waited under the shade of the patio. They had grown fatter. Mother had applied *kumkuma* powder all over and her light skin looked pink. Father's silvery beard and bull-horn moustache stood out in prominent contrast to his smooth, deep brown skin.

Mother brought out a silver tray filled with camphor, ash, and turmeric water, and conducted a small prayer to cast out evil eyes.

After the prayer, a gaggle of noisy women led me into the house where relatives and well-wishers mobbed me. There were too many of them, people whom I vaguely remembered, but also some unfamiliar faces. But every woman treated me as if I were part of her close circle. Too many painted faces, too many fake smiles, and an avalanche of advice for the bride-to-be. The pong of their moist body odour—reminding me of damp cloth stored in musty cupboards—and bad breath were suffocating. I wanted to scream: Leave me alone. My caked smiling mask was in danger of shattering with exasperation and revealing my true self: an exhausted girl who yearned for a cool bath, a cup of milk, and some sleep.

Kovalan did not sneak into the grounds, disguised as a guest, to take a peek. I sighed. He was not a spontaneous person, and had probably grown more stringent. I would not disappoint him, for I too had changed. I would be a mysterious book and an alluring fruit hanging on a branch—but not too high.

Once rested, I rushed out to seek Kovalan, but Mother stopped me. Father too stood in silent acquiescence with Mother's wishes.

"A bride-to-be does not wander about the streets to meet her fiancé," said Mother. I gave Father an appealing look, but he said,

"Listen to your mother, amah."

Did he refer to me as *amah*? Whatever happened to gold and silver, diamond and ruby, and all the other pet names? Amah!

Was I that old? Many years ago, I swore never to grow old, but time had conspired his mischief.

Disappointed, but I agreed with my parents. Kovalan would have to wait. Did I have a choice? I have to transition from maiden to married woman. Chinnamma's lessons and reminders came to the fore. *Remember.*

Looking back, I wondered how could I have done all those things with the boys: racing down the streets, climbing trees, swimming in ponds and rivers, screaming down valleys to hear echoes, and fighting? Fighting! I shuddered and hoped Kovalan would not recall my antics.

I had changed in Chinnamma's farm, but for a moment, the pleasure of home had brought back the old carefree ways.

***

My wedding day started with an early morning bath in water sprinkled with scented flowers and rice grains, and followed by a series of obligatory prayers. Discarding the damp garment, I reclined on a long seat with my wet locks of hair loosened. Sweet incense seeped through my hair and removed moisture while adding fragrance.

Under the close supervision of a matron, beauticians lined my eyes with black kohl; the rich eyeliners smarted and turned the corners of my eyes red. Then, I became a statue, with arms outstretched, and they applied henna and sandalwood paste, and coloured powder and saffron inks on my skin. A stylist combed and smoothened my hair, parted and braided it, and curled it into a heavy knot which she then adorned with strings of flowers, hairpins of gold, and precious stones.

They turned me this way and that way and layered me with silks. After which, they hung various ornaments of gold and silver. Next came the sweet-smelling garlands, by which time sweat trickled and tickled down my back.

The bridal *panthal*, a shimmering marquee in gold fabric, caught and bounced the brilliant sunlight. Billowing silks, cascading from tall frames, gave the illusion of dancing walls. More colourful buntings of fine translucent fabrics criss-crossed the high ceiling. The astrologers had chosen an auspicious day in the winter months, and a northern wind brought cool relief flowing through the tent. But swaddled as I was, I might as well have been standing over a boiling cauldron.

"Keep your head down!" Chinnamma reproved for the umpteenth time. Again, I was a little slow and felt a finger nudge my head down. I wanted to scream.

Kovalan and I, and our parents and clan members, sat facing one another. Before us were several large silver trays filled with coiled garlands and fresh fruits, rock sugar and sticky dates and savouries, and piles of fine silks. Taking pride of place among the spread of gleaming silverware were several trays of jewellery: gold and silver, all encrusted with colourful precious and semi-precious stones.

The families engaged in the centuries-old ritual of choreographed play-acting. Father and Kovalan's father, Sir Masattuvan, exchanged questions and made declarations regarding our marriage, with much nodding and approval from all sides.

My focus was on Kovalan, who sat opposite. He had grown in height and filled out. I gave him a secret smile, but his eyes shifted.

Chinnamma nudged and whispered. "Eyes down. Look demure. Be graceful."

I kept my head down but raised my eyes and peeped through the veil. Anandan, the groom's second, sat behind Kovalan. He too kept a stoic face, and I wondered whether I was the only inquisitive one in the assembly.

Forced to look down, I counted the number of bananas on the tray. Then I counted the dates, but that proved impossible, so I studied all the toes of the people: cracked nails, dirty nails, nails with silver rings, and a missing toe. What? I looked again. Yes, a missing toe. I peeped at the man and wondered how he lost his toe. It must have been painful. One woman had an additional toe attached to her little toe. It was nerveless and ugly. I snatched a look at Kovalan's toes and sighed with relief. He had perfect toes. I thus amused myself and—felt a pang. I missed my old self.

It was only at that moment under the hot tent I realised I will never be that mischievous girl, ever again. *Remember.* I recalled my aunt's whispers. Chinnamma was right. My parents were right. I agreed with adults. I had become an adult!

My wedding also served as a lavish backdrop, a showcase for our two families to display their wealth and prestige. It was a huge commercial opportunity where important merchants, royal councillors, and courtiers gathered and renewed acquaintances. They transacted business and resolved festering disputes in an atmosphere of peer pressure and political patronage and greased with a mouth-watering feast and ready intoxicants. The nobles and merchants exchanged favours and brokered many new friendships.

Lest the men outdid them, the queens, led by Mother and Kovalan's mother and their circle of fat relatives and lady friends, draped in their finest silks and weighed down by gold jewellery, floated—lumbered—for their lesser sisters to gasp with envy. The women's antics provided enormous entertainment, more than the music and song, as they busied themselves by hurrying here and there, and accomplished little else than to harass the poor stewards whose task it was to oversee the events of the day.

The five days' activities were the same, albeit with minor changes: breakfast, lunch, and afternoon song recitals, succeeded by evening prayers, and a dinner that included dance and drama.

The finale of my wedding day, managed with care, coincided with the foretold auspicious time, and Kovalan tied the nuptial *tali* string around my neck. Father engaged two sets of a dozen priests each: the first prayers in Sanskrit, in honour of the delegations from the Aryan lands in the north, followed by the more extensive chanting in my beloved Tamil.

Maha-Rajah Kari-Kaalan, his Queen, and their entourage made a dignified late entrance and sent ripples through the crowd long before they appeared. There was a great commotion as people rose to their feet and surged towards the king. Guards, their arms locked, formed a human fence and held back the crowd.

Kovalan and I fell at the feet of the royal couple to receive their blessings. After saying a few words, they departed and drew in their wake most of the people who had come to witness our wedding. How silly of the people, for when they returned, others had taken all the choice seats.

After the speeches and just before dinner, Kovalan slipped a set of elegant ankle bracelets around my feet and sang in his rich voice, evoking envious awe throughout the eager gathering.

"I bathe your feet with ancient rites
Of turmeric dust, flower-scented milk
Sandalwood paste hides shyness,
Henna tempts with magic on skin
Anklets filled with music adorn your feet
With rubies perfect, blood red within
Your virtuosity, my unbroken ancestry
Silver, gold slipped on your toes
Swearing in the temples of my father
Our Love straddles Eternity, till
Time dies, the Cycle completes."

###

6: A Stranger and a Celestial Nymph

"You are a mimosa crying touch-me-not," I said. Kannagi went silent, and that irritated me. "Say something, for my fingers crave to explore but the knots on your garments remain fast."

"Why do you vex so, Athan? Do I not give myself when you demand?"

"Yes, but only when I demand. You never give freely of yourself."

But I stopped quarrelling when Kannagi broke into tears. She heaved and sobbed, and I showered kisses to pacify her. It was fortunate that we lived on our own as I did not want Mother, ever ready to defend her son, to pick on Kannagi. As for Father, a chasm had opened between us, and it reduced even our greetings to nods and grunts.

Another night, as I watched Kannagi sleep in peace, a perplexing rage swelled within me. Earlier in the evening, we had an amorous encounter. She had cringed and made me feel as if I was a violator.

"Man's *adharma*, sins, have three roots," she said. "Desire, anger, and errors of judgement."

Her words, appropriate for philosophical discourse perhaps, flew as arrows into my bristling and brittle needs. For all I heard were accusations that my carnal rights were lust, my justified outrage was anger, and my insistence on living a conjugal life was an incorrect path. She expected me to look and admire but not embrace, embrace and enjoy but not indulge, and indulge in sweet words but not infuse life into them.

It was frustrating, and I found fault with her teachers on the farm. They had incarcerated my Kannagi, the mischievous one who loved life, and sent back, in her stead, a frigid stranger. I also wondered whether these withholdings of favours were deliberate attempts to have me dancing to her tunes.

Anandan had warned of the repertoire of wiles some women employed.

"Beware, lest you end up a *jalra*," he said, "keeping count on hand-cymbals to the music modes a woman dictates. That's why I prefer to flirt from flower to flower. No pubis hood will subdue me."

Every encounter presented a new hunt where I had to stalk, corner, and win her over and over again, night after night. It was exhausting, and all the more when the prize held no new wonders or intoxicating joys. And even after succumbing, she laid prone and did not respond to my overtures.

"You might as well live a desert nomad's life and mount a goat," said Anandan. "For a wife who lies as a log is no better than a goat which stands bleating."

Hearing him speak of bestiality, I had vomited.

"You refuse to even tease awake the wicks in the lamps, and our nights remain moonless," I said.

"Someone might see, Athan," she replied.

"Who?" I cried loud.

She meant me. And as our conversation and night ripened, often we found ourselves engaged in quarrels. But regardless of Anandan's urging, I refused to force myself on her, for it was demeaning and unworthy of any man, especially a husband. For me, when given, it is a gift of love; when taken, it is a theft committed in the shadows of the night. How apt, I thought, that Kannagi kept the lamps doused.

Whenever the pain of unreleased desires overwhelmed me, I sneaked into my private room to pleasure myself and then, exhausted but not satiated, returned to our conjugal bed. These episodes rendered me small and feeling unwanted. I did not wish to injure Kannagi, but felt myself losing my mind.

"Have the main course at home, my dear Kovalan," said Anandan, "but if you wish for something more enchanting..." He smiled, leaving the obvious unspoken. Sometimes I hated him. But most times, he was just distasteful medicine.

Anandan was right, and I knew many luminaries in the country who did just that—upright family men and stalwarts of society and patrons of the arts who harboured a seedier side. Some of these men of stature purchased and supported harlots and enjoyed exclusive access to the women. Others, succumbing to the blandishments of these women of soiled morals, brought them home and set them up in small houses quaintly referred to as *shiru veedu*, within the vast family holdings. These tenements often occupied a corner in the estate and it was possible to maintain two distinct households and for the two families, and the queens, never to meet.

And Anandan was persistent—even the king has a harem, he declared—and I would soon run out of arguments, making me even angrier. Our exchanges would escalate and lead to harsh words. And shaking with anger, I would stomp out of Anandan's house.

After one such quarrel, I broke ties with him. I did not confide in Kannagi, for she would prevail upon me to make my peace with Anandan. Worse, what if she insisted on knowing the reason for our quarrel? She was wary of Anandan's morals, but the two of them were friends too, and I would not disparage him to her.

But this was later, for the early days of our married life started off well.

Upon her suggestion, we toured temples, enjoyed one another's company, and our honeymoon turned out rather well. She prayed and paid respects to the gods, and I looked forward to our evenings. It started off as a carefree time, but as the days progressed, I noticed some strange traits. She lingered, ever longer, at every deity ensconced in the temple sanctums, and in time I ended up waiting for hours, and lost all cheer.

One evening, we were in the throes of passion and, in a bright voice, she recounted a wish to visit a particular temple. It devastated me; she was not present in body and mind. I went limp and withdrew. Later that evening, in a gentle tone, I mentioned her callousness. She expressed no regrets, but questioned my fixation on carnal matters.

After the first weeks of touring, we settled into the routine of married life: Kannagi managed the household; I focussed on my fledgling business. She did an excellent job, but I met with disappointment.

The merchants I approached, my father's circle of collaborators, proved traditional in their views and deflected every one of my ideas.

"What you propose is interesting, Kovalan my boy, but let me first have a word with your father." But I did not wish Father to intervene, resolved as I was to make my own way.

Then, Kannagi shared splendid news. She was with child. My joy was fathomless; our love bloomed again. We had love, happiness, and wealth. Those were the best months of my life. And we were the perfect couple. Alas, that was too much and the gods became jealous. They unleashed fate, and he proved cruel.

Kannagi suffered serious bleeding that triggered a spontaneous abortion. Losing our child devastated us, but more so Kannagi. With my wife miserable, I could not bring myself to leave her lonely. Therefore, setting aside my business plans, I spent all my time ministering to her needs. It brought us closer, and we tried again for another child.

But when she suffered several more miscarriages, Kannagi grew despondent and threw herself into prayers and temple visits. When I attempted intimacy, she turned cold. I had to start and hold the conversations, because she spoke little and even then only of the mundane, such as meals and prayers. I shared my love of song and music, and though Kannagi tried hard, she knew little regarding the arts and could not engage with my enthusiasm.

My dear wife withdrew into herself. Our mothers, besides making motherhood statements, were not of much help. Upon my urging, she wrote to her Aunty Chinnamma and when that kind woman replied, our situation improved. Kannagi became receptive and, occasionally, we even indulged in intimacy.

But after several exchanges, the letters stopped coming. The courier service crossed Arakan lands, which were always fraught with dangers. One day, Kannagi's father brought shattering news. Her uncle robbed and murdered on the Arakan road, and her grief-stricken Aunty Chinnamma had thrown herself on the funeral pyre and committed *sati*, ritual suicide.

The news devastated Kannagi. She collapsed and her face twisted and mouth locked open as if in a wail, but no sound ensued from her throat. I watched speechless as she lay crumpled on the floor and heaved and gasped. She was suffocating before my eyes. Fortunately, my father-in-law administered a sharp slap to her back. That shocked her to draw a quick breath. But the wailing that followed frightened and kept me awake for many nights.

Kannagi had often spoken of her aunty, and knew her as a jovial and accommodating person. But there were chambers hidden in the woman's heart that no one else was privy to. I shuddered at the thought of self-immolation. It was a horrendous practice, imported from the north, that few people discussed and even fewer practised.

My dear, distraught Kannagi wished to visit the farm. I tried but failed to stop her. But thankfully, her father put a stop to her plan; all the more when he learned she was again with child.

I offered many lavish sacrifices to the gods and contributed fabulous donations to temples. A child would save Kannagi's sanity and restore some normalcy to our lives. But alas, when she again miscarried, I lost my poor dear Kannagi and my home sank into a gloom from which it never recovered.

She resorted to fasting and took advice from lice-ridden swamis and strange fortune-tellers who filled her mind with esoteric ideas founded on magic and mysticism.

I tried hard to accommodate her unpredictable behaviour, but occasionally lost my patience. Once, I even uttered harsh and undeserved words regarding her barren womb. It was cruel of me, but I could not retrieve the words already let loose. In desperation, she even suggested adopting a child. This was unheard of and, as the child's lineage was unknown, it would not do. I rejected the scheme outright and she withdrew from me even more. Unfulfilled in love, my focus turned to commerce, but I suffered several failed ventures.

On her better days, to her great credit and ignoring her own situation, Kannagi worried for my well-being; suggested approaching our friend Anandan, who had succeeded in his trade ventures. She was unaware of our friendship-ending quarrel. Nevertheless, I put pride in a pouch and visited Anandan. When I could not meet him, I left a message for him to call on me.

Meanwhile, my relationship with Kannagi lost the spark and profundity of love. And I found little faults with her. In hindsight, these were trivial and unfair to her, but I had grown petty and our circumstances enlarged and echoed every little error. In secret, I even blamed Kannagi for our misfortunes. But in my more generous moments, the dark thoughts directed at her devastated me. I was ashamed; felt small. This guilt made matters worse. Life overwhelmed, and I sank into frequent bouts of gloom.

***

Just as matters were spiralling into the abyss, my dear friend Anandan graced my household with his long-expected visit. Heartened that he held no ill feelings, I embraced him. We clung to one another and exchanged declarations of friendship.

And Anandan had brought a companion—Telamonius! The Greek had advanced in years and looked more weathered. The thick brown hair, bouncing about his ears, had turned white, and his beard had gone straight and stiff, a dirty besom.

"How sing the anklets?" asked the Greek. "I pray their song keeps you enchanted, and your incomparable wife pleased."

The Greek mentioning the anklets precipitated pain, as they harkened back to happy days which have faded into the fog of lost memory. Moreover, the ankle rings were part of my wife's private wardrobe and not a matter for public discourse. The Greek, though versed in Tamilakam's mores, had broken etiquette. But I hid my displeasure and said,

"All is well, sir, and you continue to speak fluently our *sen-Tamil.*"

"And you, Sir Kovalan, remain generous, as I well remember."

The Greek made a show of bowing. Telamonius" abundant deference did not sit well. It reminded me of the wariness felt when I first met him. But he was Anandan's declared friend and, pushing aside my lack of enthusiasm for the Greek, I received my guests with abundant hospitality.

Talk touched on this and that topic, and meandered, and, as liquor loosened tongues, we found ourselves on grounds favoured by all virile men. Enchanting maidens. And one maiden in particular, a celestial beauty, with teasing nipples, hips of a honey bee, and a welcoming pubis.

"Accompany us, my dear Kovalan, and pay court to the king," said Anandan.

"That is the stated excuse on everyone's lips," said Telamonius, "but the main event is the fair maiden, Madhavi, descended from the heavens. By all reckoning, she is an accomplished dancer, and this is her public debut. There will be many jostling for the privilege, and pleasure, to become her patron and protector."

"Why would I want to attend any happy performance when my dear wife, Kannagi, is even now confined to her chamber and recovering from yet another miscarriage?"

"I'm so sorry to hear of your wife," said the Greek, his reply swift and insincere.

"That explains your dullness, my dear friend," said Anandan, and he placed a gentle hand on my shoulder. Telamonius intervened.

"Perhaps it is all the more reason for you to cheer yourself with dance and music, Sir Kovalan. Something to put wonderful spirit in you which, contagious as it is, you can convey to your dear wife."

"Our friend Telamonius has spoken wise words, dear Kovalan," said Anandan, "for besides music and dance, Madhavi is a mistress also of the erotic and profane, having attained perfection in these arts, rendering her an unrivalled courtesan. She is versed in science and astrology, in oratory to seduce, in the language of gestures, and knowledge enough to engage even sages and seers. And there is more, but I see your eyes already glaze with indifference."

"Her patron protector is the king himself," said Telamonius. "That is, until he confers the responsibility to another. Her beauty is storied; and some say to breathe the air surrounding her is to partake heavenly *prana*, the essence of nourishment for body, soul, and all six senses."

"You will also get to see our Illustrious Majesty, King Kari-Kaalan," said Anandan, taking over as if the two had come rehearsed, "and many accomplished men who, with a gesture, can help realise dreams, of which you harbour one or two, perhaps. Is this not the reason you wished to meet me, to rejuvenate your fledgling commercial ventures?"

I placed my suggestion on Kannagi, and to my welcomed surprise, she agreed.

"My brother Anandan is right, Athan. Go, and with new friends, recover your zest for life, for it pains me to see you so reduced." She rested her gentle hand on mine. "And upon your return, promise to describe Madhavi's artistry so I too might relish her gifts."

###

7: The Worth of a Tamil Maiden

The imposing uniformed man, seated behind the table, pulled back his sleeve and with a flourish wielded his thin iron pencil as he recorded our names on a palm-leaf. He looked up, expectant. Taking the hint, I reached for my money pouch. Anandan restrained my hand.

"Allow me, please." He handed over a palm-sized but weighty cloth bag of gold coins.

The man unloosened the draw-strings and peered inside, and his face lit up as he took a quick account of the gold.

He gestured to an under-official, one of several standing a few paces behind him, who led us into an opulent foyer already filled with men from the upper crust of Puhar society, and all dressed in rich silks and pearl necklaces.

Anandan, who seemed to know almost all the people in the room, pulled me along as he made the rounds in the tight space. Servant-boys moved about, serving silver cups of milk and watered honey. There were piles of fruit—sliced mangoes, bananas, jackfruit, grapes and more—heaped on silver trays arrayed on tables lining one wall. I drifted down the vestibule and faced a deep-carpeted corridor. Liveried guards, their lances bedecked with pennants, lined both sides of the passageway. I strolled with the slow-moving body of perfumed men.

Anandan placed a light hand on my arm and a familiar but unwelcome face greeted me—Telamonius, the Greek. There were three other Greeks whose names did not register, but I gathered they were Telamonius' workmen. After the quick exchange of greetings, I tried but failed to nudge myself away from the Greeks, for by then, the doors drew open and ushered us into the deep concert hall.

A stern official, familiar with the behaviour of the wealthy self-important men streaming into the hall, raised his voice and spoke as he would towards unruly children. His booming vocals herded the men to their seats. As expected, there was some confusion, and it took all the restrained ferocity of the stern official and his glum assistants to resolve sitting disputes, and relegate the gathering to a measure of humming silence.

The majestic doors opened again and released a retinue of ministers and courtiers in tunics of shimmering silks and turbans adorned with pearls, plumes, and precious stones, prompting the gathering to stand and bow. The officials clasped their hands and dipped their heads in choreographed unison before settling into their chairs. There was a hushed excitement. Now and then, a minister or senior courtier caught the eyes of some luminary in the crowd, and exchanged smiles and nods. Again, the doors opened and in streamed sages and teachers in scanty vestments and white tunics, and priests in saffron robes. Again, we repeated the established ritual of standing and bowing with clasped hands.

A sudden boom and blare of percussion and wind instruments reverberated around the hall. Moments later, dozens of musicians, beating drums and blowing trumpets, appeared.

The noisy procession heralded the royal couple's entrance. Maha-Rajah Kari-Kaalan and his Queen Consort entered the hall, followed by captains decked out in splendid brass armour and silken turbans adorned with dyed horsehair plumes.

The people stood up and bowed, and panegyrists recited flattering accolades as the royal couple ascended the steps to the dais. Maha-Rajah Kari-Kaalan, his chest covered in heavy gold and gleaming jewels, surveyed the great hall and, satisfied, settled on the throne.

The master of ceremony, a tall man in a heavy robe with silver embroidery, approached the royal rostrum and, after securing the king's permission, began the evening's performances.

Several poets and sages recited verses and sang ballads, praying for abundant rain and bountiful harvests, and praised the Cholan lineage, the Cholan Kingdom, and Maha-Rajah Kari-Kaalan and his Queen Consort. The people relished the elegance of the verses and tossed scented flower petals into the air.

I sensed the obvious displeasure and impatience of Telamonius for, on several occasions, he leaned to the side and demanded of Anandan.

"When will the dancing girls perform?"

Anandan counselled restraint, but the Greek remarked in a voice which carried that had he known, he would have arrived much later for the dancing girls. This elicited frowns from some men seated within hearing distance, but made no impression on Telamonius.

In the wake of the poetry recitations, several percussion and choral ensembles performed. More percussion and wind instruments followed the ensembles.

Then, it was the *dancing girls'* turn but Telamonius kept wondering aloud when, if ever, the star dancer, Madhavi, would make her appearance. The master of ceremony heard the Greek and gave him a severe look, but Telamonius did not notice or did not care. Soiled by the Greek's proximity, I cringed in shame.

A sweet melody from a lone flute filled the auditorium and held the gathering in rapt anticipation. Fine pink kumkuma mist floated down from the ceiling and the tinkling sound of several dozen anklets heralded the star attraction. A stream of light-footed maidens ran out in a single file and the line curled within itself, as would a shy millipede. Drums took up the beat, growing in vigour. The girls continued to mark time with their feet, their anklets in perfect harmony with the drums. Then, the music stopped, and the girls dropped to the floor.

All except one.

There, standing at the centre of the curling line of crouched bodies, was a lone figure, and even in her veil, one could discern her exquisite beauty and alluring sensuality. As the star of the evening, Madhavi needed no introductions.

She mesmerised with movements of graceful flowing arms, gentle swaying of sculpted hips that accentuated a slim waist, and feet that marked entrancing beats. Music from an orchestra of drums, trumpets, flutes and veenas accompanied her every step and pose, and one could not tell whether she danced to the music or the musicians played to her fluid movements. The drum beats, her jingling anklets, and her flowing limbs enthralled and enslaved. Telamonius' jaw fell open. He was a man possessed.

As each *raaga*, or melodic mode, etched and ebbed, so too did I sense the musical moods and tinges of colours. Madhavi's dance rendition brought to the fore all that was calm, peaceful, and beautiful—but always with a subtle tease and silent challenge. Her dance grabbed and painted my mind with dreams of fantasy and eroticism unrealised. She was an apsara maiden, descended from the celestial courts of the godly devas. Every man who gazed upon her saw his ideal, and she was perfection personified.

I fell in love with Madhavi's dance but also sensed that most men in the hall beheld her as no more than an object of desire. The thought stirred inexplicable anger and envy in me. A trembling hope coursed through my being, which at once warmed but also warned.

Anandan said she had been a dancer in the private chambers of Kari-Kaalan. Her artistic skills had compelled the king, the foremost patron of the arts in his realms, to share his good fortune with his subjects. He was right. Madhavi's divine gift of dance and gestures belonged to the annals of artistic excellence and public adoration, not for the private enjoyment of royalty.

Without warning, Madhavi's eyes fell on mine. I caught my breath. In a hall tight with eager faces, unwavering eyes, and opened mouths, it was difficult to tell, given the distance, whether she caught my eyes or perhaps it was someone else who held her fleeting interest—someone behind or beside me. When she twirled again, and her face swept around and stopped for a fleeting moment in my direction with her eyes locked on mine, I knew we had seen one another. My heart skipped a beat. Before I could recover and offer a secret smile, Madhavi moved away and danced, facing the royal dais. Disappointed, I waited, eager; eager for her to swivel, to catch her eyes again. Either she avoided me or I had imagined it, for she did not look in my direction again.

I sensed sharp eyes watching me with intensity and, unable to resist the temptation, turned to see Telamonius. He gave a thin smile, and I returned a stiff nod.

There was a great uproar of applause and the hall reverberated with the booming noise. The music stopped and Madhavi, her dance rendition over, bent low again and again to acknowledge the spontaneous and unrelenting cheers and shouts of congratulations. Some men stood up and tossed perfumed flower petals and coins—gold coins—at her feet. This enticed the entire assembly to rise. Distinguished men made fools of themselves, as their covert desires played out in overt displays of emotions. Some proclaimed their proposals and laughter followed shouts of:

Madhavi, Madhavi—Devi, marry me—Take me for your husband.

Other men copied these sentiments and similar calls carried around the deafening hall. Just as the clapping abated on one side, it picked up again along another wall and the rounds started again. There was so great a shower of gold coins thrown into the air, to land and spin at her feet, that it compelled an attendant to rush out bearing a parasol to protect her.

"Truly, the gods have blessed Madhavi with divine purpose," I said in a hoarse whisper into Anandan's ear. "For she is the quintessential practitioner of the arts."

"Buy her," said Anandan. "The king offers her to the highest bidder. For there is none here wealthier than you." His eyes gestured toward Telamonius. My gaze remained on Anandan, but my mind raced and turned over exciting possibilities.

Madhavi, hands clasped, bowed and disappeared behind the long flowing curtains hanging on the walls.

"Will she return?" I asked, surprised at the panic in my voice.

"No, but next comes the bidding and the world shall learn who will have the honour of becoming her new patron," said Anandan. And, as if having spied some disquiet, he added, "Enjoy the show, my dear friend, for I am sure my little sister, Kannagi, is fine." His misplaced concern only wrenched me with acute guilt.

"Perhaps our dear friend, Sir Kovalan, is enjoying himself even more than you know." This from the Greek. But I ignored the remark and the man.

The gruff master of ceremony brought down his sturdy staff on the wooden block at his feet. As the three sharp thumps sounded, people turned as one to the source. The great hall fell silent, save for a few murmurs. The large man, with robes that flowed to his feet, scanned the audience. Another thump of his massive staff and servant-girls appeared and collected the fallen coins.

"For those of you good sirs who have yet to summon your generosity, this is the last call to shower your appreciation."

A murmur of laughter rippled through the crowd. More coins flew into the air and landed near the girls.

56

With the last coin thrown and collected, the master of ceremony, after seeking the king's indulgence, summarised Madhavi's story. The king had nurtured the virginal maiden as his own daughter and brought her to maturity in the arts. It was now his duty and pleasure to welcome a patron protector to assume the great responsibility of furthering Tamilakam's art forms as personified by the peerless Lady Madhavi.

"Take her for your wife if," said the bearded man and stared hard at the eager faces following his every gesture, "if and only if, she so wishes. But by the King's Decree, you will not prevent her from practising and cultivating the arts. If you have the restraint to abide by these stipulations, step forward and make your petitions."

The biddings came fast, starting with a hundred gold sovereigns. Some men laughed and cried out in derision at the pitiful sum, but others rebuked them. But with every new bid, the stakes rose.

"Five thousand gold sovereigns!" The voice was shrill and accented.

Telamonius!

The great hall fell silent and a slow murmur rose; the recovering chitter of insects shocked into silence.

Arguments broke out, some questioning the Greek's credentials and wondering how this yavana would promote Tamil art. As voices rose and collapsed, the crowd's mood shifted, as did the ferocity in the rumble of voices. The master of ceremony's silence encouraged free rein of opinions. A yavana making a bid was unheard of and unexpected. Was there a Tamil to better the Greek's offer? The initial restraint evaporated, and the crowd gesticulated; their unruliness gained strength. The king and his consort remained stoic and expressionless.

"I am Telamonius, a Greek, yes," said the yavana, and his voice rose above the growing clamour, "but one who has lived and traded with and prospered from Tamilakam these two score years. And at age sixty-five, I know as much and even more than most men, worthy as you all are, gathered in this great hall, about Tamilakam's arts. I am husbanded to a Tamil maiden of the finest persuasion. I speak Tamil and can promote your arts in the Greek-speaking world, for peculiar as it might seem to some, I even speak Greek."

Muted laughter rose and snuffed out. Taking that for the crowd's approval, he added.

"Promoting Tamil art to the Greek world will be a prelude to even greater commercial opportunities for our two peoples. Am I unworthy of promoting Tamil arts?"

With the draw of a single breath, Telamonius debunked all the arguments boiling within the hearts and minds of his naysayers. Expecting the crowd's reaction, he had come rehearsed and prepared.

"If there remains anyone who feels my shadow will defile the purity of Madhavi, then let him step forward with coin heavier than mine," said the Greek.

With growing confidence and arrogance, he produced a large purse and shook it for all to hear. The Tamils muttered and whispered, but none stepped forth. Their hesitation stiffened the Greek and, flushed, he committed a colossal error of judgement. He veered from his script. He said,

"Now all the world knows the worth of a Tamil maiden's chastity."

There was a momentary silence, and then the crowd erupted with anger. Amidst the cacophony, demands for the Greek to forfeit his life were shrill and clear. A man standing behind slapped Telamonius' head, and he wheeled around, ready to defend himself. Other men, their demeanour threatening, stood up to approach the Greek.

"Halt! Halt, I say."

The master of ceremony thumped his staff. Some men hesitated, but others tugged at the sleeves of the Greeks, who had tightened into a knot. The master of ceremony shouted and thumped his staff, but made little impression.

I caught the eye of Anandan and he mouthed something, but the uproar drowned his words. People shoved and pushed, and some chairs toppled. Somewhere a conch blew; and fast, rhythmic steps approached the hall.

Attendants pulled aside the curtains and armed guards—with heavy swords hanging from leathered baldrics but shields held at the ready—clattered into the hall. The king's bodyguard cooled the ardour of belligerence in the men. The people smouldered, but for the moment the soldiers' presence restored order.

After the guards escorted Telamonius and his Greeks to the passage behind the curtains, renewed railing erupted in the hall.

"Silence! The king wishes to speak! Silence!" The master of ceremony thumped his staff, and, seeing the king stand up, the people acquiesced and quieted.

"Dear nobles, friends, and brothers of our Cholan nation," said Maha-Rajah Kari-Kaalan, and he gestured for peace. "Please, rest your feet and let us, as elders, resolve this unfortunate event of an otherwise pleasant evening. We find no fault in the yavana's petition for the mantle of Lady Madhavi's patronage." In a lowered and sad voice, the king said,

"Unfortunately, he has cast a slur on Tamilakam and on our women."

"For which he must die!"

No one knew from where the shout rang, but the call burgeoned throughout the gathering and elicited more demands for blood.

"Buy her," said Anandan.

My mouth went dry but, with every draw of breath, I grew excited with the prospect.

"Buy her, my friend, for only you have the strength."

I said no, my usual reaction to anything Anandan proposed, but already in my mind the sums stacked up: my share of inheritance, Kannagi's dowry.

"Decisions warped by emotions can never birth the best outcomes. Vex not just people. Embrace calm and good sense. The Greek will suffer to appear before the magistrates and allow justice full play," said the king, and he paused before continuing.

"Even if the Greek forfeits his life, and I pray such will not be the outcome, we will have to hand over Lady Madhavi to his house and inheritance. These rules are of our own making and ridiculed will we be if the pigmentation of one's skin dictates our justice, for even our gods are multi-hued from magnificent black to soft pink, and with all shades bridging the two. We can debate whether the Greek's beneficiaries would promote Tamil arts, but for now such questions remain for future conjecture; though the auguries do not bode well for Lady Madhavi to find fulfilment of her destiny on foreign shores. But then again, has destiny not already funnelled us to this juncture?"

"Her performance will draw hundreds, even thousands," said Anandan, and his hot breath discomforted my ear. "Did you see the gold collected at her feet?"

"What?" I said with quick irritation in my voice, my attention split between Anandan's urgent whispers and the king's steadfast words.

"Save Madhavi from the Greek, as that's what the king wishes," said Anandan. "Be recognised, for though he graced your wedding, he hardly took notice of you."

"Therefore, my good countrymen," said the king, "I shall hold the Greek's offer until a day; giving one of you, purebred by the soil and salt of our Cholan lands, time to step forth and redeem the honour of our Tamil women."

"How do I do that?" I asked in a confused daze. My mouth spoke even as my mind raced in all directions.

"Buy her, become her patron."

"With Kannagi ill, my time is not mine and what do I know about promoting the arts?" I spoke in a hurried whisper.

"Reward me a share of the takings and I will handle Madhavi's dance engagements."

Anandan had quick answers to my every objection, and my heart welcomed his rebuttals. He pressed his mouth to my ear and said,

"You seek new business and here the gods present you with a perfect opportunity. Grow not heavy with concern, my dear Kovalan, for I will help."

"I now ask you, kind sirs, beloved countrymen," said the king, and his words rose above the growing murmurs and reached the edges of the vast hall, "to retire beyond your thresholds and consider all that has happened here today. Seek the counsel of your wives and pray to the gods of your homes, and return with instruments and petitions to redeem our honour."

"You will help me?"

"Of course, my dear Kovalan, I will help you become a prominent personage of the realms."

"Now go," said the king, "and neither hurt nor hurl abuse on any Greek you meet on your way, for one man's impetuousness is not representative of his nation. Return in the morn with a generous heart and gentle news."

"Maha-Rajah!" I stood up and, shaking with trepidation, gulped deep and raised my voice. "Maha-Rajah. Maha-Rajah!"

The king, who had already helped the Queen Consort to her feet, stopped. The master of ceremony banged his staff and the swelling commotion subsided.

"Who calls the king? Step forward and show yourself," rang the commanding voice.

After several moments of hesitation, I stepped forward. Away from the cramped seats, I felt a sudden coolness in the air. But my knees wobbled and perspiration blistered all over my body. The master of ceremony gestured and, taking the cue, I walked to the foot of the royal dais, bowed low, and said,

"I am Kovalan, only son of Sir Masattuvan. My father is a grain merchant, pious before the gods, charitable to the unfortunate, loyal to the Cholan and righteous in all his dealings."

The royal couple reclaimed their seats, prompting the rest of the congregation to settle down too, leaving me standing alone and vulnerable to everyone's scrutiny.

"Yes, we and the Queen were honoured guests at your wedding," said the king. "And how is our good friend, your father, Sir Masattuvan?"

"My father is of good health, Maha-Rajah, and offers daily prayers of gratitude for the good fortune of your rule, for timely rains, and bountiful harvests."

"A true son of our Chola lands. He is not here today."

It was not a question and not an accusation, but a statement—the most dangerous kind. I said,

"No, my king."

The king smiled and in that tiny moment I detected, or perhaps deluded myself, a glint of approval sweep across his features.

"Let us hear your words, for your voice was shrill and urgent," said the king.

"Please forgive the impertinence of youth, my king."

The king waved away my apology and smiled, hinting that I get to the crux of whatever I wished to say.

"I wish to," I said, and paused for a deep breath and continued, "I wish to offer a petition better than the yavana's. I wish to take the responsibility of patronage to nurture and further Lady Madhavi's artistry."

"Masattuvan approves?"

"My father, when he hears of my decision, will be well pleased, my king."

"Yes, we are sure it will please him," said the king.

By now I had recovered my calm and was more perceptive, and detected disapproval in the king's voice. Perhaps he preferred the patron to be much older, one who would treat the beneficiary as a daughter rather than a—I dared not even think the thought.

"And how is your wife, the dear child Kannagi?"

It was the Queen Consort who posed the question. It was quite extraordinary for the public to hear her voice; a great honour, for people considered her the mother of all Cholan realms. But instead of jubilation, I felt a sharp prick. It was as if the queen was reminding me to tread with care, for I already had a wife.

"Resting at home, Maha Rani, for she has suffered a miscarriage. But the physicians are confident she will recover fully and quickly."

"She will need you now, more than ever," said the queen.

I understood the full import of her comment, but having rolled the dice in public, I resolved to see through the game, for failing to do so would shame me forever.

"I attend to my wife's every need and whims, my queen," I said, letting my annoyance feed my courage but was careful to keep my tone restrained. "It was her insistence that brought me to witness the debut of Lady Madhavi."

The queen's lips curved in a small smile, but her eyes did not dance with approval.

"With the king's approval," said the master of ceremony, and he bowed to the royal couple. Turning to me, he said, "Let us hear your bid, sir."

"My bid is six thousand gold sovereigns and lest there is another who would challenge, I am prepared to raise my offer to ten thousand."

A murmur of gasps and soft exclamations rippled through the assembly. The master of ceremony slammed his staff on the block and brought silence back to the great hall.

"This is no marketplace, sir, speak one price and say no more."

"Very well then, ten thousand gold sovereigns!"

I became patron and protector of Madhavi.

Later in the week, the king and his councillors, after taking care to weigh all matters of state and commercial interests, banished Telamonius, never to return to Tamilakam.

But that night, having rescued a Tamil maiden from a yavana's clutches and saved the dignity of Tamilakam, and enjoying the praise and flattery of well-wishers, I left the hall in a glow of well-being.

But my stomach churned and wild imaginations filled my mind. Pleading that my dear Kannagi was alone in the house and wishing to return to her without delay, I took my leave of Anandan and several newfound friends. Many of the men pressed gold coins into my palm to have the privilege of enjoying Madhavi's private dance renditions. Tormented by whispered petitions and pulled by my sleeves, I snatched my arms free and urged my carriage driver to make haste.

Reaching home, I found Kannagi asleep, so I took a cold bath from the deepest of the three wells and returned to bed, careful not to stir my dear wife. Before long, I woke and wanted relief, but could not bring myself to rouse Kannagi.

I sneaked into my private room and fondled myself and, as the shameful deed committed in the dark progressed, I imagined Madhavi pleasuring me. Madhavi! Not my dear Kannagi.

###

8: Kannagi's Error

My Athan succumbed to quick temper and spewed harsh words at our carriage driver and watchman. Once, he even uttered mean words to our servant-girls, and they broke into copious tears. What was the source of his ever-bubbling anger?

On our wedding night, when I sought to please him, he frowned with displeasure. Our tree climbing streaks, where he always wanted to win, and the *river incident*, where he thought my behaviour unbecoming, came to mind. *Remember.* And I recalled the words of my poor Chinnamma.

He is your lord, lover, and leader. Do not scare him, especially in matters of intimacy, for a man's ego is fragile. Do not expect him to please you. Your pleasure comes from seeing him satisfied.

I restrained myself and that won his approval. I would lay, pretending to be asleep and he enjoyed teasing and playing with my coyness. Chinnamma was right, and the first few weeks had been everything I had dreamed.

But in time, familiarity and routine crept into our lives, I supposed, and he would drop into bed, his angry sighs stifling our bedroom and shattering my peace. And sometimes he called out in the night, his voice edged.

"Are you asleep again?"

I would answer him in a gentle voice and drape an arm over his beautiful body, my fingers searching the magnificent mane on his chest. But he would shock me with violence and, after satisfying himself, roll over to sleep without even a tender kiss to seal our intimacy. On most nights, when he turned cold, I planted soft kisses on his back, but he would not yield. On other nights, I cried without a whisper, for I felt abandoned. After losing my babies, it grew worse and his rejections were hot skewers that thrust and twisted in my flesh.

Every morning, with new prayers promising renewed hope, I welcomed the bright day and chirping birds, but in the evening, the familiar disappointment revisited. My dear Athan wallowed in misery and pulled me into the whirlpool, and I struggled to stay afloat. He needed help and therefore I resorted to the one person who knew my Athan best: Anandan!

Actually, I did not wish to approach Anandan, as I did not approve of his addiction to harlotry and the debauched life he led. There was a time after our marriage, my Athan stopped calling on Anandan and did not even mention his name. Perhaps there had been some falling out between them. I did not pry, but was pleased.

But seeing my Athan's business ventures fail, I had relented and encouraged my husband to approach his friend for help. It was a decision blessed by the gods, for everything had turned out well on the business front.

After winning Madhavi's patronage, Anandan proved himself a shrewd steward, and our coffers filled. It surprised me that Anandan did not abuse his relationship with Madhavi. Neither did he dip into the till. He proved himself a reliable friend but also an enigmatic person. Perhaps he had much good within, but my fixation on his treatment of women had clouded my judgement. At my wit's end, I sent for him and, to my added surprise, he answered with a prompt visit.

"For now, I'm overseeing Madhavi's performing arts business, little sister," said Anandan. "And arranging dance programs and gathering guests; all good paying people."

"What then could ail my Athan's happiness, dear brother? I seem to know him less by the day." I scooped diced mangoes, jackfruit, and banana into a silver tumbler, and added cool fresh milk to the brim. "He does not even indulge in his songs, his one true passion. It has been weeks since he composed a verse. He does not sing anymore. The last song I heard him hum was his favourite and mine, one which has happy lyrics. But he sang in a soft voice, to himself. And it was in a sad tune."

"I harbour a suspicion and am guilty of the situation he finds himself in," said Anandan.

I offered him the tumbler of milk and *mukkani*, the three fruits, and said,

"Remove the void in your stomach, and the heat from your body, dear brother. So refreshed, share your suspicion, though I believe you are guilty of only doing the best for my dear Athan."

Anandan threw his head back and poured the thick sweet brew down his throat. He dabbed his lips with the tail of his turban and said,

"I've asked, no insisted, for Kovalan to take charge of the business."

"Take charge? But why, dear brother, will he not be lost without your help?"

"Kovalan rewards me handsomely for stewarding Madhavi's concerts, but I harboured an agenda, little sister, and shall confess. Now that I have enough savings, adventure beckons, for it has been a long-cherished dream to seek my fortune in faraway Araby. Perhaps my going away, a selfishness on my part, is the source of his unhappiness."

The news of Anandan's impending departure saddened me, for he had proven a dear and reliable feeding hand for Kovalan. But our friend too held dreams—and why not? We should not thwart his departure on our account, though Kovalan would miss Anandan's brash love and unstinting help; and I would miss his reassuring presence.

"He has to superintend the Madhavi business, but has yet to set foot in the dance hall."

"My Athan has not visited the dance hall? But why?"

"The dance hall is an annex to Madhavi's house and my dear friend exercises caution for fear of society's gossip," said Anandan. He paused, and I sensed there was more.

"And?"

"And, little sister, what might you think if he meets Madhavi, especially in privacy. She is but—"

"—a maiden who lives alone—"

"Yes."

"—but for her mother, Chitra-Vathi, and her maid servant, Vasantha-Mala."

"You're well-apprised, little sister, but some say Madhavi is a matchless beauty, and what of your fears?"

"I do not fear, for my Athan loves me dearly and is a righteous man."

"That he is, but his righteousness will move him to deny the petitions of men and corner him into unpopularity, little sister."

"What petitions, my dear brother?"

"Petitions of the kind a brother cannot discuss with a sister."

"You speak in riddles, dear brother. Trust me enough, please, and speak plainly."

"Kovalan views Madhavi as an artist worthy to behold, but most men who come to the dance hall view her only as a beautiful object."

"Say no more, elder brother, and accept my apologies for my dull approach in pressing you into such a corner. I am a silly woman judging the world from a woman's view. I forget there is a man's view too. Is that why my dear Athan avoids the dance hall, as he does not wish to confront these uncouth petitions which he will surely decline?"

"Kovalan's absence, which I encouraged until now, draws instead of driving away eager guests who fill the coffers, for the lion's lack of interest emboldens scavengers. With his presence, and their petitions turned down, there might be a substantial decline in earnings. That would compel Kovalan to make good the shortfall from his private purse."

"That was shrewd of you, brother, but was it righteous to lead men on by offering them false promises? As for money, my dear husband has a generous heart and will put coin to cost to help Madhavi realise her art to greater heights."

"You speak of righteousness, my dear little sister. We've known one another since our childhood, and you know I've no need to prove anything. Society embraces you when you're up, but even your shadow will step on you when you're down. I've no desire to attain the unreachable ideal which righteous men spew but don't practise; no need for righteous living, for I'm already living and it's enough."

Anandan's words silenced me, for he had spoken from the heart. It was not for me to judge him. He was right for now. Perhaps in time, with more love, varied experiences, and reflection, he would realise there is a greater right. And thinking perhaps to right away set him on the straight and mundane, I said,

"Marry the chaste Madhavi. Stop all amorous petitioners. She will be your beautiful wife and avoid public stage. My dear Athan saved her once from the clutches of men. You save her from the curse of the devadasi."

Anandan threw his head back and laughed. He did not laugh at me, but at himself.

"You love me as your dear brother and, therefore, overlook my wayward ways. But I'm no man of destiny. I am but a mere man-servant who tosses the spear to the hero who destroys the demon and gains immortality. And no one will recall the servant's timely intervention."

"You speak poorly of yourself, my dear brother. If what I hear about Madhavi is true, she will transform you into a man worthy, which you already are but have yet to recognise."

"But first she must *choose* to husband me. For you see, Kari-Kaalan has decreed she can select any man for a husband, but no man can impose on her. Once selected, no man shall reject her. And even if she desires a celibate holy man, and he dares scorn her choice, he will do so under pain of losing his head."

"I have decided. She will choose you before some shrivelled *sannyasi* appears."

When he heard my words, Anandan laughed and so did I. It was a strange feeling—to laugh—and I realised how much misery had taken me for his constant companion. But it was not the time to dwell on my wretchedness, and so I said,

"I will help Madhavi see you for what you truly are—a good man and my esteemed brother; and will speak to her as one woman to another woman."

"I'm not a marrying-man, little sister," said Anandan, and he laughed again. "My eyes dance when they spy a comely maiden and my head enjoys resting in the soft pearl-adorned bosoms of strange beauties. My vigour will cause grief to Madhavi or to any woman cursed enough to marry me. Would this be well-done by your elder brother? And will you, dear sister, spew into Madhavi's ears rootless embellishments? So, you see, perhaps in the twisted abhorrent life I pursue, I too am shadowing the path of righteousness. I deny innocent women my infidelity."

And he laughed ever more, and that made me feel guilty, for I had misjudged him again. Perhaps he was a good man and like all men, he had his weaknesses but, unlike most, made no pretences. I could sense the flickering flame of dharma living deep within him.

"There's something more troubling you. What is it?" said Anandan. "Come now, treat me as a brother, please."

He was right and, after some hesitation on my part and further encouragement from him, I was truthful; confessed my fears. I said,

"I trust Kovalan's correct living but also harbour a wife's reservations. Madhavi has such renowned charms, and a foolish woman's fears bubble within me."

"Let me bury your fears, little sister. Ordinarily, I would not share these secrets of men, but this fear of yours is reasonable and requires routing. In matters of harlotry, perhaps I know your husband better. On many occasions, I sought to tempt Kovalan with easy servant-girls and even brought him to whorehouses. He will not set foot in houses of ill-repute and not succumb to the easy charms of willing maidens. Instead, he always fought my wily attempts by evoking your name and his unshakeable love for you. And when I pressed, he found quarrel and even broke ties with me.

"Trust me, little sister, if I had found a flaw in his chaste armour, I would not have encouraged him to acquire Madhavi's patronage, or now suggest he steward the venture. For Kovalan and you are my friends—my only true friends—and I will promote nothing to hurt you. Kovalan beholds Madhavi as a gifted artist and a business venture, an opportunity for Tamilakam's arts to flourish to greater heights. I am poor even in this aspect, for I view her as a mere plough that provides plentiful produce. For him, the money is only a validation of his business acumen. It is the arts he wishes to promote."

"You tempted my dear Athan with harlots? How could you do this to him and to me?"

"You are right. I tempted him and perhaps risked your happiness. I was impetuous and wanted him to indulge as I did. But he is a far better man than I can hope to become. Looking back, I wonder whether I can blame fate for having guided my actions. For now, I ask, is a swami who recluses himself on a lonely mountain superior in purity to one who lives among whores but remains untouched by debauchery? Just as Lady Sita, commanded by her husband Lord Rama, entered the fires that shrunk in fear of her, Kovalan too bathed in flames and emerged pure. And for this test, I take undeserved credit, for it was not a result I expected. You have nothing to fear from Madhavi or any other apsara maiden."

"Please forgive me, elder brother, for doubting your intentions. You indeed know the full measure of the good and purity in my dear Athan."

"So, my dear little sister Kannagi, will you entreat upon your good husband to pay Madhavi a visit? Impress upon him your thoughts that her hair is black and shiny, and not a tangle of serpents; her beauty is to be relished and not ravaged; and her art is to be admired by decent men such as her patron and not parleyed for anything less. Once satisfied that you harbour no fears or questions regarding his love for you, he will embrace the stewardship of his business. He will reject the petitions of these foul men and so drive them away, for they are cane squeezed dry of sugar; and in their stead, welcome men of honour to the dance hall who, even now, stay away for fear of being tainted by the company of these others."

"Your words are correct and perhaps it is just as well my dear Athan steers his ship."

"It's agreed then. Good. If I might suggest, there is no dance event this evening, and it is Madhavi's rest day. He can go to her house and return in peace."

"I will ask him to invite Madhavi to our house as a welcomed guest and my dear Athan will never deny me, and on the day of her visit, you must join us too, as an honoured friend and elder brother."

"Careful, my dear little sister, for you might become, before your time, an old aunty trying to arrange a marriage liaison." And when he laughed, I joined in the laughter too.

After Anandan departed, I reflected on his visit. I had wronged him and that day I knew I had a genuine friend; a true brother. Anandan lived a strange life. Perhaps such are the ways of people born into poverty but strive to acquire a small measure of wealth.

I also recalled the laughter released in my house. Anandan had left behind some joy. For that, I was grateful. I resolved to help my dear poor Athan rediscover his zest for life and rekindle new joy in our hearts and hearth.

But when I suggested he visit Madhavi and see to her needs, my dear Athan proved reluctant. The poor upright man. He feared rousing my suspicion, for Madhavi was an acclaimed beauty. I had to press him with arguments, drawn from reason and his responsibility, before he agreed.

I stood at the threshold and bade him a safe journey. But as his horse carriage set off, I felt an unexplainable and fleeting pin-prick in my heart. What have I done?

###

9: Madhavi's Soft Scented Folds

The horses, their bells chiming, turned onto the soft sand covered street, and the white-washed wall surrounding Madhavi's mansion came into view.

"Tree House." Anandan had said. "Madhavi refers to her dwelling as Tree House."

I sat behind the driver and cowered under a shawl from the prying eyes of the people on the street. My face flushed with embarrassment and heart thumped with guilt as if my innermost desires were transparent for all to see.

My dear wife Kannagi had encouraged the visit to Madhavi and, protesting with reasons which grew ever weaker but in secret yearning to go, I relented; convinced that destiny has decided.

"I will be back soon," I said, and felt a strange unease. Seeing Kannagi's absolute trust, I asked her again, knowing the unfairness of the imposition, to accompany me. And I felt relieved but shame when she replied,

"I am drained and weak, Athan, and the physician suggested I need to rest."

***

From where I stood, the balcony was in full view and Madhavi was looking out, with her back to me. She remained still, as if in some deep contemplation. Not wanting to intrude into her privacy, I held back. I could not see her face, did not know her, and yet she cut a figure of loneliness.

A lovely body-hugging sari, shimmering silk with plenty of sequins, wrapped her, exposing smooth flesh at the waist and shoulders. Though I loved the richness of silk, I cared little for sequins, for they were tawdry and lent an air of frivolity to the wearer. But not on Madhavi. Or perhaps, as with most men in a similar situation, I lowered my values; adjusted my standard. On her, the sequins looked just right, or so I concluded, bringing out an allure of beauty that at once drew but also cautioned.

I was a male mantis, compelled to trade one encounter for life itself. I stepped back, wanting to flee. But my legs refused to move. My heart took control of my head. Though she continued to gaze out at the night sky, she had sensed my presence. And I welcomed the fatal attraction. I waited, and my feet became my accomplice and did not bear me away.

Madhavi turned, her deep-lined eyes darting from one small imaginary spot to another until they landed on me. I swallowed hard and felt the lump travel up and down my throat. I cursed the gods for having rendered men transparent—be it the moving apple in the throat or an aroused lingam.

We stood so; our eyes locked. I recognised the visual embrace I had felt that fateful day in the royal hall. I waited for her to say something or to come forward to greet her guest, her patron. She remained still but for a full-faced and welcoming smile.

My feet moved forward, driven by the desire welling from the depths of my heart and the twitch of my loins. Her smile, confident but also streaked with submissiveness, sucked my life. The breeze brushed past her and carried her scent, warm and sweet, to my eager, flaring nostrils.

When we were at an arm's length, Madhavi went down on her knees and touched my feet. Her hands sent a delightful shiver up to my head. She waited, folded low and hands covering my feet. I placed my trembling fingers on her shoulders and she rose on firm muscles, her movement fluid as though choreographed to perfection.

"You kept me waiting, my lord," she said, and smiled.

Her words stirred but, I refused to parry; though I wanted to say something rude. And her smile, innocent and trusting, robbed my hard thoughts.

"I dreamt with joy last night for my gallant, and today you have come and given me new life," she said. Tears glistened in the pools of her eyes. When I did not respond, some fear clouded her face.

"If you feel your presence here is a mistake, go, my lord, leave me. If fate decides that you win my trust but betray my hope, go, and breathe life to the written words."

"What terrible life have you lived, woman, to utter these strong words to your patron, who wishes you well?" My voice sounded strange and detached, rude and quite unlike me.

"You live a charmed life, my lord, one I have no part in and it be the best not sullied by tales of my sorrow."

"I see before me a young, talented, and beautiful maiden brimming with life and future. What sorrow dares befriend and spoil your happiness? Share with me your woes and perhaps I might have a salve."

My words brought out her smile and, wiping the tears threatening to spill, she said,

"Please, my lord, forgive my poor manners." She stretched out her hands in the gesture of welcome. "Let me offer you some refreshments of sweet wine so my sour matters will fall less heavily on your ears."

"And tell me, why do you call your abode Tree House?" I tried to sound casual, choosing a safe topic to start over.

"It's a silly girl's habit, my lord," she said. "Tree House, because it evokes many fond memories of my childhood."

"Child's play?"

"An uncle built a tree house once, and I spent many happy hours in it, imagining myself a princess and with dashing princes of the realms vying for my hand."

"And did they come, your princes?"

"One prince did, and he has come today."

Embarrassed, I looked away and, seeking a distraction, my eyes settled on a child's doll; its paint worn by many years of play.

"Ah, you found Seema, the first gift I received from my uncle. Seema is my dear friend who never hurts or quarrels or competes with me. You may think me silly, my lord, but I am an only child and by giving names to little things, I surround myself with little friends. They make life less lonely. Here is Seema's companion, Ranjan." The face on the second doll was identical to the first, save for a thickly painted moustache. She picked up another toy, a wooden carving of a prancing horse. "I call him Velan."

"The same uncle?"

"No, another. I recall when growing up I had many uncles, all such lovely men. They always brought gifts when they came to discuss matters with my mother."

"Where are they, your uncles, for I have yet to have the pleasure of meeting them?"

"Oh, as I grew older, they all went away."

"That's sad. But why, where?"

"I don't know, but my mother said it was not appropriate, especially as I had grown into a maiden."

"I don't understand."

"Forgive me, my lord, but let's not dwell on old cobwebbed things, for they bore. Let us discuss instead your happy visit."

"There is nothing wonderful to discuss, for I came only to ensure you were well. And now my dear wife, Kannagi, waits and I must take my leave."

The name of my chaste wife was a balm for my fevered mind. I thanked Kannagi for being with me in spirit and giving strength that few men could muster when confronted with such an alluring goddess. I rose to leave.

"Can I receive a wish from you, my lord, before you leave?"

"If it is within my means to grant, yes." I remained standing, confident that when the time came, my feet would bear me away.

"Allow me, my lord, to offer you the hospitality of some poor fare for nourishment before you set off."

"The time is late."

"It is our custom, my lord, is it not, to offer at least some sweets and drinks to a guest?"

"Very well then, I will have some water, please." My mind spun and my legs wanted to bend and set me down. What magic holds me here, I wondered.

Madhavi gave a sharp clap of her hands and a maid-servant who went by the name of Vasantha-Mala, her anklet jingling a rough melody, arrived with a tray of drinks and dried fruits. Madhavi offered me a cup, and I tasted the drink.

"It is not water you offer."

"Honour me, my lord, it is wine I selected."

"And what other skills do you hide?"

"I am a poor working girl, my lord, but stay a moment longer and I shall reveal what little more I possess." She clapped her hands again and her maid-servant brought a veena.

"You play music too."

"Poorly, my lord, and forgive any missteps."

Settling herself on a circular divan, Madhavi strummed a haunting tune on the stringed instrument, evoking some yearning of years slipped by.

I listened, mesmerised. She offered me another cup of wine and also some salted fruits. The salt was a draw and soon my hand reached for the tray as she played more music.

"Join me, my lord, please. I have been working on this piece of music for quite some time now, but lack the verses to enrich it. Perhaps you can help."

She played the music again and, requiring no further encouragement, I broke into song, fitting to the beat. Together we finished the short but beautiful song. She played another piece of music and again, I crafted some spontaneous lyrics. She played yet another piece, and I matched her music with more lines of poetry. There was a hint of competition and I rose to the challenge. After each song, she replenished my goblet, and I drained every refill. Intermingled with the songs, she weaved questions that birthed responses from me.

"Name a bloom that does not need a bee to pollinate and never fades in beauty."

"The smile that blossoms on the lips of a chaste maiden for the private enjoyment of her husband," I said. And so, the questions flew fast and teased, and I quite enjoyed the challenge.

"Bards spew paeans of praise on women of delicate beauty thus: Having created thee, Lord Brahma broke the mould. With so many moulds shattered, beauties are as common as rainbows. Is there a better beauty, my lord?" She leaned forward with a gentle smile, and I took but a moment and sang my reply.

"The Lord Brahma by his hands fashioned you, oh maiden of matchless beauty, and he then stooped to wash his hands in pristine waters. And from the flecks of his fingers sprang all other beauties of the world; rainbows included."

Hearing my words, Madhavi clapped. She behaved like a joyous child who had received a novel gift. And her unbridled joy swelled my happiness.

There were more challenges and teases, and they brought back forgotten memories of my youth, the little dares, and fights even, which I so enjoyed with Kannagi. How much I missed my Kannagi, the person I once knew and loved. I smiled, a sad smile, to myself.

"My lord."

"Yes?" I was back in Tree House.

Madhavi offered a cup of wine, and another, and some more. And the wine was sweet too. I grew intoxicated and fell into a blissful sleep. When I woke, it was already in the late hours of the night.

Resting on Madhavi's bed, it took a few lazy moments before I realised, I was undressed; naked. She was lying beside me asleep; unclothed. The kumkuma on her forehead had smeared. My chest betrayed streaks of the pink powder from her pearl-adorned breasts. Horrified by my transgression, I bolted out of bed and pulled on my vestments.

Madhavi awoke. I expected nothing but anger and outrage from her. Instead, perching herself on an elbow, she gave me a beautiful smile. Her behaviour shocked and confused, and I looked away. But felt my eyes pulled back to her full round breasts. I apologised for staring and again looked away; did not know what to say, what to do. I had committed such a gross violation, but had no memory, and her next words confounded and frightened.

"We've not done anything but as expected of normal married couples."

"Married?"

"My lord, you placed a garland around my neck."

I was speechless and mumbled words of apology and innocence. She reached out, her movement swift, pulled me to her, and pressed her lips to mine. I backed away, but she persisted. Her lips fed ambrosia, and I capitulated.

I wanted to, tried to, call out Kannagi's name, but the words stuck in my throat. And with every passing moment, I grew intoxicated as her wet lips clamped over my mouth and her tongue searched within.

With a strength of will I did not know I possessed, I grabbed a fistful of hair and wrenched her head back. She held my eyes in those half-closed windows of hers, her wet red lips parted and inviting assault.

I was on the verge of pulling away when my eyes took a second look and my lips crushed hers. We became two desperate swimmers fighting the white waters, gasping and kissing, and twisting into the unruly sheets.

"No!" With a great shout, I pushed her away and stood up, my chest heaving for breath. "No, this is not right."

"I chose you for my husband the day my eyes settled on you in the king's great hall."

"You watched the bidding, from behind the curtains?"

My voice was careless, as I looked left and right, as if searching for a misplaced article of clothing. I had to keep busy, for my eyes and limbs had minds of their own.

"No, even before the bidding," she said. "Our eyes met when I was performing. Do you not recall? I saw you and you saw me."

"Yes, I recall the moment."

"What troubles you, my lord?"

She stood close, letting her warm scent tease my senses. She searched my eyes, as if besotted, and made me feel I was the centre of her universe. Her lips came close, but I turned away, and she planted a petal soft kiss on my blushing cheek. My legs refused to budge, and all my limbs froze. Her head rested on my sweaty chest and a finger traced a circle around my nipple.

She was smooth and knew how to arouse me in ways I had never experienced. I recalled the incident in Anandan's storehouse and the servant-girl working her magic on my friend. I knew now what he must have experienced, but this was pure—and felt right. Madhavi, the angelic maiden men would die for, was the aggressor, the huntress. She gave me a thrill, which I admitted without shame I had never received from Kannagi.

Madhavi's newness, freshness, and boldness trapped me in warm sweaty embraces. Possessed, I was ready to trade my life for this one encounter. We fell on the bed and pleasured one another.

The night grew longer, and the watch cried out the advancing hours. I cursed time, willing it to slow its relentless pace.

But dawn invaded and, exhausted, I fell into a deep satisfying sleep, promising myself I would awake soon enough—but did not.

It was past noon before we awoke and had a late lunch in the bedchamber. After which, we returned to pleasuring one another.

The thought of Kannagi was always in the back of my mind. But every time guilt took hold, a small voice reminded me of the misery encountered in that house and I felt justified. There was nothing in that house but fervent prayers, outlandish rituals, and tears; and fasting, which wrecked me with guilt and prevented me from enjoying even a simple meal. And when we had physical intimacy, she made me feel as if I was a violator.

These were all gross exaggerations, but they lent a seductive advocacy exonerating my continued coupling with Madhavi. This goddess of erotica. This goddess of love.

It was late after sunset and when Madhavi and I were again replenishing our strength over a meal, small talk, dangerous talk, wandered here and there.

"You are kind, my lord, but also reserved, for you disapprove of what I do."

"I do not disapprove of your dancing. It is a beautiful art and of great divinity, it condenses the essence of our culture and civilisation, and conveys value and worth."

"You disapprove of my dancing in the public eye, my lord, but I enjoy performing for crowds of eager audiences. These people—accomplished in their own arts and fields of endeavours, famed for their power and wealth and god-given talents—appreciate the nuances of my gestures and poses. They're my peers, no, they're my masters, and it gives me great pleasure to invite their plaudits."

"So, you believe your life is more favoured when famous people fawn on you?"

"Yes, my lord, it's the curse of my art, the curse of my femininity, for my art will flourish hand-in-hand with my youth. But when age burdens me with her company, I will lose my admirers, for finite is the number of times the curtain rises for one in my position."

"Break the curse then and let one in your admiring throng take you for a wife. Dance only for his pleasure. The praises of your husband are worth more than all the accolades placed at your feet by strangers."

"Take me then, my lord, declare me your wife and I will dedicate myself and my art for your pleasure alone."

She held my hands tight and close to her chest. Her eyes pleaded, desperate with desire and dreams. I tore my eyes away from her and said,

"I must take my leave, Lady Madhavi, for my dear wife, Kannagi, waits anxiously at the threshold for my return."

"And what is to become of me, my lord, for are we not married?"

"And so, you claim again, but who bears witness to this matrimony which even I do not recall? We enjoyed ourselves as lovers, and as lovers we shall remain, if you so wish. But for the rest, did I not rescue you from the slimy Greek old enough to be your grandfather and save your honour, and the Cholan's as well?"

"You saved me from fate and already revelled in the public accolades of the people, and the private rewards of my body."

"Did I entice you with false promises?"

"Are you treating me as a whore, my lord?"

"How can you utter such crass words, especially after we shared so much wonder in so little a time?"

"We shared much, true my lord, and I wish to build a roof with you."

"You ensconce well under the roof of your mother, Chitra-Vathi, and with servants to attend to your every need."

"You embrace my words but ignore their meanings, and the woman you speak of is no mother but a fiend, and my servants are but my jailors."

"Fiend? Jailors? Truly you speak in riddles and I tire of your games, for the day is late and I have not bathed or offered my prayers, as is my practice."

"My lord, please listen, I beg you, and listen with intent, for the woman, Chitra-Vathi, who masquerades as my mother, will sell me to the highest bidder. I am an orphan who knows not my bloodline. She has nurtured me for a single purpose: to profit from my beauty and the practise of my godly arts."

"Then I shall directly go to King Kari-Kaalan and petition him to stop this travesty. Fear not, Madhavi, for all shall be well."

"There's no need to speak to the king and sully his peace, my lord, for by his decree I've already embraced you as husband and we consummated our marriage. You're now not only my patron and protector but also my husband."

"Enough!" Then, in a gentler voice, I said, "Send me off with a smile, if not a kiss, and I shall retrace my steps back to you. I cannot another night leave my fragile wife alone to face her demons."

"But is my honour not as fragile as a butterfly's powdery wings? When you rescued me from the Greek, my lord, did you not know your obligations? Am I a mere chattel?"

"Madhavi, your words are powerful and pierce my heart, but I also know that you are well-versed in the ways of argument. You will not move me. Please step aside, for I must now vacate this place."

I rose and did not hide my growing resolve, nor the tremor of anger in my voice.

"My lord, your wife Kannagi knows you're held to your obligations, for did you not say it was with her blessings you arrived? I implore you to stay this night too, and in the morning if your wife's vision calls, depart freely and turn back not to see this poor wretch."

"If I remain until another sunrise, then surely my dear Kannagi will keep her doors bolted."

"Then at her feet I'll seek forgiveness and swallow all blame and pride, and even poison, if she so prefers. Stay until another sunrise, my lord, and when the time comes for you to depart, go; and if you do not, I will myself bring you by the hand."

Years ago, when Anandan enticed with the offer of his servant-girls, the thought of Kannagi gave me resolve, and now in silence I again begged my wife to help resist this temptress.

But the more my feet dallied, the stronger grew the allure of Madhavi's bed. I relented—no—capitulated to her spell and fell over the cliff. But a desperate hope made me cling to a blade of grass even as a long-toothed rat gnawed away my resolve.

"Very well, Madhavi, for this one night more I shall enjoy your hospitality but in solitude, for truly the devil's drink has muddled my mind, and the night has conspired and turned late.

Prepare for me a chamber in some quiet corner of the house and I shall spend the night in prayer until sleep tricks me to slumber."

"Why do you treat me so poorly, my lord? Your words tear me asunder as they spew judgements already made regarding my chastity. Is this dharma?"

"Enough! It will be as I say or not at all."

"I am a poor girl with no recourse, my lord, and so it shall be as you say."

That night, I prayed, telling myself that if I could but survive the night in seclusion, I would have broken her spell, for she had indeed worked well some magic. But alas, the breeze too had its agenda and made the curtain billow and bring soft music to my ears.

Before long, my feet carried me along the petal-strewn corridor to Madhavi's lamp-lit chamber. Her door, no more than dancing drapes, was inviting. My hand pulled the curtain aside, and I caught whiffs of margosa and white mustard wafting past to ward off evil spirits, and also sweet incense to titillate the senses.

I beheld the goddess of erotica reclining on her bed, one knee raised and a hand behind her head, her eyes closed. Her shaven armpit, a clean smooth mound, set my heart thumping loud. It reminded me of more erotic secrets within the hood of her pubis, which whispered promises of blissful pleasure.

As I stood feasting with my eyes, a song escaped my lips. She heard me and, opening her eyes, smiled and held out inviting arms. In a slow and smooth movement, I allowed myself into her embrace and buried my face in her armpit. My tongue slipped out and relished her taste, and she sang her moans even as her fingers searched.

And so, it was with us that day and for many more days thereafter.

My time with Madhavi flew past at a dizzying pace, and days melded into weeks, and weeks into months and a year or more passed. In my pensive moments, the thought of Kannagi surfaced and drove me to dark corners of the house and crevices of my guilt. But again, and again, Madhavi drew me to the sanctuary of her soft, scented folds.

###

10: Attempt at Reconciliation

Anandan came to Tree House with news of his long-delayed journey to Araby.

"I'm sure you'll return a fabulously wealthy man and make a worthy maiden happy as your wife," I said.

"Well, one never knows what the bend in the path brings, dear friend Kovalan," said Anandan, and he laughed. "But for now, I shall journey to the Araby deserts and taste their sweet dates, those hanging from trees and hiding behind veils."

"Could you, Anandan Sir, grant me a favour?" asked Madhavi. "A hope cherished and dear to my heart. I hesitate, for you have already done much for me and my art."

"Speak your mind, Lady Madhavi."

"Please convey my invitation to elder sister Kannagi to visit Tree House, to receive a respectful welcome with all proper formalities. It is past overdue and I yearn for us to meet."

Madhavi expressing her wish to meet Kannagi, without consulting me, shocked and annoyed. But I hid my misgivings and let matters take their course.

Anandan, who had sensed my disquiet, said, "As she is your elder sister, as you yourself just now acknowledged, should you not be the one calling on her?"

"I fear for my reception, but inform elder sister Kannagi that my need is a mere pin's head space in the lowest realms of her big heart and I shall gladly take a distant second to her, who is and will always remain the first wife."

"You've chosen your messenger shrewdly," said Anandan, "for I love her as my dear sister, and shall do my best to entreat her with all suitable words of reason and rally. I have mustered my caravan for an early departure, but shall call on my dear sister Kannagi in the morning and send word back to you by runner."

"Trouble not your help, Anandan Sir," said Madhavi, "I shall despatch my servant, the well-trusted Vasantha-Mala, whom you're already well-acquainted with, to arrive at your doorstep before the cock crows. Take her with you and let her be the bearer of good news."

"A good plan it is. As you wish, Lady Madhavi."

We also spoke at length regarding Anandan's long journey, but I remained distracted and did not engage in his ventures.

I harboured disappointment that Madhavi had embarked on so great a potential change in our lives without my full acquiescence, and even as I faulted her judgement, my heart fluttered with hope. Reconciliation with my dear Kannagi would unload an enormous burden in my heart, rendered as it was by guilt and shame. I wanted for us—all three of us—to join as one.

And with Anandan's departure, my heart thumped. What news my dear Kannagi would send back, I wondered. And throughout the night, as I floated in a shallow stream of rocky sleep, dozens of eventualities filled my fevered mind.

***

Anandan poured honeyed water on my parched heart and I hugged the brass lamp he conveyed. It was an auspicious gift, selected with love and blessed by my Athan Kovalan, reported Anandan. My fingers glided over every part of its tall stem and broad oil skirt, relishing the thought of my husband's hands having touched the same spots.

"Surrounded by fabulous wealth, you continue to lead an austere life, my dear little sister Kannagi, keeping the fast and offering prayer and penance. And the good news is, Madhavi awaits your coming and stands ready at her threshold to welcome you with all suitable protocols of respect. She yearns to relinquish the right hand of your husband's seat and live in your shadow, to come and go as you will and wish. By Madhavi's own words, which I repeat: *Inform my exemplary elder sister, I seek but only a tiny tenement in the far corner along the rear fence beside the cow shed.*"

"She is a woman of such great virtue, and yet she has taken my husband from me," I said.

"It is Kovalan who shies and stays away, out of shame for the great betrayal vested upon you, but secretly, he wishes the better reconciliation."

"Then speak not harsh judgement, my brother, for he is my husband and incapable of betrayal, even if the exuberance of his virility has caused some mischief. We wedded with blessings from the holy fire and witnessed by the elders of our land. Our union is a seed sown to flourish a thousand years."

"Should I then send word and tell them to expect you?"

"Yes, with all my heart, yes." I exclaimed and felt even more joy than the day my Kovalan took me for his wife.

Anandan hesitated. He was shrewd; after allowing a taste, he held back the honey jar.

"Even though, as the younger, is it not only proper for Madhavi to call on your feet?"

"It is my husband I go to meet, my dear brother, and let him introduce her as spouse, partner or less, as he so wishes."

"Yet it is her house, and what will people say when they hear of her generosity?"

"It is *my* generosity people will see, but there is no contest here and my dear Kovalan is no trophy. I go to reclaim what is already mine."

"True, but there might be one or two who might say it was you who had gone begging and banished Madhavi to a spot no larger than a pin's head in her own home."

"Who speaks these untruths?"

"For one, her mother, Chitra-Vathi. I've not seen more venomous snakes. And this one, even when stripped of skin and dried moisture-less under the sun, will strike with venom more potent than the king of cobras. Perhaps, if your husband himself were to invite and escort you by hand for all to see, you achieve the same end but with better dignity."

"My dignity comes from going to my husband when he calls and this holy oil lamp is proof enough of his summons. Should I be so heartless as to cause my dear Athan to make the journey instead, for others to witness him come begging? Is his wish not my command? And as for the snakes, I shall embrace them to my heart and chase away their demons, for no creature is born evil."

Anandan called and the maid-servant, whom he had introduced as Vasantha-Mala, trusted of Madhavi, entered. Then he paused with some new thought; spoke in riddles, something new, for he had always revealed the plain streak.

"Did Kovalan not walk up the steps of your father's house, little sister, and cross the threshold when he came to ask for your hand in marriage? I recall it was a grand occasion accompanied by the blare of trumpets and beat of drums and chants of holy men."

"Yes, he came calling but I struggle to see what your question signifies, for now he is already my husband."

"Indulge me, little sister, and pray tell, what then followed his visit?"

"Why, much water flowed and as tributaries converging to the great life-giving Kaveri River, his visit culminated in our marriage and gave me new life with my Athan."

"Well said, and so, once again, you stand at the threshold of a new, albeit renewed life, with your dear Athan. How then can it be onerous upon him to come here and once again cross your threshold to take you by hand? This time also, as before, for all to witness."

Anandan did not approve of Kovalan taking up with Madhavi. Perhaps he blamed himself for the part he had played.

For myself, I wished to join my dear husband, and if it meant only another day's delay, it was well and good, for I would not let the time go to waste. I will use it to bathe in scented water, straighten and braid my tangled hair and adorn it with his favourite blooms, and wear garments and gold to please my husband. And I also appreciated Anandan's intentions for wanting to exact a small penalty from my Athan, a paltry price I would more than make good with my unquestioning acceptance of whatever arrangements he wished.

"You are a loyal friend and dear brother, and I shall abide by your suggestion."

Anandan turned to the maid-servant, Vasantha-Mala, and repeated his message, and had the woman recite back, to remove any doubts from the words or their tone.

"Wait," I said to the maid-servant and gave her a small purse of gold coins as payment for the errand.

"Thank you for your generosity, Lady Kannagi," said the maid-servant.

"Go now, and lose not a moment to relay the message," said Anandan.

He then sent the woman off, giving stern instructions to the bullock cart driver to coax the animals for haste. Having discharged his responsibility, my dear brother Anandan bowed with hands clasped.

Driven by sudden remorse, I fell at his feet and sought forgiveness. Anandan, taken aback, placed his finger tips on my shoulders and brought me up to my feet.

"What have you done, dear little sister, for you to seek forgiveness from me? You have always treated me as a dear friend and also with utmost respect as an elder brother."

"I have thought poorly of you, dear elder brother, and even blamed you for my Athan having left me for Madhavi. You brought her into our lives and even encouraged my Athan to go visit her. I hated you for placing a flame beside a cotton ball."

"We think alike, little sister," said Anandan with a heavy voice, "and every waking moment, I blame myself for the rift separating you and Kovalan. True, I was the wedge. Kovalan's return will dislodge the chock, but the scar will remain. I am the culprit for having smeared the artistry of your love, and it is I who should seek your forgiveness."

Then, he smiled a sad smile, and took his leave.

As his back receded down the path, a great pain crushed my chest. How could I place the blame on him? As I had, he too had trusted Kovalan's righteousness. As I had, he too had not suspected Kovalan's weakness. But unlike me, he took the blame upon himself. If, as a wife, I did not know my husband's frailties, how could I demand more from Anandan, even though he is a true friend, but a mere friend no less?

Anandan's journey to Araby promised to be perilous, and I wondered whether we would meet again. We must, so I could make amends. Alas, here I was, again thinking only of myself.

***

I completed my morning ablutions with haste and, even before partaking in the warm milk prepared by Madhavi, climbed the stairs and waited on the roof terrace. The vantage point gave me an unrestricted view of the neighbourhood. In the near distance, the towering *gopurams*, gateways, of many temples punched the skies above Puhar, but for once, these held no interest for me.

The sun grew warmer by the moment, and I knew Anandan would have already departed with his caravan.

The maid-servant, Vasantha-Mala, was due to return soon. I squeezed my knees together as my full bladder added to my anxiety.

Taking a long look at the street and catching no sight of the carriage, I went downstairs. On the way back, I stopped to remind a serving-man to direct the maid-servant to my presence the moment she arrived.

"But sir," said the man, removing his loose turban and tucking the cloth under an arm as a mark of respect, "Amah Vasantha returned many moments ago."

"Where is she?" I asked through clenched teeth, trying to stifle my outrage.

"With Periya Amah, sir."

"Who?" I snapped. I knew who he meant by big mother but wished to show my disdain and diminish the old woman's standing.

"Periya Amah Chitra-Vathi, sir," replied the servant, his voice now trembling.

"Enough! Seek the servant Vasantha-Mala and tell her to come to me right away. Go!"

Bowing several times, the man hurried off. Once out of my sight, I heard him shout.

"Amah Vasantha! Amah Vasantha!"

I also summoned Madhavi, who hurried after my feet. Reaching our private chambers, I wheeled, my face dark with anger.

"What is it, my lord?"

"Ask her!" I pointed with my chin just as Vasantha-Mala entered the room.

"Forgive me, sir, immediately I returned from Lady Kannagi's house, Periya Amah, waiting at the gate, prevailed that I follow her, leaving me scant choice in the matter."

"You had a choice and made your choice! Why? Is it because my whip hangs raw, and not as supple as those of other masters?"

"I'll speak to my mother, my lord," said Madhavi, who, unlike me, was much in control of her emotions. Turning to her maid-servant, Madhavi spoke with an edge, hoping to blunt my fury.

"What news do you bear from Anandan Sir? Out with it and miss not a word."

"I was not at the discussion that ensued between Lady Kannagi and Anandan Sir," said the woman, with head bowed and eyes to the ground. It was the posture of a servant in contrition but also a ploy, for it hid her eyes and her lies. She continued.

"And these are the words uttered by Anandan Sir: *Tell my friend Kovalan*—begging your pardon sir, but Anandan Sir charged me to repeat without deviation—*tell my friend Kovalan and Lady Madhavi, in this house, bereft of love and dharma, lives only seething outrage and thirst for vengeance.*"

Hearing these words, Madhavi let out a gasp of disbelief and sank into a broad chair.

"Continue!" My voice boomed, trying to hide my anguish.

"Anandan Sir said: *Lady Kannagi has given herself to entities living in the nether regions, and she demands of her husband, Kovalan, to return,*" said the servant.

"Continue!"

"Then, Lady Kannagi, her long black tresses loosened to her waist and appearing as the Goddess Kali herself, scooped sand from the foot of the plinth holding the sacred *Tulasi* plant, and threw it into the air and cursed."

Madhavi let out a soft cry and collapsed, her body prone on the divan's armrest and tears wetting her blouse.

"Continue!"

"She cursed," said the woman and added, "and these are Anandan Sir's exact words conveyed to my poor unfortunate ears: *I curse the devadasi's womb remains barren; her heart unable to give and receive love; her name synonymous with all things unclean and unchaste; and, when the full moon rises, that her lips blabber and wail in the voices of a dozen demons.*

"And she repeatedly scooped and flung sand in the direction of Tree House."

By now, Madhavi was sobbing. Servants appeared at the door, but upon seeing my fiery gaze, they froze and stepped back out of sight.

"Is there anything else?"

"No sir, but Anandan Sir looked red and broken. After charging me to repeat his message, to ensure I will not allow poor memory to alter a word, he set off silent and with shoulders drooped and head hung low."

"Did you reveal any of this to Chitra-Vathi?"

"No, sir. Periya-Amah pressed, but before I broke, you summoned me. Grasping opportunity, I fled from her entreaties."

"You lie, and you lie well, you scoundrel." I took two steps, and she fell to her knees and pleaded her innocence. I snatched her waist pouch and out spilled several gold coins.

"And since when do servants in this house get paid in gold?"

I grabbed the woman's hair in a tight fist and made ready to strike. The maid-servant cried but also exhibited a streak of defiance as she said,

"Lady Kannagi gave this gold, sir, as payment to, please forgive me Lady Madhavi, as payment to Lady Madhavi for having sold herself like a—please forgive this wretched being, I cannot bring myself to utter such profanity." The servant's defence: she had hidden the gold coins and the rest of the message because they were too cruel for the ears of Lady Madhavi.

Devastated, I slunk into a chair, for the coins bore the markings of Kannagi's family emblem, vouching for the fine purity of the unalloyed metal. But there was nothing pure in the words spilled that day.

###

11: The First Fractures

Madhavi's public performances found no favour with me, for I did not relish other eyes exploring what I considered exclusive for my enjoyment. I paid a high price for the privilege—I refer not to mere coin—and was not prepared to share her.

Word and duty bound to King Kari-Kaalan, to allow Madhavi the practise of her art, I decided she would teach instead of perform. Therefore, I erected an extra wing to Tree House and established an academy to teach fine arts.

With some reluctance Madhavi acceded, but if she harboured any lingering unhappiness, it did not cross over to our bedchamber. She gave bliss; I possessed her, and she was mine alone. Or so I convinced myself. Delusion has the power of turning into reality, and I revelled in a real world of my making.

Just as matters settled into a happy routine, during a reception—realising how much Madhavi wanted to get back on stage—I relented in a moment of silly generosity. Her impromptu performance met with thunderous applause, and the street-criers repeated stories and accolades of appreciation by various nobles and known men.

My misplaced generosity, which I exchanged for public praise and validation of my standing in Pattinam, took on a life of its own. Thereafter, at almost every occasion we graced, friends and even strangers invited Madhavi to showcase her dance skills. I frowned, but she pointed to the lavish gifts of treasure.

The invitations became relentless, turned blatant, and exploitative. Handsome rewards followed her favours. And whenever we returned home, I made rough love to her until she stopped me. Angry, I would roll over to sleep but only to awake and ravage her again and again.

Some days, I would plan to stay away from her for a night, but as the hour approached, my resolution burned off faster than morning mist under the sun. I wanted to punish her but was myself tortured; to discard her but at every excuse ran to her; and no matter how many times I had her, could not get enough. Truly, her soft scented folds enslaved me.

A delegation arrived, ostentatiously to invite me to officiate at some ceremony. My time already spoken for; I could not accept the invitation. But the leader of the group said,

"Begging your pardon, Sir Kovalan, if you are not available, would you at least allow Lady Madhavi to do us the honours?"

This had been their intention all along. It had always been Madhavi the people wanted to see. I had been the mere door-post, which allowed entry for their wishes. These scheming sons of nameless fathers! In a flush, all the hidden fears and jealousies lurking within me surged to the fore.

I went into a period of gloom and moped around the house, but Madhavi pointed to the treasures pouring in from her efforts, and said,

"Please, my lord, do not vex yourself. The income from the dance academy hardly wets the beak, for our outgoings burgeon by the day. We now have a dozen servants and assistants and their families to feed too."

"Do you not manage the finances?"

"Alas, I'm poor in such matters and even my mother—."

"Your mother?" My nostrils flared. "You mean Chitra-Vathi? What of her?"

Madhavi's stories of ill-treatment in her childhood had etched deep resentment, verging on hatred for the wretched woman. Moreover, Chitra-Vathi, who wore a large red dot on her forehead, reminded me of matrons in the pleasure houses of Maruvur District.

"Even my mother lacks the wits to cope with the household finances."

"She is incompetent or worse!"

We stopped talking; realised the course of our conversation bode nothing but ill. She filled a cup of milk, but I folded my arms and looked away. I wanted her to breach the silence, to lose the argument, and to know her place. And with every moment of her continuing silence, my anger raced towards rage. She timed it well and said,

"You're right, my lord. My mother and I are of humble devadasi stock. We've at most handled a few pieces of silver but never bags of gold."

I did not reply but boiled in infantile rage, and with nervous effort held myself in check. But I could not bring myself to put matters to rest, to move on. I could not. Never. It bewildered me, not knowing why I behaved so.

I had always felt insecure with Madhavi; insecure in her love, a security I took for granted with my dear Kannagi. Madhavi had many suitors. I seethed when she responded to the open exclamations of praise from other men. Did she not know how much it pained me? Had I not reminded her many times over of these men who, feigning artistic adoration, harboured only lascivious desires? I would not reply. I would not give in and forgive her. She had to do more. She had to grovel.

"I need help, my lord, and you're right, my mother is a silly woman and our household has grown too complex for one such as her."

"You should have listened to me and thrown her out long ago." My words were harsh and my tone a sneer.

"You're right, my lord, and I'm even now thinking of sending her among the servants, to live out her few remaining years."

"Stop taxing your thoughts. Do it! Banish her now to live with the servants!"

"As you wish, my lord."

Madhavi again held out the cup. She leaned close. The tip of her proud breast, behind sequined fabric, brushed my arm. It felt firm and inviting. But I resisted. For now.

I took the milk from her hand and the cool drink coursed down my throat and filled me with calm. Milk always had a soothing effect on me, and Madhavi, more than my dear Kannagi, knew it well.

Her touch teased, and I wanted to take her there and then. But I had my pride. I stalled. With great effort, I postponed the inevitable. I needed an opening.

"How will you oversee the household?" I asked, keeping my voice casual.

"If you promise not to vex yourself, I shall share my heart's desire."

"What arrangement do you propose so onerous that I will deny your heart's desire?"

"I was thinking, my lord," said Madhavi. She went down on her knees and held my hands. Her heavy bosom heaved. "I was thinking of asking my elder sister for help."

What a perfect woman, Madhavi. She knew my deepest desire, even if I had refused to acknowledge it.

"Kannagi?" I said, my voice disembodied. Of course, it was Kannagi she spoke of, for was there another person?

"My elder sister Kannagi is talented in matters beyond me and knows how to well administer a household befitting a man of your stature."

"And you, what becomes of you?"

"I'll hand over the keys to Tree House and gladly be sister Kannagi's footstool. We'll be a family and hold a torch to how a man and his wives can lead a happy life."

"You want her to move into your house?"

"I wish, no, beg my elder sister to reign in this, *her* house. This villa has the splendour and the space befitting your stature. I'll confine myself to the dance academy and sleep in that wing, entering the main house only when summoned."

"Come with me then and let everyone see you are not the small-hearted woman as some have besmirched you." It was a ploy on my part. The thought of meeting Kannagi terrified me.

"It doesn't matter what people say, my lord, but I fear that perhaps my dear sister might harbour some harsh thoughts and words for me just yet. But surely, she is a chaste woman and will receive you, her beloved husband."

"You heard her words as conveyed by Anandan and carried to our ears by your *trusted servant*, Vasantha-Mala, that day. Do you think she might have relented?"

"My dear sister Kannagi surely keeps her life stitched to body to await your return."

"Even if what you say is true, I fear for my reception too, Devi, for I have hurt her beyond words and enjoy only misery at the thought of her loneliness and anguish."

"Depart then with haste and end your misery; fill her life with your presence and remove her loneliness, and satisfy my craving to see our family united."

Madhavi was marvellous. She had defused my anger and aroused me. I was not a weakling; will not *take* her; but will *reward* her for her generosity. I exhaled long and loud, and said,

"Your words are generous and wise beyond your age, and reveal a path through the bramble."

"Go, my lord, and invite her with all suitable decorum befitting my elder sister, and I wager she will accede to your blandishments, if not your wish."

Madhavi had the wiles of a shrewd woman of commerce, a reputation attached to most devadasis. But she had also shown herself generous in wanting to share me with Kannagi, although she had taken that which belonged to my wife.

I found merit in her proposed arrangement but was no fool, for I too had reasons for bringing my wife here. With Kannagi managing Tree House, my dear wife's very presence would dampen Madhavi's more adventurous tendencies.

I could have two ripe mangoes in my hands—one I would plant so it would flourish, and the other I would devour until I tired of its taste. It was for me to find my lost courage and face Kannagi.

"Waste not another moment, my lord, but bid my elder sister welcome. Your journey would not be in vain and you will surely thank me all the more for pressing you."

She was right. I should have departed right away. But I had other needs. Immediate and desperate needs. I would have to reward her first.

"Let me until the morning dwell on all you have spoken, Devi, and what might become."

She reclined on the divan and rested on a folded arm placed behind her head. Her swollen lips parted, promising honeyed dew drops. My body arced over her and again I lost myself in her. I convinced myself that I had won. And so, I dispensed my favour to her. But a little voice kept gnawing away, saying otherwise.

When morning broke and tinkling prayer bells and incense fragrance reminded us to live and love, I did not go to my Kannagi. Not that day and not for many days, or several weeks thereafter. My old fragilities of guilt, shame, cowardice and lust chained me.

***

"I'm carrying your child, our love fruit," said Madhavi.

She placed my hand on her flat stomach. Her smooth skin was wet with perspiration, and her chest heaved in gentle excitement.

"I can sense our child," she said.

The news evoked new emotions. All along, I had viewed Madhavi as a plaything; a source of pleasure to discard if I grew tired; a toy embraced but only to deny others; and a bad memory to escape from when I return to my wife and the righteous path. But after her revelation of our child, my child—another pleasure that Kannagi could not give me—I felt no possessiveness but a sudden protectiveness towards Madhavi.

I had reason now, more powerful than my guilt and shame, to bring Kannagi into our lives. She had lamented her inability to bear a child and even urged adoption, which I had rejected outright.

Now there was already a child—my child—and therefore part of Kannagi too. There was scant need for adoption and no need to wager on the child's caste or lineage. These and other strange and hopeful arrangements churned and settled in my mind. I would not be the first or the last to take two wives, and so I found comfort in the company of other men, luminaries who also had two wives.

After all, if I treated both wives with equal favour and met their every need, what blame could reach my doorstep? Madhavi had already proposed a threesome. She was pushing me into the arrangement. And I was confident Kannagi would not deny me. My wife was waiting, pulling me into the arrangement. Could I resist? Who was I to resist fate?

I resolved to broach the news to Madhavi and visit my dear Kannagi with not a moment's delay. But I delayed my departure, for there were more immediate matters that needed my attention. I had to first reward Madhavi.

###

12: Kovalan and Madhavi Duel

The following morning, a day of festivities, when couples gathered by the water, Madhavi and I went to the river bank. It was an auspicious day, and I had decided to reveal my plan to visit dear Kannagi. Madhavi organised a sumptuous picnic spread under a wide canopied tree and we delighted in mouth-watering savouries and honeyed intoxicants.

After lunch, I lay on Madhavi's lap and enjoyed a nap. Upon awakening, and feeling bright, I broke into spontaneous song. Madhavi wielded the veena.

"A life-giver," I said. Before I could complete, she said,

"Water. Sing a song about a life-giver, for you are, my lord, my life-giver."

I thought for a moment and launched a verse that had been teasing me. I said:

"Rowing his boat down the mighty Kaveri
Sisters Himavathi, Bhavani, and Bedavathi beckon
What new adventures, what new joys from the kavalan."

To which Madhavi replied:

"New adventures take him away
Leaving anxiety waiting lonely
Why idles the queen, descended from the Supreme?"

Impressed, I responded:

"The poorer seek new pastures
The blessed find it all in one field
Former rolls the dice, latter remains on firm ground."

I folded my arms and awaited her response, but her words shocked me.

"The Kaveri strains against her banks
She too wishes to breach her confines
Find new husbands to make happy."

I went silent and considered her words. She broke into a teasing titter, thinking she had caught me, rendering me unable to propose a proper poem. Her glee added ghee to the flame. She continued to challenge. Growing vexed, I hurled my reply.

"She who worships all, worships none
For what worth a known price on one
Wavering loyalty to the highest bidder for mere coin."

Madhavi, unaware of my growing anger, responded with a laugh.

"As usual, you prevail
But be warned, the next time
I will not let you off so easily."

I turned dark and moody, but Madhavi did not notice, because men of wealth and repute—lovers of her art—came over to join us under the tree. The men, careful to bring their wives along, rested their eyes firmly on Madhavi.

Unable to bear the situation any further, I sprang to my feet and announced my tiredness and, without waiting for her reply, strode off.

My man-servant ran after me. He held up the parasol against the sun, and when I boarded the carriage, he asked, "Should I fetch Devi Amah, sir?"

I turned to the tree, under which lately I had sat with Madhavi, to find her surrounded by an eager audience.

Seeing how she had given herself over to the adulation of her admirers, I ignored the man's question and instead ordered the driver, "Take me home, and be quick about it."

The driver flicked his reins, and with a small jerk, the carriage started to roll away. My man-servant, who was standing on the floorboard behind my seat, had looked back, for he cried,

"Sir, I see Devi Amah waving anxiously, and now she shouts, though I discern not her words. Should we turn back?"

Sensing the driver rein the horses a little, I said,

"Drive on!"

The man snapped the reins and clicked his tongue, and the horses shifted to a fast canter.

Considering the good news that I wished to share with her regarding my planned visit to Kannagi, a matter Madhavi had proclaimed to be of great import, my outrage magnified many times. Pride and anger are the twins that bring down even the mighty, say the sages. But her callous behaviour justified my anger. My fury.

On sandaled feet, I strode into the house, and when the servants gasped at this great affront to the gods of the household, I kicked off my dusty leathers. I headed for the staircase, discarding my turban and ripping off my golden shawl as I went, and hurried up to the bedroom.

Many confused and angry thoughts continued to gloat at my weakness and goad my anger. I had enough of being a kept man. And as for her beauty and promises of pleasure, and the deep abiding jealousies in the pit of my stomach—I will quench all the pain in one sweep, endure the first few days of terrible anguish, and free myself from her hold. She could find another, for the nymph she was, and would waste herself even as men nourished her need for adulation.

As I sat smouldering on the bed, Madhavi hurried in, with Vasantha-Mala at her heels. The hand-maiden placed a basin of water and towels on a table, and with clasped hands and bowed head, stepped back and out of the room. Madhavi, who had picked up my dishevelled turban and shawl, folded and placed them on the divan.

"You left without informing, my lord, but my friends detained me and I took some time to excuse myself from their company, after which I directly hurried home. I should have known the hot day to be quite enervating. Let me undress and wipe you down with cool scented water. You'll feel better."

She moved towards the bed, but I raised my hand and stopped her.

"How silly of me, for you must be thirsty." She poured a drink. "Fresh lemon juice with honey to sweeten the bite, as you like it." She held out the drink, but I ignored her. Replacing the cup on the table, she positioned herself beside me and said,

"Here, let me knead away your stress, for your frame stands sharp and with shoulders raised."

"Who gave you permission to sit?"

"I did not know I needed permission to sit in my house." She spoke in a soft voice.

"*Your* house? You have drawn the line, I see."

I was looking for an opening, even a petty opportunity, to start a quarrel. Perhaps if anger took a better hold of me, it would provoke impulse, if not the courage, to walk out.

"My lord, I don't know what ails you, but if it's something I've said or done, I beg your forgiveness, whatever it might be, small or large. But please, do not take offence and render this auspicious evening dull." She rose and stood before me and offered the drink.

"Even before you know the error, you apologise. Is your sincerity worthy of trust?"

"Then, pray, share with me that which vexes you, so to make correct amends as best as I can. But please do not treat me as a stranger, for it breaks my heart."

"What was the meaning of your song?"

"What song, my lord, for we sang many today and gave ourselves over to much joy."

"The last song, the last verse."

"I only vaguely recall, as it was spontaneous and made no lasting impression. Perhaps if you could sing your lines, they might trigger my memory and the words to ensue."

"You wish to play? So be it, here it is then:
"Rowing his boat down the mighty Kaveri
Sisters Himavathi, Bhavani, and Bedavathi beckon
What new adventures, what new joys from the kavalan."

"Yes, now I recall, and your meaning, my lord?" she asked.

"As protector and provider, he adventures down the Kaveri and explores her tributaries, Himavathi, Bhavani, and Bedavathi. He braves dangers and rejoices in bringing home new treasures for his queen. That was my meaning."

"A lovely theme, my lord, and with deep meanings for man and woman. I recall now my response," said Madhavi.

"Speak it then."

To which she replied:
"New adventures take him away
Leaving anxiety waiting lonely
Why idles the queen, descended from the Supreme?"

"Your meaning?" I demanded.

100

"I sang in praise of Our Supreme Being Parasakthi, Mother of the Holy Trinity, and I asked Her, Mother to all, man, woman and child, but why is her daughter confined to hearth and home, when in the days of antiquity, she was his equal. Hunted and fought side-by-side with her man. Why not let her share the dangers with her *kavalan*, her dear lover? This was my intent. Is there anything wrong, my lord, in my words or intentions?"

"Let me continue with what I then sang, and it will reveal you," I said.

"The poorer seek new pastures
The blessed find it all in one field
Former rolls the dice, latter remains on firm ground.

"And by this, I meant the kavalan has to tempt danger, perhaps because he lacks blessings, for how else can he provide for his queen."

"Truly spoken, my lord," said Madhavi, "and I see no cause for annoyance thus far in what you sang or in my response."

"Thus far, you are right, but continue in its wake."

"As you wish, my lord," and so saying, Madhavi continued.

"The Kaveri strains against her banks
She too wishes to breach her confines
Find new husbands to make happy."

"You have deviated here, Devi, in flow and theme. Explain your words and realise your dark intentions."

"By overflowing her banks," said Madhavi, "Kaveri wishes to make fertile new lands, and with new rich harvests, many more households will rejoice in plenty. This was what I meant, my lord, and I don't see errors in my words or intent."

"Really? Can it not also mean Kaveri wishes to deviate from her chaste path and consort with new husbands?"

"Oh god, but that was not what I meant, my lord, but even if I did, what of it?" said Madhavi, and defiance lurked in her tone. "In the days of yore, was it not the norm? And even now, a union between man and woman is a carriage, is it not, which needs at the least two wheels and of equal diameters. If one were humbler in girth, even with all the couple's best efforts, they travel in circles."

"You think you are equal to your man?"

"I *know* I'm equal," replied the devadasi.

"My wedded wife, Kannagi, a chaste woman, thinks not and behaves not so, for even when she walks, she drops three paces behind so as not to step on my shadow."

"And I have much to learn from her," said Madhavi, unwilling to yield, "younger as I am, to remain your shadow and enjoy your misplaced steps."

We fell into a heavy silence. It was only at this stage that some sense seemed to have crept into her, for she quickened to make amends.

"But let us not pursue this discourse, my lord, for I fear the path augurs not well ahead, and even if you discover pebbles where I meant pearls, please treat my turn of words as a tease, as you know how guilty I am in spontaneous humour."

"Humour? You, versed in the classics, do not see that what you propose contradicts our culture, our values, our chaste morality?"

"Oh, my dear lord, truly you're poor in humour," said Madhavi, and she laughed, making light of the matter. But to my ears, her laughter was not an innocent sound but one of derision. And my suspicions multiplied tenfold when I heard her next words.

"But open in our deepest intimacies and frank in our long discourses, as we've always been towards one another, my lord, you must agree men exercise two sets of moral codes: one for women and one for men. Women, as the mighty Kaveri, should not break her banks, but men are free to explore her sisters, Himavathi, Bhavani, and Bedavathi. Society accuses the former for losing her chastity but fetes the latter his conquests. And here you are, consorting with me, and we are truly both chaste."

"Indeed, here I am, as you say, consorting with you, Devi, and we are both chaste."

I took the drink and Madhavi, pleased, in one smooth motion regained her spot next to me. She placed a soft hand on my shoulder, and I felt not a shiver of excitement, but revulsion.

I regained my composure for, my decision already made, it would not be decorous to exchange more harsh words. She had insulted our relationship and questioned my morality. After all, she was a devadasi. Her ilk was ostentatious in their dedication to temple service but danced in the public eye for all to leer; and surreptitious in service to their gurus, and also allowed into their sanctums any man who contributed coin.

"Are you feeling better, my lord?"

"You have satisfied my curiosity."

I rewarded her with a brief emotionless smile and stood up, not only to escape her touch but also to hide my face from her scrutiny. Trained like all women of her ilk, she could read a man's intentions from a mere twitch of a muscle.

"Madhavi," I said, making my voice soft, "you often beseeched me to visit my chaste wife, Kannagi, a matter I had wished to discuss earlier and only now found the opportunity. Do you continue to embrace this wish, that I visit my flawless wife, Kannagi?"

"How delightful, and yes, my lord, and with the impending birth of our child, she is very welcome to join in our joy."

"Yes, those were my exact intentions and I shall directly make haste to visit that peerless person, my wedded wife, Kannagi."

"Now, this very night? But why the haste, my lord, for would it not bode better to rest and recover, and make your vital visit under a gloriously bright sunlight? To call on her under the veil of the night, would it not diminish the significance of this welcomed event?"

"It is an auspicious day, Madhavi, and I should cross the threshold there before the sun hides and extinguishes all that is good of today." I turned to her. A mistake, for she right away read the intentions lurking behind my eyes.

"I too cannot bear being separated from my dear elder sister, Kannagi," she said, and held my arm, her grip tight and possessive. "But the suddenness of your errand troubles me, my lord. Please, rest the night and after the morning ablutions, take the holy kumkuma from our altar and smear it on her forehead and escort her back with all proper rites and respects."

"Madhavi, I have been fair to you, treated you well and, unlike most men who shackle their women, I have not put you in a gilded cage. I have given you the freedom, free as the bird, to return to the perch as and when you wish to, have I not?"

"Yes, my lord, in this and many other aspects, you have gone against the grain, but, though your tone is soft, your words are daggers with twin edges."

"Would you have me chained, Madhavi?"

"Only with my love, my lord. And, why again, *Madhavi*? What became of *Devi*?"

"Would you have me chained?" I persisted; intent that she answered to my satisfaction and not lead with her questions.

"No, my lord, never."

"Good, and shackle your hesitation, especially since you have often chided me for not visiting my dear blemish-free wife, Kannagi. I need to go to my wedded wife and see how she fares and attend to her comforts, for I have neglected her more than any decency allows."

"Your words are correct, my lord, but do not go just yet to steal a visit in the night, as though you were a thief. There is only a fingernail sliver of a moon for guidance and even that under the gloom of a foggy night."

"Steal a visit, you say?" I snatched my arm free of her hold. "Is my wife some devadasi to receive nameless men in the stealth of the night? How dare you, a woman of known value?"

"Oh god, why do you speak so harshly? You know that's not what I meant."

"Enough!" I raised my hand. "My heart is set, woman, and if you now dread my departure, is it because you fear the bonds of your love not strong? Who waits in the shadows you fear your heart will invite, to steal a visit as some thief, when I am gone?"

"Oh, god! How can you speak such words to me? You're the only god I've had sight of, my lord. There is no one, no lurking shadow."

"Enough! Wish me well then, and speak no more, for from your own reckoning, there is no alarm. Goodbye, Madhavi. I go now and there is no need for rest or sleep, for I am invigorated and awake."

I moved to the door with Madhavi hurrying behind. I picked up my pace, but she, a well-trained dancer, matched my steps with ease. As we went down the stairs, she spewed much, but I did not care to hear her words, for they were water falling off feathers; and this dove would spread its wings and be free again. By the time we reached the threshold, the servants had appeared at windows and doorways to bear silent witness.

Madhavi dropped to the floor and grabbed my sandaled feet. She was crying, a scene I had sought to avoid.

"I fear, my lord, you've decided to exclude me from your life. Please, I beg you, take me with you. All I need is a place at your feet and that is enough wet love for my heart."

"The wet love you feel now, Madhavi, is only vapid blood weeping from a vented neck long after the heart had stopped thumping."

"Don't discard me, my lord."

"If you are a chaste woman as you claim to be, do not cross the threshold and sully my pure wife Kannagi's house, for that is a holy abode. Remain! Stay!"

Then, as she clung to my feet, I wriggled out of my sandals, leaving them in her hands, and stepped out and onto the free sands of fate. Behind me, the wretched woman's wails pierced the night. Whereas a day earlier, a sniff from her would have ruined my day, now I felt nothing.

I had finally broken from her hold. I was free to return to my dear Kannagi. Free! I breathed deep and exhaled. The air was brisk and sweet.

As I calmed, an unexpected fear gripped my chest. Kannagi. My dear Kannagi. Oh god! Will she take me back?

###

13: Kovalan returns to Kannagi

I fashioned the turban with the tail end wrapped across my face, and only my eyes exposed. Thus disguised, I paid the bullock cart driver the last piece of silver I had with me, for I did not wish to take even a copper coin from that woman, lest it soils my new beginning. As for my share of the earnings, well, let my money be the going-away gift, the end of a sorry relationship, and a price well-paid for a lesson hard-learned.

I erred. I succumbed to weakness. Lust imprisoned me. The burden of blame is mine to bear alone. But another voice within laughed. The burden had always been on my blameless wife, Kannagi. Oh god. What a wretch I had become. But I thanked all the gods for having given me sight.

The bullock cart trundled along the streets in the night's silence, the wheels made sharp sounds as they crushed stones and left behind bad memories, and the soft tinkle of bells hanging around the necks of the beasts heralded new promises.

Then a thought stroked and sent a chill through my being. What if Kannagi was not at home; what if she had long gone to her parents' house? I felt trepidation even meeting her, let alone bearing the shame of facing my in-laws, or my parents.

But no, I knew my dear Kannagi would never resort to such a venture. She is my wife, my best friend, and though it has been about two years since I left, she would await my return to our house. Our house. How strange, but correct, the words sound. Our house. No, her house. And so, I argued and debated, and sank into the troughs of doubt and shame, and kept raising my eyes to the peaks of hope and reconciliation.

The bullock cart turned the corner onto the familiar street. I was glad it was late at night, for the lights in the bungalows had doused; there were no people about on the street or servants lounging at gates to catch up on gossip. The families had retired behind closed doors; the children fortified with meals to face the fast overnight, tucked into warm beds; and the husbands and wives enjoying their intimacy.

Suddenly, I felt acutely homesick and yearned for my wife's platonic company, without the overhanging feelings of guilt. A guilt I had banished to the depths of my mind but knew its ever-present indictment.

Yes, I enjoyed Madhavi's company, her music, her body, and the unfettered carnal pleasures. But looking back, I was not a fortunate man, for the feeling was one of emptiness, devoid of all divine and societal approval. Bliss in that house was an illusion requiring the shroud of darkness to vindicate and bring to life. Whenever I ventured out with that woman, I felt the staring eyes, disapproving behind masks of fawning smiles. It was mere rapture that I could have purchased for a handful of coins from the doorways which exuded cheap scents in the narrow alleys of Maruvur District.

True happiness could only come from the embrace of one's wife. I knew that now. And I again thanked all the gods who had nudged me to the right path. I had behaved as a child, ever demanding for the new toy that caught my eyes. New toys did not give new pleasures. For pleasure hid in every toy and relied more on one's imagination to bring it forth.

Though we had lost dozens of full moons, my dear Kannagi and I could look forward to a long, loving, and happy life. I owed Kannagi an immeasurable debt; and even if she poured anger and disappointment upon me, I resolved to take all her venom. For truly, I would be a deserving recipient.

Engrossed so, I mumbled a silent prayer as the bullock cart pulled up in front of my house. I gazed at the all-too-familiar gate. The driver said something, but I waved him away.

There was no watchman, and I wondered whether he was away on his rounds. I waited but soon realised there was no one on duty, not even a stray cat. I jiggled the heavy lock, but it demanded a key to come free.

I yearned to call to Kannagi but decided against it, lest the neighbourhood roused too. It annoyed me that the devadasi had been right. Perhaps I should have waited for light. I stood there under the black sky, glad the moon was too thin and too shrouded by clouds to expose my foolishness, for I was indeed a fool sneaking back to savour the true love I had abandoned.

The night turned frigid but, in my anger and hurry, I had forgotten a warm coat. Another mistake, a miniscule error of judgement, one of a long string of missteps, but none bigger than the ones committed against my dear wife. I deserved to suffer the cold already cutting through the fabric to the bone. I deserved whatever punishment the gods showered down upon me.

Curling into a tight ball, I pushed myself into a corner of one of the stone pillars standing sentinel at the iron-gate. Sleep did not come, but memories kept me company. My conscience jeered, but above the noise I heard a little encouraging voice to keep heart, and to trust my dear wife, Kannagi. I promised to redeem myself by providing Kannagi the life she deserved, so her sacrifice, her fortitude, and her faith would not go to waste. She deserved the best, much more than I could ever give, even if I lived a hundred years and devoted every moment to making her happy. But henceforth, nothing would discourage me. I would dedicate my life to my wife.

Throughout my troubled sleep, I startled awake whenever a night bird flew past, its wings flapping, or when a dog, disturbed by things of the night, howled. I did not know whether devils or demons wandered, but if there were, perhaps they left me alone because I was under my Kannagi's protection.

Sleep must have overtaken me, for I woke in the morning, feeling the pain of stiff joints. I peered over the wall and spied the family Tulasi plant on the plinth. The slender green was flourishing, and it pleased me and gave me hope. It meant Kannagi would appear to water and circle the plant as she hummed her morning prayers. And perhaps she would take me in before the neighbours stirred. I was not ashamed of what people might think of me, but was afraid of the injury she might suffer from cruel words hurled by others. For this reason, I did not wish for queries from curious eyes.

A small light came alive within the depths of the house and sent my heart thumping. The light was not from the bedrooms, which were on the top floor, but from one of the smaller rooms below. Was it Kannagi or a servant who had woken earlier?

The front door cracked open and a faint shaft of light fell on the ground beyond the threshold. A lithe graceful figure emerged, her steps soft and careful, as if not to cause injury to earth-mother. Parting the misty swirls of dawn, she approached the family Tulasi plant.

Kannagi came to offer morning prayers. My heart pounded and hot tears dripped down my cheeks and wet my tunic. She was engaged in venerations and, not wishing to intrude, I remained hidden.

She looked serene but sad, and my silent tears continued to flow. Her presence and prayers were cleansing me. I was ready to accept her anger and, the gods forbid, even her rejection. Yes, if she so decided, I would go away and attach no blame to her.

Kannagi, after her prayers, went back into the house and even as I debated how best to make my approach, she again emerged, holding a roll of banana leaf and a tin pail. She drifted to the low wall behind which I cringed, opened the gate, and unrolled the banana leaf on a plinth set outside the gate. Retrieving several small bundles of hot cooked food from the pail, she arranged them into a little pyramid. Satisfied her charity would feed some poor for the day, she turned but paused, alerted by some sixth sense.

My legs straightened, as if on their own accord, and I stood up.

She stood speechless, and I moved forward with a swell in my throat. Immediately, she ran forward, went down on her knees, and touched my feet. Her hot tears blotched my dusty skin, and it wrecked my heart. I knelt down with her and we held one another and sobbed. With trembling hands, I took Kannagi's weight and pulled her up with me.

"Athan," she kept repeating. "Athan." And she said, "You are rain for my drought. A life-giver. A good man. I knew you would return."

I withdrew my hands, afraid to hug her, afraid my embrace would sully her purity. But she would not have it. She wrapped herself in my arms and I stiffened. She looked up, gazing into my eyes.

"Do you not wish to hold me, Athan?"

Tears welled, and I blabbered some incoherent words of confused contrition, and together we cried.

***

I was back home but felt very much a visitor, a stranger who could not muster the nerve to wander the house at will. I needed to gather myself and also give Kannagi time to get accustomed to my presence.

The living room looked the same but stripped clean of furniture. Even the swing chair I sat on, though polished, lacked cushions. A solitary oil lamp, statuesque and of gleaming brass, stood in solemn silence. It was a recent addition; one I did not recall.

Kannagi brought a tumbler of warm milk and I asked her to take a sip, but she refused; insisted I quench my thirst. I decided to please her and reminded myself to do anything and everything as she wished, no matter how miniscule. I threw my head back and, as was the custom, poured the milk down my throat.

When I handed the tumbler to her, Kannagi took the receptacle, turned aside, and drank the tiny residue left behind. She closed her eyes and swallowed with satisfaction. What a fool I was for having emptied the cup.

"I'm so sorry, my sweet, I drank it all."

"All the more I can taste your sweet saliva, dear Athan," she said.

We spoke about many things, safe matters that skirted my indiscretions. As the morning gave way to noon, I asked about the state of the house. It was neat but empty. Bare, save for a few kitchen utensils, sleeping mats, and the oil lamp.

"The oil lamp has an aura about it," I said.

"You selected a worthy family heirloom that provided light in my dark nights." Seeing my expression, she said, "My brother Anandan, before departing for Araby, conveyed it to me as you directed."

"Yes," I said, hiding the truth that I knew nothing of the lamp lest it hurt her. "It gleams, but what calamity, my sweet, has swept through our house and cleaned it so bare?"

"Please, Athan, vex not yourself. I caused our poverty. This cursed woman before you carries the blame and will gladly suffer any punishment you deem fit."

"Cursed? You? No, never you! I committed grave errors, unforgiveable wrongs, and will not add to the store. But there is

110

treachery here, I suspect. Tell me, my sweet, share the story without fear. Who or what has brought this disaster upon us?"

###

14: Fortune lost to Folly

How am I to tell my Athan the truth? There is no gold, no silver—not even a copper coin. How could he not know? Surely, he knows it was by his will I sold everything to send him money. He must know. Even our house belongs to moneylenders.

He has many dreams and shared many eager plans to rebuild our life. Cursed I am to break the truth and dash all his hopes. The genesis of our doom took root after my brother Anandan sent word to my dear husband to come and fetch me to Tree House. Alas, my dear Athan never came, but in his stead, another did.

Madhavi's mother, who identified herself as Amah Chitra-Vathi, came unannounced. Vasantha-Mala, the maid-servant, accompanied the old woman. When my servants brought the news, I did not know how to receive the elder. There were no established customs. How would a wife welcome the mother of a woman who had taken away her husband? Outraged and offended, and forgetting hospitality, I kept her waiting. I refused to set eyes on the woman, for only an evil being could have given life to a daughter who would steal another's lawful husband. But in time, I relented because I could not disparage my parents by displaying poor behaviour fed by anger. I decided to receive the woman and if she proved to be a disagreeable person, so be it. For she is not my mother and not my teacher, and from my manner, she might learn how a chaste woman lives and conducts herself, and how my parents and teachers nurtured me with correct mores.

Our meeting started off wary, but the woman had a fetching way that dispelled my worst fears.

"It's a house of great splendour," said the woman, marvelling at the high ceiling and heavy drapes. Her eyes flitted over the furniture and their intricate carvings, and the flawless sheen of the brass artefacts. For a moment, the surroundings engrossed the woman, but after regaining her presence, she said,

"You're fortunate that your husband, Kovalan, has ensconced you in such a lovely gilded cage. And which love-bird will find cause to complain?"

Amah Chitra-Vathi spoke of many other things, but for the most part I remained silent, except for adding a soft word or two so as not to show overt rudeness, until she touched the kernel of my concern—Kovalan, my dear husband.

"We were all distraught when Kovalan decided not to fetch you to Tree House," she said. "It was such joyous news from your brother, Anandan, and conveyed flawlessly by our trusted Vasantha-Mala. Your sister Madhavi had been persistent, at the risk of incurring Kovalan's disapproval, in encouraging him to take you back and acknowledge you as his first wife."

"Tell me more, please, for what could have frustrated my brother's happy solution?" I asked with unhidden excitement. Noticing my enthusiasm, the woman grew verbose.

"Alas, Kovalan, possessed by things fascinating and frightening, neglects his business and indulges in the devils' drinks," said the woman. "He has gathered around him a coterie of hangers-on, the kind not allowed past any decent threshold, but what can I, a poor wretched old woman, do? He is a frequent visitor to pleasure halls where nymphs with wasp waists and deep honeyed breasts swarm, ever ready to suck the vitality of wealthy men, and returns inebriated, past the midnight call. Please forgive me, my child, it's not for me to disparage anyone, and especially your beloved husband, and if I speak ill, may worms infest my tongue and cause it to wither and drop."

"And what of Madhavi, did she not help my dear Athan find his way?"

"Alas, your sister Madhavi, that foolish girl, loves him with her pure heart and has offered to help pay for expenses your husband incurred. She has agreed to exploit her talents in return for crass coin. But Kovalan, ever full of pride and quick to anger, will not hear of it. Meanwhile, moneylenders, like stray cats and rabid dogs, appeared at our doorstep, claiming your husband had ransomed his indulgence with borrowed money. So here I am, having shamelessly climbed your gilded steps, my flickering strength drained, even as fear gripped my weak heart at the reception you would give one such as myself."

"Dear Amah Chitra-Vathi—"

"There is no need for such formality, my dear, for you are queen of this vast and wealthy palace. Please, a simple *amah* will do, as even a bent old wretch infested with lice deserves that."

"You are no wretch, mother dear, and as you wish, amah, please forgive my reluctance just now for not having quickly received you. I was angry, but remembering all good things taught by my family, I cringed. And if you will now allow me to make amends and redeem my worth in your eyes, I shall remain always grateful and with ready hospitality."

"Yes, I can see correct upbringing in you and what a lucky man, Kovalan, to have you for a wife. If he could treat your sister, Madhavi, with but a fraction of the consideration a man accords a mongrel."

"What do you mean, amah? For I know my husband well and he is not any such sort."

"He is not, except he curses your sister Madhavi for not having coffers filled with gold and silver to give when he stretches out his hand. He always chides her that if it were his dear Kannagi, he has to but blink and she would pour gold and silver in his lap, prompting him to hold up his hand and cry: Enough, enough. What can one say? We're women, are we not, and suffer a woman's lot." She exhaled. Then, placing a hand on my shoulder, she said,

"I empathise with how you miss your beloved husband, for I too, at about your age, suffered the same fate when my husband, a good man, left saying he was going away to seek his fortune, to give me a good life, though the only life I yearned for was to be of service at his feet and find pleasure in his embrace. My husband was a good man, who wished the best for me and my daughter, Madhavi, all of one-year-old then.

"My husband having gone away, the years passed and my despondency grew heavier. I waited at the threshold for his happy return but knew in my heart that either bandits or wild animals had taken my poor husband, a good man. So, I did the unthinkable and became a dancing girl. Society spewed ill and painted smudge while relishing my wincing body. For what does society care, my dear child, Kannagi? I had a cursed stomach to feed, and also a suckling child, dependent as a desperate hatchling in an exposed nest. There were predators all around, men with gold in their pouches and lust in their eyes. Should I sell my daughter to these upright men of society? Would that have gained better approval? Or should I have pressed her into slavery or let her loose to beg on streets? Or would you have me work in a house of ill-repute and play a poor role model and hasten my daughter's own demise?

"Therefore, I danced till my soles flattened and grew calluses, sang till my voice went hoarse, and smiled till my face grew stiff as clay. I eked out a miserable living, collecting copper coins from men who fashioned themselves generous even as they tossed with one hand and grabbed my femininity with the other. It was a terrible life not even your worst enemies deserve. We women bestowed with beauty, supposed gift from the gods, know it to be a curse. Men view us not as equals in a partnership but as mere playthings; toys they discard when our beauty wanes and withers. We give our youth to men, but only to die before death catches us. Not a day went by without some man offering vulgar proposal. These are matters which I cannot bring myself to speak, not even in my advanced age, having nothing more to hide, nothing more to give, for men had seen it all and stolen it all. For when these memories overpower me, in moments of my weakness, I run and hide in shadows and weep in shame for what I had become. But I told myself, it was me or my daughter, and so I gave myself over to things no woman brought up in a loving home and correct path, as you have been, should give your ears to.

"I did not wish for my daughter, your sister Madhavi, to endure the echoes of my wretched life and when she suggested performing in the dance halls to eke out a living to support Kovalan, I felt my entire body suffer the unbearable agony of lasciviously licking flames. I confess I grew in hatred for Kovalan for what he had brought upon my precious child. Please, forgive my candour, but this is a mother's heart bleeding to you, and as a woman I seek your understanding; as entwined as we are in the greater sisterhood of our lot. As women, my dear child, we're but toys for the whims and amusement of men."

Hearing the old wretch's wrenching words, my tears flowed, and I placed a hand on hers. She grasped mine as if it were a lifeline. I saw in her my mother, and many soft feelings tugged me.

"Your husband, Kovalan, born to riches, behaves as a child and, with Madhavi unable to give him gold and silver, laments that you, Kannagi, would never deny him."

"Did he say that, dear amah, did he mention my name?"

"Why, of course, my child, no sun sets in our household without Kovalan mentioning your name at least a dozen times or more. Hearing him speak so well of you in praise and more, your sister Madhavi becomes desperate to fall at your feet to receive blessings. But alas, he forbids her to cross the threshold. It is so sad, for what a joy it would give my faltering heart, fast depleting its store of finite beats, to behold two lovely and loving sisters unite into one, both serving the man they love so dearly."

"Is sister Madhavi a person of so much kindness and love towards me, even one whom she has not met?"

"Who is to tell, my dear child, whether you have already met in another life, perhaps she as your slave and you as her mistress?"

"No, dear amah, if I had been so blessed, I am sure we were sisters and no less."

"But forgive my wicked eyes, for I see something troubles you, my child, something about your sister Madhavi."

"Forgive me too, amah dear, I have been selfish, harbouring a woman's heart, a wife's hurt, and filled with ill feelings towards my sister Madhavi."

"But the blame is not yours, for those who spin tales juicier it is to embellish with half-truths and full-lies, my daughter dear, though my womb is not worthy to have borne one as chaste and generous as you."

"Please do not judge yourself harsh, amah dear, for no womb is unworthy to bear life. How can I help? Show me the way."

"As I just now mentioned, my poor daughter and your sister, Madhavi, does not want to be a burden to anyone, most of all you. And Kovalan, claiming to have so much wealth it would last ten generations, he said, has also forbidden her to dance in the public eye. But we cannot take his money, all the more for society already views me as a woman without morality. You, foster daughter to this poor old hag and sister to the blameless Madhavi, you would understand. For you're so pure, your purity blinds me; for you're so chaste, your chastity makes me drop at your feet."

And without warning, she touched my feet. My toes withdrew in shock, and I bent down and pulled her up. I wiped her warm tears and hugged her tight to my bosom. I comforted her, but our embrace also comforted me.

When she had collected herself, I said, "Wait here, I'll be back soon."

Grabbing two bags of gold coins, I re-joined the poor woman and placed them in her reluctant hands.

She kept saying no, as if afraid someone might discover the bags on her person and accuse her of thievery. But I kept pressing the pouches into her pale palms.

"Oh, my dear child, one cannot speak of the things I did; certainly not in polite company or high society. But I've never lived on charity. I've always worked, had to work, for every miserable bowl of salt-less gruel."

"Amah dear, dwell not on the past but look at the present and to the future."

"But my dear child—"

"Not another word, please, amah dear. Please. If you love me as your elder daughter, take the money and let's not hear another word about the matter."

"You chain me with your love, leaving me compelled to receive these but even then, only upon your insistence."

"On my insistence then, please," I said.

"May all the gods shower good things upon you in this life and many more."

The old woman took the gold and gave it to her hand maiden, Vasantha-Mala. Then, grimacing with pain, she rose and said,

"This gold will last until a month, but I'm sure by then your sister Madhavi would come up with some new plans."

"Inform my sister Madhavi not to stray from the path of dharma. Ask her to do as Kovalan says. Do not cross the threshold. Fear not for coin, for there is more where these came from. What use is money stored and not used?"

"Wise words from one so young," said the woman. "And if ever the need arises, I'll, as you wish, dispatch Vasantha-Mala and you can drop a copper coin or two in her palms."

Before bidding her farewell, I presented the old woman some kumkuma in a small silver container, for though deserted by her husband, in the sight of the gods, if not society, she remained married and wore the holy tali around her neck.

Over the months the hand-maiden, Vasantha-Mala, came calling, for it was plain my dear husband's appetite was insatiable and I handed over more and more treasures. There was no unhappiness on my part. It was, after all, his, and it gave me great joy knowing my dear husband was living without need. The visits became more and more regular and at shorter intervals.

First the gold went, then the silver, and before long there was no more, not even a copper coin. After which, I sold all the valuable paintings, the bundles of precious books, wood carvings, and exquisite furniture. I sent repeated word to my dear husband, wanting to know which pieces of furniture to keep and which to sell. Should I sell his favourite swing, the one he likes to sit on when composing songs? How about the divan in our bedroom, where, during happier days, he sat and sang songs and lulled me to sleep? According to Vasantha-Mala, my dear husband wished to sell everything. Everything! She further reported he was engaged in commercial ventures and for me not to worry. He hoped to recover all our spent wealth. The news gave me heart. It meant he had distanced himself from his debauched friends and turned to his business interests.

But the maid-servant continued to appear, an itch that would not go away. Yes, an itch, because with passing months, she grew haughty and even discourteous. But with my dear Kovalan persisting, I had to endure even a servant's subtle insults.

The woman would enter uninvited into my home and, without a word, sit in the living room. Silent. Brooding. Demanding. She behaved as a debt collector, leaving me to hurry and gather whatever meagre articles of value overlooked.

Finally, and at wit's end, I borrowed against the house and now the moneylenders own it. Unable to maintain the household, I had to let go the servants one after another. There was much emotion as these people had served us well and their livelihoods depended on us.

All this, I related to my dear Athan. He listened with a patience I had not seen in him; after which, he sighed and said,

"Knowing we were on the road to reunion, the witch Chitra-Vathi had the maid carry lies about the reception you promised. The news stopped me from coming to you sooner, my sweet. Then, having bought the time, the witch well exploited it."

"Was Madhavi a confederate in the scheme?"

"I don't think so, but please do not again mention that name in my presence."

"As you wish, dear Athan."

"Let's leave this fraud buried and never let it come between us. I do not wish to be a public fool, and therefore will not seek restitution from the swindlers. The people who wilfully cheated us will have money enough to erect their tombstones."

"I know well your temper, dear Athan, and already rejected all help from my parents."

"And never will I return as a failure to my father's house."

"Then we have nothing, dear Athan."

"I have you, my dear blameless wife, and you are treasure enough."

"You could call on our dear friend Anandan, who sent a message of having returned from Araby. He has grown wealthy by all reckoning and promised to visit after settling his immediate affairs."

"No, my sweet," he whispered, "let us not sully his success with our sorrow."

My Athan embraced me tight and long, and our shoulders turned dark and wet with tears, and our eyes drained.

"My ankle rings, Athan."

With nervous excitement, I removed them from my feet and placed the pair in his hands. He studied the ankle rings, and his fingers traced their perfect curves.

"But they are yours, my sweet." His voice was a whisper.

"Please take it. Sell it, Athan, and with this seed rebuild your honour."

"I will not sell them, ever."

I remained silent, did not wish to nag, for he would arrive at a wise decision.

"Perhaps," he said with some hesitation, "perhaps, I can pawn one piece and rebuild our lives with the money. And as soon as is possible, redeem the pawn too."

"A wonderful suggestion, my dear Athan."

"But not here, my sweet, not in Puhar." After a few moments, he said, "We will directly adventure to the Pandyan's Madurai, the ancient city of ramparts; and free from knowing looks and snide whispers, seek a new life."

"When do you wish to leave?"

"Now, my sweet, right away, before the sun rises and brings with it ridicule and painful gossip."

###

15: In the West lies Fate and Fame

Kovalan was eager to leave. He worked through the night writing several letters to our families, Anandan, and to the moneylenders. Leaving the palm leaf letters on the family altar, where a visitor would find them, we bundled several necessities for our journey: food and water, thick cloaks and rolled mats for sleeping, and a few incidentals.

My poor husband removed the rope, the only piece we had, from the well and tied it around the brass lamp to better carry it. The lamp was heavy, but he said it was an article we could use to barter. He planned to carry all the load but, wanting to share the burden, I would not have it. He agreed without question, and his meekness saddened me. Ever since his return, he agreed to all my requests, large and small. Defeated and subdued, he had withdrawn into himself. I resolved to help recover my dear husband's past vigour and confidence.

Well-provisioned, in the early hours of the morning, we stepped over the threshold. As stated in his letter, I left the household keys in the tall plinth where grew the family Tulasi plant. Clasping my hands, I went around the magical plant several times in silent prayer. Satisfied, we took a last look at the house and grounds and, with heavy sighs, opened the gate and let ourselves out onto the street.

In the distant dark, a dog barked, but otherwise only the buzz of insects wished us well. High in the heavens, in the sheet of deep, unrelenting black pin-pricked by stars, the thin moon smiled. The nights ahead promised to grow brighter and it would be another week or more before the sky darkened and hid the dangers of the land. To keep out the morning cold and the heat which would bathe us in the day, Kovalan wrapped a turban about his head and I pulled a shawl over mine.

Hunching under the heavy cloth bundle and lamp, Kovalan set a steady pace, and I three steps behind. Every hundred paces or so, Kovalan turned to review my progress, and I rewarded him with a moment's smile. It wrecked my heart, seeing him thus. He was of gentle persuasion, not drawn to physical prowess and unaccustomed to deprivations. After he turned several times, I assured him I was holding out well, and not to waste his energy and rhythm by stopping to check on me.

Kovalan, not used to carrying heavy loads, shifted his bundle from shoulder to shoulder. I wondered how long more before his skin rubbed raw and bled. I consoled myself that much of what he carried was food and drink, and with every meal stop, the load would lighten. But in his bundle was the oil lamp, a heavy burden but an indispensable need.

We crossed the large swathe of green and shady trees of the Naalangadi Market. The first itinerant traders were already setting up stalls, rolling out mats, and displaying their wares. Kovalan picked up his pace, and I understood his intention. We navigated turns, entered side streets and alleys and, with some relief, exited the City District.

The closer we reached the city outskirts, the poorer the neighbourhoods we passed. Humble structures made of mud walls and thatched roofs replaced palatial houses. The air carried whiffs of humanity: the foul smell of detritus and the overpowering tang of animal dung. The streets, unlike the well-swept roads in the richer districts, had turned disagreeable, riven with open sewers and spotted with animal faeces, and the ever-present red spittle from chewed betel leaf and areca nut.

We left the city gates behind and followed the tree-lined road. Soon, the eastern sun caught up with us. To keep the slanting sun from scorching his head, Kovalan thickened his turban with a second piece of cloth. The sweet man cut some Palmyra leaves and fashioned a parasol of sorts, which he held up for me. I knew before long his arms would tire but, seeing how much he worried for my comfort, offered no protest. The road extended ahead and the city walls disappeared behind; and the well-arrayed trees yielded to haphazard growth that melded to wild vegetation and forest.

Kovalan had never made this journey and therefore relied on my memory of the route travelled several years ago. He was not one to allow me to take the lead, but had transformed; treated me as an equal. I welcomed his confidence, but the responsibility overwhelmed me. What a difference between the current venture and the carefree joy of travelling in the company of my parents and a full complement of servants and armed escorts.

Madurai lay to the south moving west and about a hundred leagues away as the pigeon flies. Depending on the road conditions and detours, it promised to be a dangerous and taxing adventure but, defeated as Kovalan was, I dared not share my apprehensions with him. If we kept to the road, with luck, we might encounter a passing caravan; people who will not recognise us. Perhaps the caravan master might be a kind man, like my father. Father. My dear, loving father. My diamond. My ruby. My pearl. All those pet names. For a few moments, my tears welled. But I hardened myself. I have to remain strong. I will remain strong for my husband.

After several hours and seeing my dear Kovalan tire, I suggested a rest break.

"Athan, I need but a moment to catch my breath but will recover soon."

He moved fast to help unload my bundle and, having settled me under a shady palash tree, poured a measure of water. I plucked leaves from the tree and fashioned a plate, a skill acquired on Chinnamma's farm. The thought of the poor woman's fate made me pause, but I shook myself free. I reminded myself to remain strong and resolute.

"Take your time, my sweet," he said, having spied my momentary lapse of focus, "for we have set out even before the cock crowed and the day stretches long before us."

Opening several containers, I scooped some cooked rice onto the leaf-plate. Rolling a ball of rice, I placed it in his palm and added some pickles and a shallot for taste. Though it was poor fare, Kovalan enjoyed it with unhidden pleasure: reminded me of the young Maravar escorts who, years ago, ate with gusto from my hands. But I hid my welling emotions. I will not cry. I cannot let my husband see my tears.

Upon his insistence, I ate my lunch too, relishing the closeness of his company. He mixed honey in water and we enjoyed a refreshing drink.

Though it was only mid-afternoon, the trip had already proven arduous. I wondered how much longer our endurance would last, for I too was wearing out. I blamed myself for the ills befallen us: encouraging him into Madhavi's arms, losing his wealth to that scheming old woman, and being unable to give him children.

As these thoughts wrecked my mind, a light touch landed on my hand. Kovalan smiled and said,

"I am much recovered, sweet, and if you are refreshed, let us press on."

I realised he had been holding back on my account. Perhaps I had underestimated his inherent male strength and should worry more about my ability to make the journey.

We had long lost the outskirts of Puhar, and I had become less certain of the route. With every step, we were leaving civilisation and entering the unknown. After talking it through, we decided it was best to keep to the tree line but within sight of the road. The plan worked well until the first fork on the road.

Trees grew thick and without man-made markers and cultivations, something we townsfolk took for granted, I lost my way and grew distraught. The sun did not help. It seemed to set faster than usual. When I suggested we camp for the night, Kovalan did not complain or question.

Tired and overwrought, but after a good night's rest, and with clear minds, perhaps we could better plan the next steps. We ate a cold dinner of cooked rice, fresh mangoes, and bananas, and washed the meal down with milk. Daring not to light a fire, for fear of attracting attention to ourselves, we wrapped ourselves with kambali shawls, and the woollen garments kept us warm. I placed my arms around Kovalan and snuggled close, and overcome with fatigue, I fell asleep.

The morning found me chilled to the bone and aching all over. Kovalan, also worn from exhaustion, snored in deep sleep. I lit a fire. When Kovalan awoke, we sat close and soaked in the meagre warmth of the small fire.

After washing ourselves and having a breakfast of milk and rice, we set off again with the sun on our backs.

I had become unsure of the way, but my dear husband did not complain or find fault with me. Instead, he took the lead and said,

"All we need is to follow the western sun."

He was right, but whenever we confronted a fork in the ill-defined path, he pretended to consult the sun and shadows. Though altogether lost, he played the part of confidence for my benefit, and I grew more and more worried. We came upon windswept terrain and, with no human constructs for guidance, the featureless land was difficult to read.

We travelled with hope and prayers. On the third day, we encountered craggy hills and thick, forested swathes of green. The latter was ideal Arakan habitat. Many years ago, seduced by risqué dreams, I had wished to meet these wild people, but not anymore, not now.

More than once, Kovalan gave vent to his fears and wondered whether he had been too hasty in setting out without thinking through our journey, and the challenges city folks such as ourselves would encounter. Though worried to distraction, whenever he expressed doubts, I voiced small words of encouragement.

"I should have sold the oil lamp and purchased a buffalo cart," said Kovalan.

"That would attract tigers and bandits for sure, Athan. We're faring well and as you planned, all we have to do is follow the sun heading west."

By the fifth day, we were saving our energy and conversations for the rest periods, which we took with increasing frequency and length. The sweltering sun, the burden of the bundles on our backs, and meagre meals continued to deplete our store of strength.

The further we travelled, the wilder country we encountered. Kovalan beat the bushes with a wooden staff to flush out hidden rodents, whose startled bites could be fatal, or worse, serpents, which might strike without warning.

During the rest periods, he foraged for fruits and flowers. We ate the fruits and licked nectar from the flowers. These tiny drops of floral honey were a welcome source of energy. Foraging also helped husband our depleted store of food, for we never knew when the land would deny us bounty.

When Kovalan spotted animal droppings or fresh spoor, he did not remark or point, but would take a wide circling detour.

I did not question these strange manoeuvres but, sensing my unease, he would say,

"As long as we follow the sun, we're going in the right direction." And so we kept moving ever westwards.

One late afternoon, we came upon a small stream and took a welcomed bath. It was medicinal and rejuvenating. Having grown bolder by the day, Kovalan lit a small fire using virgin neem twigs and I dried my hair over the smoke.

"Should we not press on?" I asked, looking at the western sun. "See the shadows but only a few leagues away, their jagged points pushing darkness towards us."

"You are right, my sweet," said Kovalan, "and let us best be going."

"What was that noise?"

Before he could answer, the bushes opened and revealed dark men with frightening eyes. Some wore garlands of bleached bones, and others had curved horns protruding from thick fuzzy hair. The bull shouldered men circled and tightened around us. I clung to Kovalan.

Every so often, a frightening man snarled and lunged, and when we cringed, the gang hooted with glee.

"Arakans!"

###

16: Beast-Men of the Hills

The tight, shifting gang of Arakans yielded to a man, a chieftain of sorts, as he pushed through to the front. He was thick in girth, with veins protruding proudly on muscular arms, and around his neck dangled a gory garland of bleached bones. The beast-man growled in a thick voice, then cleared his throat and repeated in a gentler quality.

"Are my words too strange for your ears? I said, you look like Poom-Puhar."

"You speak Tamil?" I blurted, half in relief and half in fear, as I pulled Kannagi closer.

"You squeak with a woman's voice," he said, and there was a hint of mirth. "And why not Tamil? This is Tamilakam and we're all Tamils, are we not? Though your kind views us as lowlier than the low."

It was some dialectical Tamil the beast-man spoke, and his rolling words and merging pronunciations were difficult to grasp. But with some concentration I understood, if not all the individual words, at least the intent behind his words.

"Begging your pardon, sir," I said with a gulp. "Truly I am sorry but assure you I meant no offence."

"Surely you did, Poom-Puhar," said the Arakan. "But I understand your predicament. This lot would terrify me out of my wits too if I came across them in the jungle."

There was a stunned silence, and the man threw his head back and laughed, his voice starting as a distant rumble which grew louder with each syllable.

The shocking outburst spread to his cohort and guffaws erupted all around us. I did not know what to make of the jolly giant and his followers, and wondered if it was a strange feint, a prequel which bade ill for us.

"I'm Savaali and the talkative one here is my brother, the Silent One." He pointed to another massive but stern man who had a high tuft of hair knotted on his head. "We mean you no sinister harm, Poom-Puhar, but what compels your footprints on our lands?"

"I am Kovalan, sir, indeed, from Puhar. This is my wife, Kannagi, and we are on our way to the Pandyan Madurai."

The Arakan turned to his people and muttered. "Kovalan." My name carried from one to another in the group and received smirks and hints of derision. The Arakan said,

"You're *Kovalan*, king, and which realms do you lord over?"

"My husband is *my* king, sir, and he rules me, his kingdom."

Kannagi had interceded, and her voice carried a hint of defiance. It was unlike her and though she had been outspoken in her youth, ever since our marriage and especially in public, she always held back and let me do the talking.

"And with a touch of anger too," said the Arakan. "And does she also carry your spear, Poom-Puhar?" He laughed at his sexual innuendo, and the Arakans roared.

"You are uncouth, sir, and it befits you, as after all, you are Arakan." Again, and before I could intervene, Kannagi had spoken, and in unconcealed anger.

"I only jest, little sister, don't reduce me to cinders with your so very fiery eyes. For don't you know, our chieftain too calls himself a god, Eraivan, but he is quite Arakan."

"Thank you, sir, and now we will be on our delayed way," I said, not wishing to prolong the conversation. I stooped to gather my things, but the Arakan, *Savaali*, placed his foot on one edge of my bundle.

"Well, Poom-Puhar, if you keep to this direction, you'll reach your Puhar. Perhaps it's a childhood pastime you indulge in, travelling in circles."

I wondered what new mischief the man planned. I tugged the bundle. But Savaali's foot remained firm. I looked up, and he grinned.

"If you speak correctly, sir, point in the right direction," I said. "It is a late sky and we plan to find shelter, for ill-equipped we are to spend another night in the wild."

"There're no traveller's hospice, why, not even a wayfarer's shed in these parts, but there's our Arakan village and a welcomed fireside for you to share your interesting story."

Kannagi touched my hand, and her eyes urged me to accept the man's invitation. I frowned, but she was right. I straightened myself and conceded.

"We are glad to accept your kindness, sir, and my wife and I thank you."

"Good, and we'll sup on the flesh of a young boy, or, perhaps a gurgling baby." And he roared with laughter.

Aghast, my jaw dropped, and I wondered what horror lurked behind the beast-man's invitation. Kannagi's hand tightened on my wrist and I sensed her courage, like mine, melt.

"But is it not in keeping with what you townspeople believe that we of the kurinji hills are cannibals?"

"I know not of such accusations vested on your people, sir."

"Oh? And yet, I horrified you when just now I suggested feasting on the flesh of a baby. You believed it true. But the same offer from a townsman, you would take for humour and seen through the jest."

"I did not know Arakans jested, sir."

"Why is that Poom-Puhar? Is it because you think we Arakans are less than human and delight only in wanton killing?"

"Indeed, my dear uncle fell victim to murder on these roads," said Kannagi. "And my aunty, grief stricken, threw herself on his funeral pyre and met a gruesome death."

"You so quickly lay the blame of your uncle's death at our threshold," said the Arakan. "Your aunt's death is horrendous. But what civilised culture is it of yours that compels a woman to take her life in such a dreadful manner? Why treat your women as firewood when they are fruits of life? Or perhaps there's another reason, a vile one; perhaps widows are irksome claimants of their dead husbands' inheritance. Seek the source, little sister, and quench your questions."

"But sir," I said before Kannagi could respond, "all we know is that many travellers lost their lives in these parts, and their mutilated cadavers brought back to Puhar."

"With such irrefutable evidence, it becomes easy to hang the deeds on us, for we're diabolical, are we not? The unhappy rumours spread by your bards and court officials have given our

Arakan heritage synonymous notoriety with cannibalism, human sacrifice, and all manner of demonic deeds."

Kannagi grasped my arm and looked into my eyes. I knew her meaning. She had spoken in anger and regretting it, and wanted me to rein my quick inclination to win arguments. She was right. I fought hard and held my tongue.

"Forgive me, sir," I said. "I spoke in haste."

"Be aware, Poom-Puhar," said the big man in a gentler tone. "Murders committed in these parts, not by Arakans but blamed on Arakans. When jackals and vultures tear apart cadavers left in the open, the Pandyan also blame these natural acts of nature on Arakan cannibalism.

"The Pandyan king's soldiers hunt and kill my people for crimes not of our doing. And when you return to your civilised life, it behoves you to speak well and spread the truth to your brethren."

"You have explained well, sir," I said, "and I shall dwell on all you have argued, but for now the light fades and we best consider your offer of village. We, my dear wife and I, are of feeble heart and surrender ourselves to whatever you have planned for us."

"Melancholy fills your words, Poom-Puhar, but I don't think your heart is frail. Not versed in the mores of physical arts perhaps, but not feeble. And your slight wife, she's a deep one. I'm sorry for your loss, little sister. As for the rest, we do not intend our fierce demeanour and scraggy weapons for innocent wayfarers such as you."

"Why then frighten us so, and especially my dear poor wife here?"

"I am not afraid, my dear husband," said Kannagi, "but I am tired and wish for rest."

"The little sister betrays no fear, Poom-Puhar, and has some magical powers which elude my understanding. My hunters and I have been away for many days from our fires. We, too, are eager to return to our round women. The people of kurinji never write offers on shining sheets of water. If you agree, we shall venture to my village, where you can satisfy your rest. Let us now make haste, for the night brings its own special dangers."

The Arakans grabbed our bundles, including the heavy oil lamp, and set off in a run; in absolute silence. Kannagi and I could not pace the swift hunting party, burdened though they were with our bundles and several carcasses of wild boar and deer.

The beast-men kept to a rhythmic lope in a single file. Savaali brought up the rear, urging us on with some persistence. Moonlight peeped through gaps in the darkening canopy, but the band was running into deeper jungle, into increasing blindness. I grabbed Kannagi's hand and struggled to keep sight of the white soles of the hunter before me. Soon, I lost the hunter to the black darkness and Savaali stopped.

Kannagi and I, drenched in perspiration, and with hands on knees, coughed and panted. The Arakan waited with patience and I knew then he meant no ill towards us.

Once we caught our breaths, Savaali, without a word, scooped Kannagi onto his back. She protested, but he ignored her and set off, leaving me with no choice but to keep pace. I ran in a red haze of heart-burning pain and almost collapsed from exhaustion.

When we neared the village, Savaali let Kannagi drop to her feet. She lashed out at the liberty he had taken for having touched her, to which he replied,

"Your words betray you, as my actions reveal mine."

He walked away in confident strides, and I grabbed Kannagi's hand and spoke soothing words for her calm, even as we hurried, afraid to lose sight of the Arakan.

The village was not of thatched huts but caves and pitiful holes burrowed into hillsides. A warren of narrow and dim passages, scraping tight for full men, connected the hovels. Some of these tunnels turned into corners that led to deep pits. Hidden within these damp pits, as we learned later, were several cunning traps filled with poisoned spikes to maim and kill unwelcomed intruders.

We followed the broad, taut frame of Savaali, who carried a lit torch, our heads lowered to prevent colliding with the low rough ceiling. As our eyes grew accustomed to the dark of the warren, I discerned slight movements of people darting about or peering out of passages which branched in all directions. Every time the bodies darted or ducked, they caused shifts in the dim glow from burning torches not yet come into view. There were dark shadows silhouetted against shadows less intense. And the smell! A permanent odour, which we could not escape, filled the warren. The smell of stale air, unwashed bodies, and wood smoke tickled our throats and made our eyes water.

A gentle curving passage led to an open space so vast that the opposite end hid in darkness. An enormous bonfire in the centre did not help, as it caught our attention and blinded us. We were in the village centre, an immense crater carved into the hill. The gouge was a natural freak; its walls and floor were hewn smooth by divine hands. Above our heads hung the sky and the moon, and dark outlines of flourishing trees fringed the cusp of the skyline.

A thick crowd of people, who were swarthy, pot-bellied, and frizzy haired, closed around us. The blaze illuminated tattooed faces with bone fragments that pierced ear lobes and noses. The women, bare breasted, wore animal hides. But these wrappings were for decoration, not modesty. The children were naked, even the girls of age.

The crowd parted and allowed us a spot near the fire. All their eyes were on us. Occasionally, we felt a tug on our clothes and, turning, spotted a child with a finger in its mouth and a shy smile. Adults too touched our garments and even our hair. Then there was the silence. The people did not talk or make the variety of noises, coughs, and sniffles that accompany an assembled crowd. They were silent; waiting in a state of heightened anticipation. Only the sound of the crackling fire, as the wooden logs strewn on the flames splintered to heat and settled to burn, filled the vast chamber.

A movement, as if by some telepathic signal, and the crowd turned as one. A path opened. Heads bobbed above the crowd and several massive men, their shoulders built like bulls, strode up to the bonfire.

The leading Arakan wore an impressive leopard skin headdress, its jaws gaping in a snarling smile and its hide flowing down the man's back for a heavy cape. He carried a tall spear; the wooden staff smooth from use. The Arakan's thick black hair glistened, as if soaked in animal fat, and cascaded in bouncing waves down his chest to the waist. His large teeth, white and well formed, peered through the rough beard covering his entire face. His body was bare other than a strip of hair running down the middle from his chest to a sunken navel at his waist belt. He wore a deer skin, wrapped around his waist. The man's bearing and his imposing presence made clear he was the clan's headman.

"He's Eraivan, the god I spoke of, the village chief." Savaali whispered beside me. It was then I realised he had disappeared and now re-joined us. Caught in the heaving mass of smell and muscle, I was grateful for his reassuring presence.

"He's one of my fathers," said the beast-man.

I assumed he meant the man was an elder, but Savaali, reading my mind, made matters clearer. He said,

"I'm the son of his body, for my mother, before her death, told me it was so. Though she slept with many, surely, she said, it was Eraivan who impregnated her. I suppose a woman knows such things. And he acknowledges me as his son, as do another elder or two." My face betrayed horror, for he said,

"You look appalled, Poom-Puhar. But why, when in your custom, several women share one husband, do they not? Is it so peculiar in our ways, several men share a woman? A child nurtured by a village has the blessings of many guides, does it not? Now listen to the Arakan, who will also be almost human if not a god."

The Arakan king, Eraivan, stood in front of the blazing bonfire, giving us to appreciate the full measure of his magnificent physique.

"I am Eraivan, king of my people and I welcome to our fireside Kovalan from the Cholan Puhar, and his angry wife, Kannagi." His eyes darted to me and then to Kannagi. "Our guests are tired and I am famished too. The hunt has been bountiful and our fleet-footed huntsmen, gone for days, evaded the king's soldiers and returned safe with not a broken limb. For this great favour, let us offer thanks to our gods and prayers to our animal brethren, for each beast gave its life so we mere Arakans can live another day."

Eraivan stepped back and an old skeletal man, a priest of sorts, wearing a garland of bleached bones, chanted prayers in some ancient tongue while another frightful looking man beat a small drum. The priest dipped a bundle of leaves in a pot of milk and blood, and blessed the carcasses which the hunters carried forward. The bony man and his assistant went into some crude spasmodic dance accompanied by guttural chants, which the crowd echoed. This went on for some time. On and on. Repetition after repetition. Then, without warning, they stopped. The dancing, the drum beats, and the chants. All stopped. The abruptness magnified the silence that followed.

The prayers and thanksgiving completed, Eraivan raised his arms and said, "Come people, let us now feast without care, for tomorrow's promises remain fickle."

A loud cheer broke out, and the celebration ensued. Women jumped straight and high; men pranced about like simians, landing on all fours before exploding into the air again. The full village sang, their voices throaty and interspersed by what I can only describe as screeches and screams from the women and children. The beast-men brought out drums, and a great clamour begun. Their music and singing were rhythmic, haunting, and enchanting in a raw manner.

The men passed around gourds that spilled some strange opaque liquid. Savaali thrust such a drink and motioned for me to partake. I did not wish to, and moreover, the container could do with a good wash. But, upon his pressing insistence, I obliged. I held up the gourd and poured the drink down my throat. Palm wine!

The drink stung, and I spat out a foul spray. Instead of taking offence, the big man and his compatriots laughed. Savaali slapped my back, and I almost lost my balance.

"Drink! Drink some more, Poom-Puhar, and this time— sip!"

He helped tilt the gourd and drenched my clothes. I grimaced with disgust and swallowed. Seeing eager faces, I was happy to offer my drink to one within reach. The Arakan snatched the drink but, apprehensive, he studied Savaali's reaction. My host laughed, and the Arakan relaxed and emptied the potent liquor into his mouth, with heavy spills escaping and streaking down his shiny chest.

The strong sweet tang of roasted meat rose from the fire pits, and as the night stretched, we grew accustomed to it, as we did with the other strange odours in the air.

But one aspect of their culture, if these people had a culture, shocked me: their carefree and flippant approach to coitus. As the feasting and intoxication progressed, men carried away squealing women—their naked legs kicking—into the night. Women too pulled men by their hands into the dark. No one cared. No one reproached. It was all so very scandalous and uncivilised. Men and women indulged in physical relations with anyone of their choosing. Savaali had already shocked me with the revelation regarding his parentage. Women chose their partners. Men accepted without quarrel, or so it seemed. Perhaps given quieter moments, I might study their fascinating family arrangement and discover some sense. But for now, with the noise and pushing crowd and the celebratory mayhem, it was too overwhelming to accept. Kannagi grabbed my hand as if to instil caution—to hold my tongue—and we decided not to take notice of the people's unfettered debauchery. For that was what their practices were—devoid of all morality and chastity. And yet, there was something innocent and free about their behaviour.

As the night wore on, we confined ourselves to fruits and warm goat's milk and, feeling more tired than full, looked forward to sleep. But it was not to be, for we found ourselves seated with Savaali at the great circular fireside. A thick press of Arakans, their bellies bloated with meat and liquor, gathered around us.

It was then I noticed, in the glow of the waving flames, the full measure of the green, red, and black beauty spots and tattoos on the Arakans. Intricate etches of demon gods and wild beasts adorned their chests, arms, and backs. All their foreheads carried some markings which rendered the Arakans even fiercer. The men sat about, legs wide and leather skirts parted, letting their manhood hang loose. Kannagi averted her eyes, keeping her resolute gaze on the flames. The women too sat without shame, but thankfully, fat thighs covered the privacy of their hooded cobras. I too looked away from the round breasts of the young and the thin flat flaps of the old.

It was story time, and as we were the newcomers, their expectant faces turned towards us. If we had no stories to tell, they wanted to know after our situation, and I repeated a tale already rehearsed, which revealed enough to satiate their curiosity.

Then, Eraivan joined us and, without ado, grasped my arm and said, "Your flesh is as soft as a maiden's but your bearing radiates boldness. And you travel the wild country alone, Cholan, and added foolishness to ignorance by bringing along your small wife, who is a temptress."

"It must be the habit of my position, sir," I said in anger, for his unwelcomed description of my dear Kannagi.

"And what position is that, Cholan, and why the unprovoked ill temper in your voice?"

"My position as husband and protector of my precious wife, Kannagi, and she is no temptress to men who live correctly."

"Ah, I see now what pricked your anger, or was it pride, or possessiveness? Say then, Cholan, who are these men who live *correctly*."

"Men who live correctly, sir, will behold my wedded wife as daughter or sister or mother, and accord the respect and protection her position demands."

"An excellent answer, Cholan."

"Do you, sir, live correctly?" I asked, letting my combative nature get the better of me.

"My praise must come from another, should it not?" said Eraivan. "But your question demands proof. Do you wish to hear my story or prefer to fall forward and feed the flame?"

"We are weary, sir," I said, and straightened myself, "but will try to be polite guests for a moment more at least, for we wish to hear your words."

"Lean back then and listen. Yes, my people live correctly and the proof comes from the earth beast which has left us unmolested for many generations."

"What earth beast do you speak of, sir, for I know of no such wonderful creature?"

"It is a serpent, Cholan, of the fire breathing kind. She lives in the bowels of the earth and seeks openings afforded by evil deeds of man. And when the last grain of sand tilts the balance, the serpent will burst forth and devour all in its path before disappearing into the ground again. Many ages ago, even before time started his endless journey, the serpent devoured these kurinji hills, and we who inherited these realms know better than to pursue incorrect living."

"How will one know when the earth beast is about?"

"She will cause tremors under your feet and send shivers up your spine, Cholan. But the Pandyan fools ignore her warnings, for already she makes her presence felt in Madurai even as you are relentless to reach her."

"Madurai promises repair to my fortune, sir," I said, "to provide my wife with a befitting life."

"Fate draws you there, Cholan, and your fiery wife."

"I appreciate your hospitality, but my dear wife, Sir Eraivan, is the gentlest creature ever walked on this earth. She is the wellspring of abiding love and fathomless forgiveness, and I care not about your interpretation of her gentle nature."

"You misunderstand my import, Cholan, but it is what it is." With unbridled curiosity, Eraivan studied Kannagi. She cast down her eyes. But as his gaze persisted, she looked up. They locked eyes; remained oblivious to the people watching them. After several long moments, he broke off and said,

"As my son Savaali discovered, your quiet wife is a deep one and I see it too. Our ancients, having gained the third eye on account of their severe fasts and deprivations of many sorts, foretold that amid our darkest days, a well-being would appear from the east to right matters gone asunder. As the fowls fly west and serpents slither away in fear, she will release the earth beast to shower flames and split the earth underfoot. She will churn the eager soil so that new shoots may sprout. *She* it is, for the well-being is of the feminine divine. And she will destroy the evil, even now closing upon my people, and save us."

"Are your people in danger, sir?"

"Yes, Cholan, for a new breed of Pandyans, filled with ever-growing avarice, committed wanton atrocities on Arakan lands, often on their own people. But they attach the blame to the Arakan. These are but excuses to force the king's hand to drive out my people. For these scheming men covet our lands. Thus far, we have prevailed, but their forays grow audacious and persistent. These are dark times for my peaceful people."

"You allude to matters beyond us, Sir Eraivan, and we appreciate the words, but not the situation you speak about. We, my wife and I, wish not to prolong your hospitality but to continue our broken journey in the morning. We spy eager faces seeking news but plead weariness for being poor guests with a yearning to rest our heads in sleep."

"Say no more, Cholan," said the Arakan chieftain with a deep sigh, "for tiredness sags your eyes and robs interest of the dangers facing my people. It is what it is. And we have been ignorant hosts and detained you beyond hours. We shall leave you now. I suggest you sleep here by the fire, for it will keep you warm. My people will bring you some wools to make it even more so." Eraivan slapped his thighs and stood up and said,

"Good! I will see you in the morning before you depart with a suitable escort."

###

17: The Edge of Civilisation

Kannagi stirred, and I sat watching her in the half-light, as has been my habit since we embarked on our journey. Marvelling at her unblemished beauty, my heart filled with leaping joy. But fearing that even my tender gaze might wake her, I stole away and sat on a tree trunk, axed to serve as a bench.

With brightening light, the village layout grew clearer. The centre was a vast hole cut by the hand of nature into the hill, for all around us were high cliffs. Caves pockmarked the steep slopes of hardened rocks surrounding us. The vast chamber was the epicentre of a long dead volcano. Shrubs covered the mouths of caves and, for a casual observer, the hill slopes looked serene and uninhabited. Trees had taken root on the cusp of the volcano's yawn. Seen from the lowlands, the village centre was only a copse of trees on a hilltop.

I sat there gaping at the ingenuity of nature when Kannagi turned with a smile. We exchanged tender words of greetings and after which addressed the matter at hand.

"The people are wild but friendly enough, Athan. But let us not dawdle, for Madurai beckons and we have many leagues more to trace."

"You are correct, my sweet. Please wait here while I seek the best of their lot, Savaali, and secure water to wash and something to eat before we set out."

Before I could venture forth, the Arakan king, Eraivan, approached out of the mist. He carried an earthenware pot of coarse bread and fruits and, under his arms, two ewers, the larger filled with water and the smaller with fresh goats' milk.

"My people continue in their late slumber and myself prepared this selection. Wash and refresh yourselves, good people, and I shall directly return with an escort to guide your onward journey." And without more to say, he turned and disappeared into the misty haze of dawn.

"And what did he mean last night, Athan, by studying me with such curiosity even as he spoke of a feminine wonder from the east to save his people?"

"It intrigued me too and is beyond my understanding, but let us not dwell too much on words fuelled by intoxicants, and instead make our preparations to depart."

We completed our morning ablutions and fortified ourselves with the breakfast well-prepared by the hands of the Arakan king himself. Their customs were extraordinary. A king who prepared breakfast for wayfarers. There were no servants in Arakan families, but what of his wives? And Savaali's mother has had several husbands. Apparently, so did many of the women in the village. All strange and even outrageous practices. But they claimed it was the way of our forebears. But Kannagi was right. We will have time enough to pause over such matters, for now Madurai awaits us.

When we had packed our few belongings, Eraivan, who seemed to have good timing in such matters, again appeared. Savaali, his brother the Silent One, and an armed group followed in his wake.

"Here, a small parting gift of smoked honey," said Eraivan. He handed a jar carved from wood. "You have set your mind on Madurai and I wish you well. Make your fortune, good Cholan, and pray quickly depart Madurai on your fleet feet. For evil lurks there, a city once exemplary and stain free, and blind men will release the locks to the nether world. And out will spring the fiery she-serpent."

"My wife and I thank you, Sir Eraivan, for your generous care and hospitality. We shall accord due weight to your counsel."

"Go now, Cholan, for my Arakans are restless to guide you to the hilltop, the one we call *The Edge*. For, it is the edge of civilisation. But move with impatience, for in these lands the day grows old fast, and before a blink abdicates to its darker cousin. From the Edge, you will gaze upon Pandyan country. Their roads are well-pressed and patrolled by their king's cohorts. No welcome for Arakans, but welcome enough for you. Go now, and may all the gods and goddesses you pray to look after you and keep you and your good woman safe."

Once more, with Savaali leading, we walked through low, tight tunnels. Torches, plunged into sodden walls and others wavering in hands held high, lit the way. I now had a better measure of the village. As I had already discovered during the night, the village comprised caves, holes, and hovels in hillsides, and all connected by the work of nature and the hand of man. The warren of passages was in places walls of earth and, in other portions, hard stone. Murals and strange markings adorned the stone walls. Much of the vulgar art depicted animal hunts, men with oversized lingams, and couples in various acts of rough coitus. There were also scratchings of gods and fanged demons.

Again, we avoided abrupt bends and pike filled holes until a faint patch of light greeted us in the distance. We heard birdsong and soon exited into the forest on the outer slope of the vast hill range, and the fresh morning greeted us.

As the day before, with the Silent One in the lead and Savaali bringing up the rear, we struggled to keep up with the Arakans as they moved through the forest. They ran in an easy lope, jumped over fallen tree trunks, and scaled up and dropped from boulders, and always landed on sure feet. Their movements were fluid and the cohort always silent, gliding through the bush like ghosts. There was not even a grunt when they dropped from a height and the air punched out of their lungs.

Kannagi and I tired early in the journey and the tribesmen offered to lift us on their backs as if we were children riding play horses. My dear wife dithered but I, almost fainting from fatigue, urged her to discard all inhibition. Seeing me clamber on a man's back, she, too, did likewise. When one man tired, without hesitation, another took over the burden of our weight and kept the unbroken pace. No one complained, no one slowed, and so they carried us until the next exchange.

We made respectful distance and within hours, the trees thinned and we broke into the open. And a glorious day greeted us. We stood under an expansive sky filled with cotton clouds floating in a sea of brilliant blue. Waving grassland dipped and raced ahead, and paths snaked alongside mountain streams. The Arakans did not seem the worse for the journey, but the run had exhausted us.

The day was already mature when we reached the small spur on the hill—The Edge. Savaali pointed and said,

"See that hill there in the far yonder, skirted by the line of trees? Beyond the crest lies the village of *Puranchery*, gateway to Madurai. Seek Gayathri, a widow. She will provide lodging for you."

"Is this woman known to you?" I asked.

"No, but wayfarers mentioned her kind heart and a clean hut," said Savaali. "It is a steep path and will devour the better part of your day."

When Eraivan referred to the lookout as *The Edge*, the edge of civilisation, I had assumed we were *entering* civilisation. But I learned from Savaali, his king meant we were *leaving* civilisation.

"We part here, Poom-Puhar," said Savaali, "for any sightings of Arakans will raise a terror and entice soldiers to hunt us down, for they hold no ready respect for our lives."

"You have been kind my friend, all of you, and I dread it will be well past the daylight hour before you repair to your homes."

"Think nothing of it, Poom-Puhar," said Savaali. "The gods go with you."

"My husband's name is Kovalan, sir," interrupted Kannagi, "if you please." The huge Arakan with the abiding humour laughed and said,

"If you wish me to address him as king sir, so be it, *Kovalan Sir*. The gods go with you too, fiery little sister. Take that path leading away to the left, for it is a sly one and bends behind the enormous boulder you see on your left. You cannot miss the village."

I followed Savaali's outstretched hand. He was right. An unsuspecting traveller would have missed the path.

When I turned to thank him, Savaali was gone; and so were all his men. One moment they were there, and the next moment we stood alone. Kannagi looked just as amazed.

"Remarkable people, these beast-men," I said.

"Men, Athan, not beast-men, please."

"Yes, my sweet. Men."

"Come, Athan, let us not waste the haste made by these selfless souls, for the horizon sucks away sunlight fast. It is best we seek shelter for the night in the village before we lose what precious little daylight remains."

***

The thatch-roofed huts of Puranchery had low doors and were identical in construction, made from bricks of mud and rice straw, and slapped with flat cow-dung cakes to soak up the heat. Each house had a little garden. And a flimsy fence, made of weaved coconut leaves, marked out individual plots. The dirt streets, though well-swept, betrayed little invasions of grass sprouts here and there, hinting at the ever-ready forest waiting to reclaim the land.

The people were trusting and welcomed us with shy smiles, and children gathered and formed a small procession in our wake. As it was a woman we sought, it made sense for Kannagi to make the enquiries.

"We seek shelter with Amah Gayathri," said Kannagi.

Immediately several hands pointed the direction. Some children offered to show us the way and others ran ahead, excited and calling out the woman's name.

By the time we and the party of gambolling escorts reached our intended destination, a woman of indeterminate age and her daughter, a few years younger than Kannagi, were waiting to greet us. They were of a pleasant disposition and, as was the custom, clasped hands in welcome. The woman, clad in the white garments of a widow, addressed Kannagi.

"Welcome, please," she said with reverence, "I am Gayathri, and this is my daughter. Who are you, nice people, come to seek me and for what purpose?"

"Hello, Amah Gayathri, I am Kannagi and this is my husband, Kovalan. We are lately arrived from the Cholan capital city of Poom-Puhar. Some good people we met on the journey, upon learning our need for affordable lodging, suggested we seek your hospitality."

"I see the tali around your neck and so he is your good husband, as you say. Pardon me for speaking plainly, but we are two women, my daughter who has come of age and I, and with fate having taken my dear husband, we live alone. And society demands many precautions before allowing anyone, and especially men, into our humble dwelling."

Suspecting Kannagi might become defensive, I said,

"All you say is correct, Amah Gayathri, and it is for my dear wife Kannagi, for whom I seek shelter. An arduous journey has ravaged her health. For myself will sleep in a small corner of your veranda outside the locked doors of your house."

Throughout the exchange, the entire village, it seemed, gathered in a tight knot around us and scrutinised our every gesture and weighed our every word.

Unfortunately, the people were not passive onlookers and several men interrogated us, as if duty bound to prevent any inadvertent occurrences and gossip. I felt myself growing annoyed at the implications that smeared my integrity but had the good sense to conceal my discomfort.

Only after gaining the approval of the people, Gayathri found her voice to grant us a room. I did not have to sleep on the veranda.

I took out the gleaming oil lamp and handed it to Kannagi, who offered it to our host.

"Please, Lady Kannagi, keep your family heirloom for now," said the woman. "You wear weathered garments, but below the dullness, I detect fabrics of high quality. Your words are subdued, but your bearing hints of one who had once lived as a queen. My daughter and I are blessed to have you and your husband as our guests. You are welcome to stay as long as you wish and partake of our meagre meals. When you depart, pay us what you deem fair, for your offer now is far too excessive."

Gayathri led us into the house and we lowered our heads to enter the door. The air in the cottage smelled of flowers, and the dirt floor was clean. An arrangement of rocks served as a stove, and there was a small pile of stacked firewood. Several clay pots and receptacles cluttered one corner. There was little on offer, but more than we could have scavenged on any jungle trail. Most of all, since we departed Puhar, this would be the first night under a proper roof.

Our room was dim, lit by a dull light from a small window set below the roof. The window let in breeze while providing a measure of privacy.

I sat on a welcomed rope bed which had a mat covering, and Kannagi lay on another mat on the floor next to me. Weariness won, and we fell asleep.

###

18: Spend Lies to Save Lives

The Captain of the Royal Household Guard, a tall, muscular man with purpose in his stride, escorted me to a large room. Rich, sandalwood furniture and silk-covered cushions populated the opulent room.

Two men, of evident importance, luxuriated on divans and awaited my approach. The man of years was of slight frame and had a full head of hair and bleached beard. The younger man was rotund and bald, save for a ring of black hair that went around the back of his head from ear to ear, and had a thick bullhorn moustache. He was pale skinned, as if the sun had never set sight on him, and nursed a bandaged arm in a sling. The captain said,

"Honourable Prime Minister Sir, Esteemed Royal Jeweller Sir, this is Kovalan of Poom-Puhar." Turning to me, the captain said, "Please pay your respects to Shree Sagasana, Prime Minister and Grand Counsel to the Great Pandyan, and Thiru Pillay, Royal Jeweller to the Crown."

The older man, introduced as the prime minister, stood up and took my hands. It was a warm and assuring welcome. I was grateful and took a quick liking to him. But Thiru Pillay remained seated, and I sensed he was no friend.

"Thank you, captain."

With a polite gesture, the prime minister dismissed the soldier and guided me to a chair no less splendid than his own. An attendant appeared from behind the drooping drapes and served honeyed water.

"Dear sirs, I think there has been a misunderstanding and your soldiers committed a grave error in identity. They mistakenly—."

"Please, Sir Kovalan, refresh yourself first," said the prime minister with a soft smile.

"And we will do the questioning, if you will please," said the royal jeweller, his voice raspy, to which the prime minister lifted a hand to stay the man's words.

"What my good friend and eager colleague, Thiru Pillay, meant to convey was," said the prime minister, "for now, time is a premium for all of us. You see, we have a foreign delegation visiting, an eagerly awaited event but one that has lent disruption to our routines."

I liked the prime minister's conciliatory tone, but the royal jeweller, with his hooked nose and dark-ringed eyes, sat hunched as a vulture. The prime minister said,

"Therefore, to resolve this misunderstanding, as you so rightly pointed out, allow me to recount what we know, and then you can share your knowledge regarding the matter at hand and educate our areas of ignorance."

"Yes please, Sir Prime Minister," I said.

"You, Sir Kovalan, having lately arrived from Poom-Puhar, presented an ankle ring to an artisan goldsmith, hoping to raise money. Is this correct?"

"It is as you say, prime minister."

"All would have been well and no need for this interview if not for the artisan having recognised the anklet as one uncannily similar to another he had once marvelled. You see, Sir Kovalan, the artisan you met, and handed over the anklet to, is in Thiru Pillay's employ. The man is one of a select few tasked to polish and restore the lustre of the queen's ornaments, a job he had undertaken several times.

"As fate would have it, on the most recent occasion, there was a tragedy of sorts. You see, when transporting the chest of royal treasures from the palace to the manufactory, under suitable guard and with Thiru Pillay himself supervising the transfer, a runaway wagon jostling and thrashing about behind a crazed bull ploughed into the carriage carrying the royal trunk, spilling the contents, including a pair of the queen's anklets, onto the street.

"Thiru Pillay, even after suffering a fractured elbow which he is still nursing, had his men throw a cordon around the affected area. They combed the place and turned over every grain of sand. Thankfully, the searchers rescued all the scattered ornaments, save for one anklet belonging to the queen."

"I fear the import of your story, sir," I said.

"How did you come by this anklet?" The prime minister spoke in a soft voice, but his eyes were as alert as a hawk.

"Your question intrigues me, but I did not come by this anklet. It is mine, or more accurately, my wife's, the chaste Kannagi. It was part of my wedding dowry to her."

"So, you claim it as yours in the first instance," said the prime minister, "before it became your wife's, which by the laws of our Pandyan realms, and even by your Cholan mores, remains ultimately yours. Therefore, my question remains, how did you come by this anklet?"

"Very well, and since it will bring this sorry matter to a close, I bought the ankle ring from a trader, a Greek by the name of Telamonius, in Poom-Puhar." Noticing a defensive tone in my voice, I caught myself.

"When, may I ask?" said the prime minister.

"Why, several years ago and before my marriage rites."

"And where is this Greek, Telamonius, now?" asked the prime minister.

"He once travelled in trade between his Achaean homeland and Tamilakam, but because of an insult given to the womanhood of Tamilakam, my Cholan king had the man banished, never to return. I know not where he is now."

"And what a stroke of good fortune that." Thiru Pillay muttered; his tone derisive, and he looked away with disdain. But the prime minister, ignoring the man, said,

"Sir Kovalan, you place us in a rather difficult position, you see, and I need to speak frankly, if I may. This anklet which you claim belongs to your wife, to you, to your family, well sir, it is remarkably similar to another belonging to our Queen, Kopperun-Devi. Indeed, it is identical to that which has been missing for some time now."

"I understand your thrust, Sir Prime Minister, but it does not sully the truth I speak."

The royal jeweller snorted and his behaviour provoked my anger. My face hardened, and I went still. The prime minister raised his hand for calm, and said,

"Please, Sir Kovalan, perhaps my words come across as surprising. Nevertheless, we do not intend to stoke flames but to resolve the matter, which I am quite sure, as you have already advised, is all an unfortunate misunderstanding. After all, your Cholan craftsmen are as skilled, if not more so, as those in our Pandyan realms. Why, with enough money, anyone can commission a goldsmith to craft an exquisite anklet fit for royalty."

"Esteemed Prime Minister of the Pandyan court, sir," I said, "if you already believe my truth, I do not understand where this talk goes, for it instils a great foreboding within me."

"Please, Sir Kovalan, to assist with my quest, allow some leeway to present my piece and you will surely receive relief."

"You mean inquest."

"There is no inquest here, sir, for do you see stern judges and disbelieving faces arrayed against you? Certainly not," said the prime minister. His tone betrayed a tiny edge. It was evident he was an accomplished advocate, but restrained himself well. He said,

"What you have here is an expert witness and artisan well-versed in the fashioning of gold adornments, the esteemed Royal Jeweller, Thiru Pillay, come to assist so we can better understand the situation presented us. And I, an old man who has committed his life to upholding justice and good governance.

"Therefore, and please indulge me, may I enquire after your story, for your bearing is of one once accomplished and successful, and yet lately fallen on dire times. Any such revelations as you share will better enable us to appreciate how you came about owning such a treasured ornament and the need compelling you now to exchange this extraordinary heirloom for ordinary money. And why journey to Madurai for this sorry exchange, risking Arakan lands even, when Poom-Puhar is renowned for her men of means?"

"Very well, Sir Prime Minister, and your observations are correct, for I am an adventurous sort, especially in commercial matters. As the only son of a successful merchant, I hope to one day at least touch my forehead to the long shadow of my esteemed father, Sir Masattuvan. My father is a grain merchant. He is upright and hails from a long line of forefathers equally accomplished and in the service of the people of Poom-Puhar.

"Alas, I met a courtesan of great beauty and talents, and even greater wiles, and admit having foolishly given credence to a misplaced sense of duty to her, and trapped by shameless lust, found myself on an intoxicating path. Having lost my fortune to folly as just rewards for betraying my betrothed's love and trust, I returned to my blameless wife, Kannagi, and here I stand reduced by poverty, unable to face my dear parents, relatives and friends in my country of birth.

"My dear wife, chaste woman, she is, handed over her anklet, so I can redeem my fortune and honour, and once again walk among men of accomplishment. It is her wish. But for myself, my first and last purpose now is to provide my wife with a life I have so denied her. It wrecks my peace, but my pain is a grain when compared to the heavy heartache caused my dear wife, Kannagi.

"So, I sought Madurai, to quietly and unrecognised go about my plans, but now a breath's pace away from being accused of some alien crime."

The prime minister listened, attentive, as I expanded my unfortunate story. He asked a question here and there, but always displayed a keen interest in my words. I felt peace envelope me, for his manner was of one who had seen much pain and tragedy in his own long years.

But throughout the interview, I also discerned the disquiet and displeasure emanating from the royal jeweller. From his constant interruptions to the flow of our discussions, it was obvious he had already whispered confusion and conflicting evidence to the prime minister. When I had no more to say, the prime minister said,

"We have here our royal jeweller, and he swears—."

"On my children and children's children I swear," said Thiru Pillay. The thick green vein went taut on his bald head.

The prime minister threw a sharp look at the man, bordering on a rebuke, and said,

"As you see, Sir Kovalan, the incident agitates our royal jeweller for the king holds him responsible for the loss. Nevertheless, he will hold his peace as we resolve our predicament as expeditiously as possible."

The prime minister locked eyes with Thiru Pillay, who held the older man's gaze for a moment before breaking off.

"It is possible, Sir Kovalan," said the prime minister, continuing as if nothing had happened, "through some freak of fate, you had come across this valuable anklet."

"Fate brought this fabulous ankle ring to my hands, sir, but not of the freakish kind."

Suddenly, the royal jeweller protested angry words, but I did not hear him, for I too responded with hot words over the man.

Our exchange flew back and forth before the prime minister raised his hand again to stall the quarrel.

"Good sirs, please, hear the words of a wearied old man who has witnessed much in life," said the prime minister. "Fate brought us together today." Shifting himself closer, the prime minister took my hand and said,

"Kovalan, dear son of a loving and esteemed father, if you agree to having committed an unfortunate mistake, we, the royal jeweller and I, will petition our king and try utmost to prevail upon him to let the matter rest. And you can go about your life."

"The king will not accede, for he has already ordered the criminal's beheading," said Thiru Pillay. He heaved and his nostrils flared like a short-tempered rhinoceros. But the man's displeasure was incomparable to the intense indignation I felt.

"How dare you, sir, how dare you imply I am a thief?" I blurted and stood up.

"Please," said the prime minister, unperturbed, and stretched his hand with an open palm, gesturing for me to sit. "Please," he repeated, and I dropped back into my seat. He then turned to the royal jeweller and said, "The king had issued no such decree." Turning back to me, he said,

"What my colleague meant was, you see, it is the law of the Pandyan. Thieves forfeit their heads to the executioner's blade. But only after digging to the core of the matter and only if found guilty. For now, these appraisals are in their infancy and yet to uncover any guilt." Thiru Pillay nursed his injured arm and said,

"Prime minister, do not implicate me in any scheme other than the truth."

"Dear Thiru Pillay, we will together inform the king that our guards tried to apprehend a thief trying to sell the jewellery in the market, but he eluded capture and made for Arakan lands. We then sent out a party to search for the thief. But the thief, being resourceful, completed his escape. By which time, the good Kovalan here, on the road to our Madurai, picked up the anklet, presumably discarded in panic by the thief, leading to the present misunderstanding. Pleased that his queen's treasure returned, the king's vexation would cool, and the case closed with no bloodshed."

"And the artisan and soldiery privy to the discovery, how will they view your tale?" asked the royal jeweller.

"They know not the circumstances before Sir Kovalan presented the ankle ring to the goldsmith."

"And you will lie for this man?"

"We are court officials, Pillay my friend, and we must spend lies to save lives."

"Not I, sir. I do not feed such fodder," said the royal jeweller in a triumphant voice.

"You have always been a man better than I can ever aspire to be. I shall go to the king and let the penalty be on my head alone. All I need is your promise to hold your silence. You owe me, dear Pillay, you owe me."

The royal jeweller exhaled sharp and loud and, after a long moment, nodded in agreement.

"Thank you, my dear friend, Pillay. Thank you."

"What of me, sir? Not only will I lose the value of my dear wife's anklet, I shall return to her a thief."

"Kovalan, my dear boy, and please allow me, an old man advanced enough to be your father, to refer to you thus. As compensation, I will myself give you gold from my private purse, so you can return to your beaming wife and gaze at the *kumkuma* on her forehead. Would you not prefer to see her dressed in silk saris, weaved in the colours of her choice, rather than in the cotton white of a woman who has lost her husband?"

"Is my life worth more than my integrity?"

"My dear Kovalan, is your wife's happiness not worth more than anything?"

"Sir Prime Minister, I have already neglected my duties and betrayed the love and trust of my dear Kannagi. Even now, I labour to repair and rebuild my store of merit in her eyes. A false duty of care for a cur, and emotions and ego, led me astray once, but if I were to do what you now suggest, then I do it with full faculties in attendance. Can there be a better betrayal?"

"Most men relish the flesh of the mango and disregard the seed, dear Kovalan, but you see, if one plants the seeds of our errors, new wisdom flourishes, for from the swamp sprouts the lotus, does it not? I seek what is right and just, for the alternative leads to pitiful spilling of precious blood that does not wash away guilt, but plants and nourishes it."

"But it wouldn't do at all," I said, "for how long before the whispers reach the ears of my kith and kin?"

"What we speak and decide here, remains within these deaf walls. It is how we shape secrets and save lives." The prime minister studied Thiru Pillay for his response and again the man nodded.

"You see," said the prime minister, "all good men bend when lives, innocent lives, are at stake. As agreed, we shall—."

"Wait!" My voice stunned the prime minister and surprised me, too. He paused and said,

"Take a while then for a better plan, but I pray you arrive at an agreeable decision."

"When I purchased the anklets from Telamonius, the Greek, my sworn friend of six lives, Anandan, was in attendance. He is a successful merchant and a man of good repute. Send word to him in Poom-Puhar and he will come to vouch for my innocence."

Again, the prime minister remained engrossed before he said,

"Perhaps your plan holds some merit and we might yet put the genie back into the bottle."

"Preposterous," said a red-faced Thiru Pillay. "The return journey to Poom-Puhar will be until ten days or more and even that at full belt and through Arakan lands. And even if by some miracle this *Anandan* prevails in his haste, the king expects redemption of the lost treasure before the Roman audience."

"You see, dear Kovalan, as I mentioned, we are expecting Romapuri," said the prime minister. "What you might not know is, the winds have been good, and we received news lately that the senatorial delegation arrives earlier than envisioned. Already our carefully arrayed preparations to receive the deputation are in utter turmoil. You see, the king will now honour the Romans sooner than slated." Then, seeing his explanation made no impression of understanding, he continued.

"Her Majesty will also grace the event. And the queen, dear Kovalan, will insist on decking herself with these special anklets, valued gifts from her husband, the king."

"I am no villain, sir, and will not perjure the truth."

"The king will not wait until the days you seek." So forceful was the royal jeweller, his spittle flew as he spoke.

"You see, Sir Kovalan, I will share some confidence, and only because you are well-apprised of the situation confronting us," said the prime minister in a gentle voice.

"The king recently took a courtesan and fell out of favour with his queen. Yes, it is your story too. That as it is, the king adores his queen and never lost his love for her. But after failing in several attempts at reconciliation he has decided, presumably from hints gathered in their many quarrels, that the queen will be more receptive to his overtures if he can but produce the lost ankle ring to complete her wardrobe.

"Apparently, the queen wishes to relish the chase of youth and has challenged her king to embark again on the hunt. You see, for a man, the hunt expires when he catches the game, but for a woman, it is a never-ending game. As you would do anything for your wife, so too Nedun-Cheliyan, our king, for his queen, his beloved Kopperun-Devi."

"But my friend Anandan's testimony promises the secret to my redemption and, if you ensure the collaboration of time, a happy close to this unwarranted accusation."

"Perhaps you are right and there is a way out of this maze." The prime minister shut his eyes as if in meditation. Having decided, he said,

"Sir Kovalan, I'll send a rider to Poom Puhar to fetch your friend, Anandan, while I try to prevail on the queen herself, for I have known the princess when she was but a child who played on my lap." The old man smiled and his eyes glazed as he drifted into some old memory. Recovering from the lapse, he said,

"Now, she is a kind mother to us all. I will ask her, no, beg her, even on bended knees, to give you the time. But if all else fails, you must confess to having picked up the anklet from the dust, and bring this sorry episode to a safe and bloodless coup."

"I just now thought of another idea, one far superior to the long journey to Poom-Puhar and its attendant delay," I said. "My dear wife, Kannagi, holds the second of the pair of ankle rings. Allow me to return to her and bring the twin, and it would be evidence enough to redeem my integrity."

154

"And where waits your wife?" asked the prime minister.

"In Puranchery, a village half a day's journey away."

"We know where Puranchery lies," said the royal jeweller. "But we will not allow you the freedom to leave, lest you never return."

"Please, Thiru Pillay, we can clear the confusion confronting us in a day, if not less," said the prime minister.

"We cannot let him out of sight, not even under armed escort," said Thiru Pillay, his voice resolute, "for one never knows what trickery or dangerous allies he plans to summon."

"Very well then, but not because I subscribe to your suspicions, Thiru Pillay," said the prime minister. "Sir Kovalan, we shall fetch your wife, the chaste maiden Kannagi, with all proper respect so she might present the evidence to prove your innocence."

"You leave me little choice, but to agree, for the matter demands haste and resolution without fail."

"Yes, without fail, Sir Kovalan," said the prime minister, as if speaking to himself.

"An enterprise so vital requires the best of your servants, prime minister," said Thiru Pillay, his voice having acquired a conciliatory tone. His shifting moods were enigmatic and worrisome.

"Yes, I shall right away make available my rider," said the prime minister. "He is a trusted man of many years in my service."

"Thank you, Sir Prime Minister." And I bent down and touched his feet in a mark of gratitude and respect, and the old man gave me his blessings.

"Thiru Pillay," said the prime minister, "do we have your assent?"

The royal jeweller, who had been in some deep reflection, agreed but pressed for his earlier condition: that I remain in the custody of the Royal Household Guard.

The prime minister summoned the Captain of the Guard and said,

"This good man, Sir Kovalan, as you know, labours under an unproven cloud. Hold him as your guest with all the required respect and considerations."

When the captain held up a coil of chains, the prime minister shook his head and said,

"There will be no spectacle. Take him also by the secret passages."

"As you wish, prime minister." The captain bowed and stretched out his arm, inviting me to follow him.

"Thank you, Sir Prime Minister," I said. "Thank you, Sir Royal Jeweller."

The prime minister gave me a warm and reassuring smile, but the royal jeweller returned a blank look.

The captain and his soldiers escorted me down a long corridor, the walls adorned with colourful livery and paintings depicting the great deeds of the Pandyan kings. A narrow door concealed in the wall led us down a tight, winding flight of steps and into a dark passage.

The soldiers lighted torches, and we turned corners and navigated bends, but always kept going down a steep gradient. The air grew stale and life-less, and I detected burnt camphor and thin incense, as if we were entering the chambers of an old temple. I soon learned that in one small but significant aspect, I was right—it was a temple of sorts. A temple of death.

We arrived at a portcullis, beyond which was a spacious chamber, and cut into the stone walls were several cubicles. It was a small jail, and all the cells were empty.

The captain invited me into a cheerless cell and a guard lit an oil lamp. Another man brought a rolled mat, an ewer of drinking water, and a woollen blanket.

"We don't lock the cell gates," said the captain, "but I'll post a guard outside the door you just now passed. He'll attend to your needs." The captain pointed to the passage leading deeper into the cave, and said,

"The last cell has an altar, if you wish to pray." Then, he added in a voice devoid of emotion.

"It is also the execution chamber."

###

19: A Scorpion's Trap

The days in the subterranean cell crawled, and the nights were late in coming, but one afternoon, I had a welcome intrusion from Thiru Pillay, the royal jeweller.

"It is good to welcome you, Sir Royal Jeweller, and please forgive my poor hospitality. I am eager to hear gentle news from your lips to cool my burning heart."

"I have some bad news, Sir Kovalan," said the man. "The prime minister's rider could not locate your wife, Kannagi, in the village."

"What? I don't believe you, sir! Is this another scheme to deny me due justice? My wife is a chaste woman and will never cross the threshold without my permission."

"I am confident she is everything you say, Sir Kovalan, but she is not in Puranchery."

"Where could she have gone?"

"The people in Puranchery were not privy to her plans," said the royal jeweller.

"I wish to see the prime minister."

"Please, Sir Kovalan, I am also the bearer of good news," said the royal jeweller, happy and self-assured. He took a step forward, as if he was sharing some secret, and his flabby frame reeked of foul sweat and stale perfume. He said,

"When the rider returned with the sorry news, the prime minister, ever conscious of the desperation posed by slipping time, in my presence directed his rider to make all haste to Poom-Puhar to fetch your friend, Anandan. The man took four fresh horses from the prime minister's stable and even a swift homing pigeon.

"And having lately visited the palace, providence led me to meet the prime minister in the long corridors. He was hurrying to answer the king's summons and, knowing how eager you will be for good news, tasked me thus. His rider, on fleet hooves protected by the gods, reached Poom-Puhar."

I was wary of the red-faced man with dark-ringed eyes, but as our encounter matured, my guard relaxed. I paid eager attention to his next words.

"The message the pigeon carried and the prime minister had me commit to memory was: *Friend Anandan located. Returning to Madurai.* The prime minister said: *Tell Kovalan, I meet the queen tomorrow and am confident to win the time to prove his innocence.*"

"It is wonderful news, but do not pause. Tell me more from Poom-Puhar. Did my dear Anandan reveal my innocence?"

"No more news to add, sir, and as you can well imagine, it was not for the rider to make such enquiries, tasked as he was only to locate and beseech your friend to hasten to Madurai. In both these tasks, he succeeded well."

"Though the news is meagre, it is good, and thank you, sir. Please forgive my poor manners when we last met at the prime minister's chambers. I was distraught, but that lends no excuse for my uncivil behaviour." I clasped hands and dipped my head.

"It is a sack long discarded, Sir Kovalan," said the royal jeweller with a wave of his hand, "and think nothing more of it, for in your situation I might have behaved likewise or perhaps even torn out my heart in shame and fallen lifeless on the opulent carpets."

"Yes, sir, the urge took hold of me. Better to extinguish than to flourish under a cloud. But that scheme condemns my dear blameless wife to white shrouded widowhood. And she deserves better than what I have given her thus far."

"Enough of dark talk, Sir Kovalan, for you need to live for your wife, and you will. Any man worthy of his wife will do so even if it meant forsaking other things of importance to him." He paused, as if mulling some thought, and said,

"While you relish the welcome news, Sir Kovalan, I also have a good suggestion to rid the predicament which restrains you here."

"A good suggestion, sir? But with the good news already received, what more could decay the obvious fortunate outcome? I see sunlight but if there may rise dark clouds, please tell me your plan for I have drained all schemes and none reveal better promise of success."

"Allow me your ears, Sir Kovalan, so I can apprise you regarding the situation confronting us. I came to the Pandyan Court as an apprentice to learn the art and skills of working with gold, silver, and precious stones. My guru was the peerless artificer, Guru Nallathamby. Does the name trigger a thought?"

I shook my head and the royal jeweller looked curious, as if I was hiding some secret knowledge. Then, he told a story.

"The prime minister, Sir Kovalan, has a special interest in your welfare. He and my guru, having grown up together, were bosom friends. One day a few years ago, while on a river expedition, the prime minister's son, a fine young man he was, accompanied my guru. As fortune would have it, my guru slipped and fell into the river, and the prime minister's son bravely dived into the raving waters. Amidst frantic shouts and calls, the boat turned around, but it was too late. They saved my guru but never found the boy. His death devastated the prime minister. The tragedy broke my guru's heart too, and he travelled to do penance in the Western Ghats. Unfortunately, he never returned, for he fell prey to the wild Arakans in the hills. The king sent his formidable household guard to track and punish the foul killers. But grief once rendered always leaves a scar.

"Anguished though he was, by the loss of his only son and a dear friend in such proximity one to the other, the prime minister remained steadfast to his duties. He proposed, and the king agreed, for my humble self the privilege of carrying on my guru's work as royal jeweller. A great honour, for which I owe an everlasting debt to the prime minister, but an immense responsibility too, sir; one which I struggle with my immature skills."

"A heartfelt story, but why share this confidence and what of your suggestion?"

"It is no special confidence but a tale well-known throughout Madurai, and I related the story so you would better understand the store of love the prime minister holds for you. He considers you as the son he once had the joy of embracing."

"And I am grateful for it, and hope to repay his deep trust and kindness. But you were about to suggest a solution, one to unhook me from my predicament."

"Yes, but let me share another story, the last I assure you, about how an artificer jeweller gives birth to a work of art," said the royal jeweller, and threw a glance behind him before continuing. His eyes, passionate, danced with excitement as he invested in the story.

"First, the artificer tests and selects the purest of ores to blend the base metal, though base it is not, be it silver or gold. Then, he chooses the gems, and it requires a sharp eye to check for flaws lost even to light. And he cuts the stone. There are veins often not visible to ordinary eyes, but the cutter senses and splits so the jewel gives along the natural breaks, yielding blemish-free facets and edges proud and unchipped. Then comes the most challenging task of all—the mould. Craftsmen roll the ankle ring from a beaten sheet of gold or silver, then curve the tube and fuse the joints. The craftsman polishes the vein on the outer circumference, but the fold inside remains, and it distorts the music made by the jewels within. Therein lies the weakness, the ordinariness of all ankle rings."

The royal jeweller kept looking over his shoulder, as if fearful of eavesdroppers, or perhaps, as one expecting an intruder. And his behaviour intrigued but also exasperated me.

"But for the queen's anklets, my guru used a mould," said the man, his voice having softened as if he spoke a rare secret.

"Yes, not a sheet, but a mould to cast the cylinder; an unheard of and arcane technique for a tube," he said. "He then cut grooves on the inside diameter of the tube, another secret skill he had developed. The width and depth of these grooves determined the eight modes of music. The queen loved a specific tone; for that reason, my guru fashioned the grooves to capture the tone. How did he fuse science and music? Only he knows. These mysteries died with him in the Arakan jungles.

"The perfect ornament comes not only from the stones but also from the mould which must be flawless. This is where most craftsmen are impatient and therefore fail. It takes a master, not only a master of craft but also a master of patience, to extract perfection at every stage of his creation.

"My guru, Guru Nallathamby, was such a master of craft and controlled calm. There was none other like him, Sir Kovalan, and his creations have no imitations for, after crafting the queen's ankle rings, he broke the mould under the king's expressed orders."

The royal jeweller stopped and searched my face with his accusing eyes. Receiving no response, he said,

"And here you are also with an ankle ring, Sir Kovalan, of an identical build and perfection but claiming some imposter fashioned it."

"I made no such claim, sir, only that I purchased it from Telamonius the Greek. But what does it matter who I bought my anklets from? I am accused of having stolen the queen's anklet. Of this, I am innocent, I swear."

"But do you not see? They are the one and same charge levied on your life."

"And when my dear friend Anandan arrives, he will corroborate my story."

"And he is a *dear* friend and will *say* anything to save your life. Sir Kovalan, can you not weigh how feather-light his witness is on the scales of justice?"

"But truth is truth. That as it is, what will you have me do, sir, and I remain piqued by the mysterious suggestion you harbour but yet to reveal."

"The prime minister and I are sympathetic and concerned for your life, Sir Kovalan, for no piece of jewellery, no matter how exalted, is worth the price of a man's life."

"It is the truth, Sir Royal Jeweller. I did not steal the queen's ankle ring."

"You did not steal the anklet, Sir Kovalan, and so I am convinced, as is the just prime minister. But someone has stolen the queen's anklet and you, sir, had in your possession a treasure the likeness of which is an uncanny twin of the lost specimen."

"Your words confuse and in a certain light instil fear, Sir Royal Jeweller."

"They need not, Sir Kovalan, for I was turning over in my mind how to satisfy the king and save your life. My king is an honest and upright man, and if it were up to him alone, he would release you in the blink of an eye. But consider the precedent so planted, and the flood of wild petitions his favour will set free. The governance and justice of any nation teeters on a fine needle-point balance. Once tilted, it will take great effort to regain its equilibrium. A king who loses his moral fortitude to govern will be a fool to press his rule by the point of a spear. As you can well imagine, there is more at stake here than an accused's life, more than the fate of one man."

The captain of the guards arrived and presented himself. It became apparent the royal jeweller had soaked up the time to await the guardsman; and I wondered for what purpose. The royal jeweller turned to the seasoned soldier and said,

"Captain, with all the great demands on your time, thank you for honouring us with your presence."

"I am but bound by the prime minister's wish, and he has made clear I must accord priority to any requests concerning Sir Kovalan. But I will be frank, royal jeweller, I am busy with not even a moment's rest break."

"Yes, and the prime minister has been generous with the time not of his, but thank you, captain, and with it, my apologies. A man's life hangs on a spider's silk and you will be proud to see justice done." Turning to me, the royal jeweller continued.

"Here is confirmation from the Captain of the Royal Guard, himself descended from a foremost *Kshatriyan* family of warriors and a flawless witness, that the prime minister remains ever vigilant for you to receive justice."

"And found innocent," I said.

"But of course, and found innocent," said the royal jeweller.

"I am grateful, sirs, to all of you who continue to humble me to my rightful place even though I harbour doubts about your intentions, sir. Please forgive me for asking again, but tell me what you propose and what I must do."

"Confess, Sir Kovalan, as suggested by the prime minister, and with my agreement also, and acknowledge the anklet is not yours to claim."

"No! No sir, how can I take the blame when I am blameless? No!"

"Please, Sir Kovalan, I beg you to hear the admonishments of reason. Disclose that you did indeed pick up the queen's anklet from the street somewhere and, having given in to some moment's weakness, kept it for your own. On my part, I will take the blame for my carelessness and suffer whatever punishment the king deems fit. Let the consequences of my shoddiness be my price for not having better husbanded the jewellery entrusted into my care.

The prime minister and I will plead on your behalf to our king who, righteous as he is, will find sufficient grounds to set aside the death penalty without tilting the scales of Pandyan justice."

"Your suggestion does not differ from the prime minister's, which I have already declined. No, sir, I thank you and am grateful but cannot and will not—."

"Please allow me your indulgence but for a moment more, Sir Kovalan." As he spoke, the man chopped his palm for emphasis. "If you continue to insist the anklet is yours, it will only cast aspersions on the prime minister, for going to such lengths to secure your release. Our Pandyan soil does not relish blood. Sully it not with your precious lifeblood. What do you hope to gain from this continued intransigence?"

"My word challenged, sir, my honesty mocked, and integrity stripped naked."

"Yes, mocked and naked, and even our king Nedun-Cheliyan has detractors who mock his effigy on stage and street dramas for having taken a mistress. It is unbecoming but comes with the freedoms we enjoy. And we have great sages who live their lives unclothed. It is not the end, sir, to stand naked and mocked. It adds to our merit, even as we shake the dust off our feet and journey on this grand adventure called life. Please, do not allow whimsical notions to distract your safety when graver matters continue to twist and tighten around your throat."

"My notions are not whimsical, Sir Royal Jeweller, for what else makes a true man if not his integrity?"

"Is it integrity, sir, or perhaps pride in play here? But what does this or any other word matter? These seductive words are the playthings of bards who gather in sangams, gatherings of sorts for the privileged, to fashion verses and spout erudite arguments. All for coin, base coin, even as they poke their fingers in the air about this and that exalted ideal.

"But in this harsh cell deep below ground, so close to the centre of the trembling world, and listen how the earth-mother sighs," said the royal jeweller, and he made a dramatic show of listening with a hand to ear as a dull rumble rolled under our feet, "we confront realities of life, we face the imminent dangers of your situation. Death, sir, has foisted himself on you as your constant companion, and it is he who mocks your helplessness and will strip naked your life."

"Death Sir Royal Jeweller, , is welcome."

"Welcome, yes sir, go, welcome your poor dear wife to new life, renewed life, for as you said, she waits with bated breath for the safe return of her garlanded husband. Should she drape herself in fine silks or flesh devouring flames on a funeral pyre? Should she now receive the headless cadaver of a proud man? Will this be done well of you; done well of any husband?" The man grew more and more passionate and he said,

"You know her great sorrow because of your little indiscretion. Yes, and please forgive me for I too was no paragon in my youth. I too took the same path you, and indeed most young men take, to cross to maturity. The thrust of my argument, and one of good sense, is why, pray tell, why? If you insist on your current intransigence, surely you will scale the executioner's scaffold, and worse for your blameless wife. Compromise, confess, and masquerade, for all life is a play, is it not? Resolve this sorry trouble. Take back your life and return to your wife. Live, and thrive with your wife."

"Your words are seductive, Sir Royal Jeweller," I said, "but they will not move me to lie. If one resorts to fanciful words to unlock forbidden doors, then one will embrace more of the crooked path. The first lie always looks harmless, and I speak from experience. But once surmounted, with each new lie, it gets easier, and the slippery slope and abyss awaits at passage's end. I am born of this beautiful earth-mother, eaten her salt and fattened on her milk, I cannot and will not now ransom my life for a lie."

"It is not a lie, Sir Kovalan, for how can you be so sure, how can you remain so adamant that the ankle ring belongs to your wife? Is it not possible, is it impossible, even if you consider the possibility remote, that you could be mistaken, that the anklet belongs on the feet of Queen Kopperun-Devi? A slim possibility, yes, and as thin as a ray of light perhaps, but is it not possible?"

I was growing exasperated with the royal jeweller's unrelenting effort, and it reminded me of Anandan and how he would try to wear me down against my wishes. The memory of my youth stiffened my resolve: bullied into leaving my father's house; bullied into attending Madhavi's dance debut; bullied into going to her; and bullied all my life by my own seductive reasoning. I also suspected that the royal jeweller, though his words carried the trappings of logic and good sense, did not mean well. Below the surface of his reasoned arguments, I detected a trembling fear harboured.

Suddenly, by the grace of all the gods that my dear wife, Kannagi, worshipped, a thought struck. This man, this jeweller, had probably stolen the anklet and was exploiting my predicament as a key to his escape. I stopped. In a flash, the mist lifted with jaw-dropping clarity. Questions bloomed and stacked and cried for answers. Yes, he was the culprit. He must be. But I locked away my suspicions. Come my day in court, I will reveal my doubts. I will again ask the prime minister, in open court, to fetch my dear Kannagi. She will produce the second ankle ring and all will see the other half making the pair belonging to my queen, to my Kannagi.

But a new doubt clouded my hopes. Why would the royal jeweller steal the queen's anklet? He was a wealthy man himself. Who then was the thief? Not my charge to discover but, without a miscreant, I remained in their eyes the primary suspect. No matter, I consoled myself, for with my dependable Anandan's testimony and my loving wife's appearance with the twin, justice will save me.

"Please, we are friends here, all of us, are we not, captain?" asked the royal jeweller, but the guardsman's face remained impassive. "Do you not understand, Sir Kovalan, your life is in peril? Speak the truth and at least you might find clemency at the feet of the king."

"Enough, sir!" I said in a raised voice.

"There is no need to raise your voice, Sir Kovalan, but I ask you again, is it not possible the anklet might fit another woman, and not just your wife?" The jeweller's tone had become a little stringent. "Of course, if I suggested this woman could be a harlot with a known price—."

"Harlot?" My voice barrelled loud. "You dare use that word in the same breath as my chaste wife—."

"You know that is not what I meant. Please. If a woman of ill-repute laid claim to the anklet, I could understand your outrage. But we speak of the queen. Concede at least that the anklet could have, once, many years ago, adorned her feet."

"Hear me, and hear me well, sir, no woman, and I mean no mere woman, can wear my dear Kannagi's anklets."

"*Mere* woman, sir? We speak of the queen here, the Maha-Rani, Royal Consort to Maha-Rajah Nedun-Cheliyan."

"Do you not hear me? I said no woman, because any woman who wears the anklet is my wife and it can only fit someone as chaste and pure as Kannagi, and she is my wife."

"Any woman, sir, you say if it fits a woman, she is then your wife? Are you saying the anklet will not fit the queen's feet?"

"No, unless the woman is my wife." I shook in fits of outrage.

"I think your confusion leads you to spew anger, Kovalan. Are you saying, and pause before you reply and I warn you I am a loyal subject of my king and queen, if the anklet can fit the feet of my queen, Kopperun-Devi, then she is no more than your wife?"

"Not no more, sir, she can only be my wife because no other woman has the dignity, the chastity, and the purity to wear my wife's divine anklet."

"Are these then your last words, Kovalan?" The royal jeweller thundered.

"To you, Thiru Pillay, yes, these are my last words!" I matched his thunder with mine.

Then, afraid that he might misinterpret my words, I wanted to recant but could not bring myself to bow. Not to this low-born man. Not to this thief. My shaking anger and stubborn pride would not allow an ignominious retreat. Instead, I lowered my voice and said,

"But I will have more words for your king when the rider returns with my dear friend, Anandan. Please convey my humblest respect to the prime minister." I folded my arms. The royal jeweller, his face grim, addressed the Captain of the Guards.

"The culprit has again rejected our offers of clemency and you have borne witness to all that has happened, and I hold you to it."

"If there is nothing more, I have to go, royal jeweller," said the captain.

"Thank you, captain," said Thiru Pillay.

The guardsman gave me a curious look; of great pity, I thought, and left my presence.

"Think carefully, Sir Kovalan, of all we exchanged, and wisely decide."

I could not allow this thief to get away with his guilt; could not let him win. I had to triumph with my last word.

"Esteemed Royal Jeweller, tell me please, all these secrets of the ankle rings which your Guru Nallathamby used in his craftsmanship—how did you come to know of them?"

My question stunned the man, and the green vein on his bald head bulged. His chin wobbled, and I wondered whether from outrage or terror. It did not matter what unsettled him, but it pleased me. He swayed a little, as if the earth shook under his feet, before hurrying off.

But my elation was short-lived when a sudden sharp pain pierced my chest with despair—I had sprung the trap too soon. What a fool! When would I ever learn to cage my anger? Now that the royal jeweller knew the flaw in his scheme, what would he do? My first reaction was to call for the prime minister or even the captain. But who could I trust? I had no choice but to wait for my day in court.

I had stumbled upon the missing piece to the puzzle. It was not for money the royal jeweller had stolen the queen's anklet. He wanted to learn his guru's secrets. And how better than to break open the queen's ankle ring.

Another fear gnawed on itself and grew. My chaste wife would not have crossed the threshold. Where is she? Where did she go? I suspected treachery. I even feared for my dear Kannagi's safety. O gods of my father's temple, what have I brought upon my poor innocent wife?

Something tickled my ear and, looking up, I saw a thin stream of dust pour down from a crevice in the ceiling. The crack was not there before, or perhaps it had been, but I missed it. Then, the earth did indeed tremble under my feet.

###

20: Almost an Arakan Woman

Ever since my dear husband returned to my embrace, the old predictions of the astrologers had kept me constant company; sometimes giving hope, and at other times thrusting fear into my heart. If the augurs were to come to pass, if I was to gain fame as foretold, how else could it be without my husband? He had to prevail and his ventures must meet success. And when his wealth and fame bloomed, as a tide lifts a boat, I too would rise with him. But I remained troubled. Some unknown fear gnawed away at my calm. Once before, I bade him farewell and lost him to Madhavi's arms. Now, that same dread of loss closed around me.

It had already been several days since I last saw my Athan's back. Meanwhile, food had lost all taste and sleep eludes me. Every sunrise, with hope, I watched the morning grow; and every sunset, with dread, I watched the day die, leaving me yearning for my husband, who was my thumb and beak.

Gayathri and her daughter failed, yet again, to entice me with food and, stifling the dull pain in my stomach to keep alert for the sudden arrival of my husband, I went to bed.

Sometimes the earth quivered as if it was a slumbering beast shivering to shake off the torment of ticks. When I asked, the kind woman, Gayathri, said,

"It's the nature of the beast to remind us to live correct lives, Lady Kannagi."

Upon enquiring further, Gayathri related a tale handed down for generations, part of the local lore, and similar to the extraordinary story told by Eraivan, the Arakan king.

"It's a fire-breathing creature of immense proportions and power which lurks beneath the earth, its fiery tongues always probing, seeking a fissure. And once found, it'll escape to the surface and fly high into the clouds and rain down fire and smoke and ash for days on end, the likes of which we witness but once every ten thousand harvests or more."

"Will it surface here, in the village?"

"The village is safe, Lady Kannagi, but the wise ones say where evil reigns, the beast will discover an exit and surface to devour and destroy."

It was a superstition of people who lived close to nature, and therefore, when the ground moved again, I ignored it and turned to relieve the numbness on my side.

But this night a gentle weight rested on my arm and rocked me back and forth—and I woke with a start. Blinking into the dull dark, I saw eyes! I cried out. And immediately a hand clamped over my mouth.

"Little sister."

The voice was familiar, and the hand over my mouth released, followed by a whisper.

"It's me, Savaali."

I smelt Savaali; he had the smell which followed the Arakans.

"We have news of your husband, Kovalan Sir."

"Kovalan?" I whispered.

He said yes, and rose in one movement, pulling me up to my feet. He held my hand and guided me in the formless dark, and we eased out the door and into dim light.

"Where are you taking me?" I twisted my hand free.

Savaali held a finger to his lips. Grasping my hand again, he ducked and crouched and, tugging me in starts and stops, weaved and darted from shadow to shadow as we navigated past silent houses and opened windows. When we reached the outskirts of the village, I pulled my hand free again and demanded.

"What news about my husband, Kovalan?"

"Not here, little sister, for the wind had risen and the dogs will sniff us. Come, I'll carry you so we can make better haste."

He squatted and this time, without protest, I climbed on his back. And as he trotted off at a brisk pace, he said,

"I meant the dogs will sniff *me*."

"Where are we going?" I clung tight and bounced on his back, and my words pumped out one at a time.

"To the edge, where Eraivan awaits you."

"My husband, what news of him?"

"Eraivan waits, little sister, though for now I don't know what the news."

Savaali was already slick with sweat and I had difficulty holding on to his slippery shoulders.

"Wrap your legs around me and press tight," said the Arakan.

"Your girth is too wide."

"Not as wide as my woman, little sister, do you remember her?" said Savaali. "And if you continue to slip, brace yourself, wedge your toes into my waist belt."

I did as he suggested and that helped to hold my grip. I remained worried for my husband, but Savaali's presence instilled confidence. Blind hopeful confidence.

"My woman, do you remember her?" Savaali asked again.

The big man's effusive cheer proved infectious. Surely, nothing can be amiss. Not with my big brother around. Thus, having assured myself, I said,

"Yes, how is she, your woman?" I recalled a huge black woman with pendulous breasts, frizzy brown hair, and a ready smile.

"Which one?" There was mischief in his voice.

"How many women do you have?" I asked.

"One, but she's so huge that I sometimes think I sleep with two. She has a round belly with a deep sunken navel." He laughed.

"You make fun of your wife."

"She's not wife yet and for now sleeps with whoever she chooses. I too have enjoyed *kalavu*, pre-nuptial love, with her. Perhaps one day, I'll marry her and keep her for my own."

"You're an upright man, Savaali, but tell me, why would you marry a woman who already knows other men?"

"You speak with the head of a townsman, little sister, a city dweller corrupted by the insatiable need to possess another. But so be it, I'll tell you why."

But he did not. We reached the meandering paths, and Savaali picked up speed. After waiting a little longer, I burst with impatience and cried out.

"Tell me, Savaali, for your silence is the tease."

"You betray a hidden anger, little sister, and it smoulders. Fearful is the day men will cringe and shiver, and soil themselves when your anger erupts."

"I do not know what you speak of, but tell me and test me not any further: why do you prefer a known woman?"

"I wanted to just now say but noting how risqué it might sound, let it pass, but since you've instilled awe in me with your hidden anger, here it is, my story. One day, I made a terrible mistake. It was a moonless night. Intoxicated, and to render my enjoyment complete, I rolled over and penetrated my woman. What is the word you cultured people use? Coitus." And again, he laughed.

"Yes, I had *coitus* with the woman, but she was not one who ordinarily slept with me. It was a terrible mistake made in black darkness."

"Oh, god, what happened?"

"You ask this of me? Of course, I enjoyed myself and she too I believe."

"I meant, silly man, what happened, as in what were the fruits of your error?"

"Silly?"

He stopped and twisted to lock eyes with me. A silence fell, making me regret the liberty taken. He had always been a jolly man, but now, alone under the hazy moonlight, I feared him. Rallying my courage, I said,

"I meant no harm but only jested with my brother, who I suspect has great affection for his little sister."

"Even with an elder brother, you're wont to jest?" Savaali leaned back, bringing his wet cheek so close I felt the heat from his hard-set face.

"Well, yes," I said and, having detected a softness in his voice, pointed a defiant chin at him and continued, "especially with my elder brother, for only he has the wisdom and patience to brush off irreverent words of a mischievous little sister and spy the love within."

"I'll think more on these matters of wisdom and patience you claim to see but they have themselves hidden so well from me." Savaali made a face and said, "For now, what troubled you so much, little sister, that you let spew such irreverence at me."

"Silly?"

"Not the word, *the question*, silly." He roared with laughter and set off again in a fast trot.

Savaali had set and sprung the trap. For a moment, I welcomed his thoughtfulness; feigned annoyance and whined; and gave playful kicks, making him laugh even louder.

"I meant, what happened next, after that terrible mistake with the woman of the night?"

"Oh, in the morning, I did not know who the woman was, and no one made a petition against me. But I was sure she was not my woman."

He hopped across a dip in the ground. He was carrying my weight and running, and I, bouncing on his back, remained conflicted. It was as if I ate bitter gourd with payasam, for one part continued to worry for Kovalan and another part thanked Savaali for the fleeting distraction.

"But I learned something from my error," he said.

He did not finish his story. It became clear now. He was deliberately diverting my attention from all talk regarding my husband. Surely, Kovalan is safe. If he was not, this kind brute will speak the truth. And so, again, I found confidence and courage. But I was abrupt. I snapped.

"Finish it then. What did you learn?"

"You see, you see, you see—anger!"

"Savaali, please." I made whining noises as restitution for my rude response.

"You're as eager as a hatchling in a nest, and here is the juicy worm. That day I learned intimacy feels the same no matter with whom. I can take another woman, and another and yet another, but at the moment of release, the sensation is the same, is it not? That's why my woman, heavy and jolly as she is, gives me total pleasure, as complete as any fading beauty of round breasts and ginger waist. Why then should I hurt my woman's feelings and let her grief fill my heart? I've since kept my discipline."

"That's very generous and decent of you," I said.

"I always say, water quenches thirst. And it matters not whether drunk from a gold goblet or a raw gourd."

"Is that what you always say?"

"No, I just now thought of it and said it." And he laughed that eight-waved sound of his.

As we progressed into the half-moon shrouded terrain, I marvelled at how well he had distracted me, with his tales and laughter, from my worries over Kovalan.

Savaali stopped, and I sensed that exhaustion had got the better of him. But I was only somewhat right, for shapes emerged from the night. Arakans.

A huge Arakan, who wore a stern face and a tuft of hair, approached. The Silent One. The brothers greeted one another by colliding with force as if they were wrestlers in first contact.

After a whispered conference, a burly young man carried me. And the group set off again, in a fast run, with Savaali, tired as he was, keeping pace. The path climbed in a steady slope but our small party was relentless. Perspiration oozed from my every pore and I exerted all my strength to hang onto the humping back of the man; he too, like Savaali, wore a necklace of bones. The group pressed with their forced run; entered and embraced the pit darkness of the forest.

The steep gradient tired my carrier and they transferred me from one man to another, all the time pressing ahead at the same tempo. It shocked me that like an Arakan woman, I too embraced so many men. What was I doing? Where is my dear husband? I recalled my dream many years ago of an Arakan bearing me away with Kovalan giving chase. Many disjointed thoughts surfaced. Then, exhaustion overwhelmed and I fell into a concussed sleep, my head bouncing on the muscular shoulders of my carrier.

I do not know how long the men struggled, but when I awoke, with my arms aching and legs bowed with pain, there was already a hazy blue fog about us. And the first glimmer of dawn greeted us.

The Arakans stopped and lowered me next to a tree stump. Grateful, I sat down, happy to retire from the world of aches. A heavy woollen cloth draped over my shoulders. I pulled the blanket around me and looked up into the grinning face of Savaali.

"We made good time, but you've grown too weak," said Savaali. "And so, I've sent a runner up to The Edge to fetch Eraivan down to meet us here instead. You rest and regain your strength, little sister. Here."

He placed a bowl in my hands. Hot goat's milk warmed over a new fire. He placed another bowl beside me. Pieces of honeycomb, juicy with raw honey.

"Here's a piece of ginger, and there's also water here for you to wash, and change clothes."

It was then I realised Savaali had taken a bundle of garments from my room. I chewed the raw ginger and gargled with water. All around, Arakans, young men who had carried me in turns, collapsed from exhaustion. Seeing them thus, sapped by their selfless exertions, my eyes grew wet. I turned away for, if they saw my tears, it would hurt them even more.

By the time Eraivan arrived with his entourage, the long, searching fingers of sunlight already encroached on the valley below. He had timed his arrival, so I was well-rested, washed, and presentable.

Several of his men carried a stretcher; on it, a body covered by rough cotton cloth. I jumped to my feet and rushed to the stretcher.

"Oh no, my dear Athan."

"It's not Kovalan, little sister."

Savaali stepped forward and scooped me off my feet and turned, so his body blocked my view of the stretcher. "Not Kovalan." But something else seemed to trouble him.

"Who then?"

"We've a guess, and only because he told us before his life escaped through his terrible wounds," said Eraivan, as he came closer.

Forgetting decorum, I ran and hugged him tight. My reaction took him by complete surprise and he stood transfixed for a moment before circling his massive arms around me. His touch was light and reminded me of dear Father holding me in his arms. I looked past the Arakan king at the stretcher, now laid on the ground. It was a man under the brown stained shroud. I searched Eraivan's face.

"Who is he?"

"He claimed to be your elder brother and also a friend of your husband."

"Anandan!" The name escaped my lips.

"That was the name he claimed as his. Say he is the one, before I present further news concerning your husband."

"My husband, my dear Athan, is he safe?"

"He is, little sister, he is as of now."

Taking my hand in his massive paw and placing another hand on my elbow, Eraivan guided me up the small rise to the leafy stretcher.

He gestured, and an Arakan knelt and removed the flap of cloth covering the face. With my heart thumping to escape my chest, I stepped forward.

It was Anandan. My knees buckled, and I collapsed with a cry, with Eraivan holding and following me down to the ground.

Anandan had grown older and thicker, but a smirk, as if mocking the god of death, etched his face. I melted into copious tears and lamented my friend, my grief feeding on itself and driving me into greater despair.

Eraivan, after waiting in respectful silence and seeing me tire, sat me on a thick protruding root close to the prone body of Anandan.

"He perished not by our hands, little sister," said Eraivan. "We put herbs and such-like miracles of the forest to soothe his last hour. Your brother died easily with a look of contentment, especially after he finished this, a letter addressed to you." He handed over a roll of old hide, cut from an Arakan coat, and said,

"Do these words hold meaning to you, little sister?"

"Yes, but it is difficult to read in this poor light."

"Bring the light." Eraivan ordered, and several torches converged around me. "Is it our little sister you grunts wish to roast?" His hoarse voice had an instant effect, and the torches tilted back a little, like unfolding petals.

The light better, I read Anandan's words, written by a shaky hand as his life bled away:

Our dear Kovalan stands falsely accused and under threat of execution for having stolen the Pandyan queen's anklet. Summoned to Madurai by their prime minister, Sagasana, to bear good witness, but I am betrayed. Dally not. Save your husband ~ your loving brother Anandan.

While I read Anandan's message, the Arakans brought forward a man, his hands bound behind his back but not otherwise harmed. They forced the man to his knees and stepped back.

"This is the canny coward for having fallen with a cruel knife on your unsuspecting brother," said the Arakan king. "And an unknown villain stoked him."

Eraivan threw a look at the Silent One, who grasped the man's head and pulled it back. The Arakan drove his knee into the man's back and placed the edge of a knife on his straining neck.

"You turning your knife on Sir Anandan, when his attention diverted, was no chance quarrel occurred on the ride," said Eraivan. "Was it Sagasana or some other who charged you with robbing this innocent man's life? Speak and be quick with it."

The man, his eyes blazing defiance, sneered and spat.

"The rider is a slave," said Savaali. He stepped forward and, with one tug, ripped off the man's tunic. "See the old whip wounds like withered branches on his back. He knows pain and will not speak in haste, though it is inevitable he will, but do we have the time for such a show?"

Savaali gestured and the Silent One cleaned the flat of his knife on the man's cheek.

"The one who holds you to his blade is my brother," said Savaali. "He's not as charming as me but he will part your tongue down the middle from throat to tip, and render you the snake you have been to one who trusted you. And if you still do not blabber, split as your tongue will be, you will annoy my brother greatly and I dread to think what next he conjures up." He leaned down and whispered. "The Silent One has a nasty imagination."

The man studied Savaali and spied the blade from the corners of his eyes. Part of him counselled reason, but another part, the stronger, seemed defiant. The rider looked away but at the last whisker's moment, changed his mind and said,

"I plead mercy for a servant merely completing a task under pain of death."

Savaali smirked. He and the Silent One gave their attention to Eraivan. The chieftain stepped forward and said,

"Who paid you to steal the life of Sir Anandan? Reveal the name, you wretched man, and you'll go free. Was it Sagasana or another snake slithering in the palace mulch?"

"Sagasana."

"Wise decision." Eraivan gestured, and the Silent One manhandled the rider to his feet.

"You promised my freedom," said the rider.

"That I did, but I also did not say when," replied Eraivan. "You'll remain our guest until the little sister here redeems her husband's freedom. Meanwhile, you'll regale us with tales of your other adventures, of all the innocent lives you stole and put blame on us."

"You promised his freedom, Sir Eraivan," I said, "but how will I seek satisfaction for my poor brother's murder?"

"Is it blood you thirst, little sister?" asked the Arakan king.

"My heart cries out for justice."

"Know yourself, little sister, for it is revenge you clamour to quench here, not justice. But if it is justice you seek, she awaits you in the Pandyan court."

"How long will the murderer be your guest?" I asked.

"The rider holds many dark secrets, little sister," said Eraivan. "This is not the first time we spotted his bloody act, but the first time we snared him. We will coax him for answers regarding other murders, but you focus instead on your store of energy for the challenges ahead." Before I could say more, Eraivan cut in and said,

"We'll make ready the Pandyan horses, and Savaali and the Silent One will ride with you to Madurai, where you'll have time enough, I pray, to plead your husband's innocence."

The Arakan king was right. It was a half day's ride to the city gates and I could not waste another moment. The men brought four horses; fine, well-fed beasts with sturdy legs.

"These are the prime minister's horses, if you believe the rider," said Eraivan, "worn from recent hard riding, but much fight remains in them. You take turns riding with the brothers and with two spare mounts, you'll make good time."

Even as Eraivan was speaking, and the brothers fussed with their horses, I pulled the hem of my sari between my legs and tugged the tip into the back of my waist. I then stepped on a rock and, swinging a leg over, settled on the saddle of the nearest horse.

"I learned to ride on my Chinnamma's farm."

Surprised but admiring looks greeted my declaration as I leaned forward and patted the mare's neck to calm the startled animal.

"Which way, Sir Eraivan?" I asked.

The Arakan chieftain, wearing an amused smile, pointed.

"Thank you," I said and wheeled the mare and, nudging its sides, set off down the gentle incline. A loud cheer erupted from the Arakan ranks and the frightened horse neighed.

Looking back, I noticed Savaali and the Silent One watching my progress with delight. They exchanged looks, and Savaali burst into his customary laugh. They too mounted their horses and, with more cheers urging them, galloped down the slope, even as I dug in my heels and took off.

By the time I reached the flats, Savaali had caught up and, leaning down, grasped the reins and brought my charger to a slow gait.

"You'll burst the poor animal's heart, little sister," said Savaali. "Trot, and that's strenuous enough, not dash."

The Silent One, who had the spare horse on leash, caught up and for a moment all three of us rode abreast.

"We can't enter Madurai; my brother and I," said Savaali. "At best, our appearance will create mayhem. At worst, we'll squander many lives. We'll leave you a short distance from the city gates." He studied me with renewed interest, and when I betrayed shyness, said,

"Forgive me, little sister, for staring so, but in the dark you'll terrify me more than my brothers."

"How can you jest when my dear Kovalan faces his desperate situation?"

"Be gloomy if you must, but I see not how that alters his situation."

"We should make more haste, brother Savaali, for the horses are strong."

"Even at a trot you'll deplete them."

"I will take the spare and race ahead and if disaster strikes, you and the Silent One coming behind can put matters right."

"Seeing you ride more expertly than us, perhaps your scheme holds much merit."

Savaali turned to his brother and the Silent One handed the spare leash to me. As I readied to gallop off, I asked,

"Why do you say I will terrify you in the dark?"

"Your black clothes fluttering in the wind, fierce eyes, and dishevelled hair; why, you're almost an Arakan woman."

"Only *almost?* Am I not good enough to be Arakan?"

"You're too bony."

He roared, letting out his eight-syllable laughter. And leaning to his side, he gave my horse's rump a sharp slap. Instinctively, I dug in my ankles and the horses took off.

###

21: Avatar of Death

Nedun-Cheliyan, the Pandyan king, swung his cape over an arm as he hurried down the gleaming corridors. His queen, Kopperun-Devi, tired of her games and satisfied that she had chastised him enough, had sent word. Upon hearing the invitation, the king dismissed his counsellors and, lips pursed, strode to the queen's palace wing, eager to mollify and win back her graces.

The Maha Devi, a fickle woman, had on an earlier occasion, also summoned the king who had bustled forth. But her trusted handmaiden, the old hag, had stopped the king at the threshold of his queen's chamber.

"The queen has taken ill," said the old hag, with a triumphant glint in her dead eyes.

"What poison have you fed her this time?" said the king, his eyes blazing with fury.

"Only that brewed in the slippery honey pots of your whores."

Nedun-Cheliyan grasped the jewelled handle of his dagger, but the witch pushed out her shrivelled chest in a dare. The king, his chest heaving in anger, flicked and rolled his cape over his arm. Turning around, he hurried away, fearing his rage would better his reason. And the crone cackled in his wake.

I, Thiru Pillay, trusted Royal Jeweller to the Crown, spied it all back then, and watched the same drama unfold again.

The king and queen did not know the old hag worked for me and, thus alerted, I intercepted the royal. So, here he was again, rushing after the hag to meet his first love, the Maha Devi, determined that nothing would frustrate him.

Just as he reached the turn to the queen's wing, my desperate voice rang out. "Maharajah! Maharajah!"

"How dare you! Be gone, Pillay, unless you yearn for death."

I sank to my knees and touched my forehead to floor, even as the king's steps receded. I held up an embroidered silk cushion. Resting on it was the exquisite rarity.

"The queen's treasure, my king, I found the anklet!"

Upon hearing the news, the king stopped in mid-stride and turned.

"The queen's anklet, my king. And please forgive me for having lost it."

The king hurried back and reached for the anklet. After a blink, he snatched and examined it.

"It is unblemished and none the worse for mixing with dust."

"And so it is, my king."

"Rise, Thiru Pillay. This will be a welcome gift to your queen. You're forgiven, and thank you."

"I did myself apprehend the thief, my king, when he came to my manufactory to sell it. The thief now awaits his fate in the subterranean cells."

"Ensure a fair enquiry befitting our Pandyan legacy."

"He denies his guilt, my king, but admits to another even more onerous."

"Oh?" The king raised his eyebrows.

"My, my lips quiver, my king, to even think, let alone give voice to the man's impudence."

"Speak up, man, or would you rather we stand here and grow old?"

"The thief claims the anklet as his own, his wife's rather," I said, and swallowed hard. "And he further claims it cannot be the queen's anklet, for it fits only his wife. If it fits another, even if she is the queen, then she too must be his wife."

"What? How dare the scoundrel!" The king paused. "Or is he a mad fool spewing nonsense?" He caressed the anklet with his thumb, and that calmed him. "Perhaps you misunderstood him, a dangerous mistake. We don't doubt your sincerity, Thiru Pillay, but question the power of your recollection."

"The Captain of the Royal Household Guard was witness to the travesty, my king."

"Very well then," said the king. Looking down the corridor, he commanded. "Who's there?" An attendant, standing in an alcove, stepped out and bowed, and the king said, "The Captain of the Guard, before our presence. Now!"

"Right away, my king."

The man hurried off and somewhere far away, in the endless corridors, voices called, reverberated, and echoed.

"Recollect with care, Thiru Pillay, were those his words? A life is at risk here."

"My memory of what took place is unassailable, my king. Our esteemed prime minister had already questioned the thief at great length and, discovering no innocence, had the man incarcerated in the dungeons."

"My king," said the old hag, her voice a dry croak, "time slips and with it my queen's enthusiasm to receive you."

"My king!"

The captain snapped to attention and saluted. The king ignored the crone but turned to the guardsman and said,

"The thief you hold in the subterranean caves, what spoke he regarding the queen and the fitness of this anklet?"

For a moment the captain looked confused, but in those blinks of an eye, and seeing me, the royal jeweller on my knees, his memory flooded back.

"Out with it, man, and be quick about it!" said the king, having remembered his queen's summons and become impatient.

"My king, the queen——," said the crone.

"Silence!" said the king, and he pointed a finger at the hag who slunk back.

"Captain?"

"Yes, my king, the accused Kovalan declared, and these are his words as my memory reminds me: She, meaning the queen, can only be his wife because no other woman has the dignity, the chastity, and the purity to wear this divine anklet."

"Your words vex me and I find them hard to believe, captain, and yet am compelled to, because your reputation for honesty is as unwavering as the morning sun." The king grasped the anklet tight and the muscles on his forearm tensed.

"Thank you, my king," said the captain. Emboldened by the king's praise, he continued. "Those were his words, but——."

"Should I inform my queen," said the old hag, speaking across the guardsman, "that the king has more important matters to attend to; matters regarding a common thief?"

The king glared, but the wretched witch did not wait for a rebuke. She wheeled and glided away on swift feet hidden under the sweeping hem of her white sari. The king turned on the captain and said,

"But what, captain? What?"

"Begging your pardon, my king—."

"Yes, yes!" said the king, interrupting the guardsman.

"In my humble opinion, the prisoner's words might lend another meaning. Moreover, he said he had words for your ears and requested an audience."

"Does the accused not trust the integrity of our prime minister?" The king threw a look at the corner around which the old hag had vanished. He turned to the royal jeweller and said,

"We've heard enough. Thiru Pillay, are you sure of the man's guilt?"

"On my life, my king, I am very sure."

"It will be on your life, Thiru Pillay," said the king. "And what of the prime minister?"

"I cannot speak for the prime minister, my king, but he found no hints of innocence and had been relentless in asking the thief to confess the crime."

"Should we summon the prime minister's presence, my king?" asked the captain.

"No, he is hosting the lately arrived Romans," said the king.

He fingered the anklet and again looked towards the petal covered corridor leading to the queen's private wing. The hour was late, and he needed to appease her to sit next to him when the Roman senators presented their credentials. Having arrived at a decision, he pushed out his chin and spoke in a commanding voice.

"And whatever fanciful interpretations you ascribe to his words, captain, they apprehended him with the queen's ankle ring and, therefore, guilty enough. Furthermore, I am sure the prime minister offered him clemency in trade for a guilty plea."

"He did, my king, but the Cholan ingrate rejected our Pandyan generosity," I said.

Knowing it prudent not to add further, I turned to the captain. And so did the king. Thus prompted, the captain, having no choice, said,

"I heard Thiru Pillay offer clemency on behalf of the prime minister, but the man declined. He insisted his innocence and claimed he had no need for clemency."

"Very well then, captain, you know the penalty for stealing from the king. Do your duty!"

With that, the king, holding the anklet high, as a child having found a bright new toy, hurried along the flower-strewn aisle. His feet shot out and crushed the soft petals, which wept their fragrance, to overhaul the old hag before she fed mischief into the queen's ears.

The captain saluted after the king and threw me an accusing stare. But his ferocity remained caged by oaths of loyalty to crown, country, and commands.

For myself, with head bowed, I retraced my steps. The prime minister said as courtiers we need to *spend lies to save lives*. A noble ideal, but one that will make us all liars. What good is a law if not pressed to the hilt and what use a courtier not versed in statecraft? And I am an erstwhile student of statecraft—perhaps even better than the good prime minister. What's more, history will thank me for saving the secret of the ankle rings, a secret that my Guru Nallathamby, a selfish man, was intent on taking to his grave.

***

The execution chamber was at the end of the corridor and similar in layout to, but larger than, my cell. An altar dedicated to Yaman, the God of Death, occupied one corner of the room and a stone dais stood in the centre. A stone slab, about the height of a man's knees, stood erect on the dais.

"Give me a moment, Sir Kovalan, while I attend to some matters," said the executioner.

"I wonder aloud, how will you wash the blood of a blameless man from your hands? The hands that grasp the heavy blade soon to be wet with the blood of the faultless; will those same hands caress the love of your woman and cuddle the innocence of your child? How do you bring yourself to be a fearful demon here and tender husband and doting father there?"

The executioner ignored my words. He completed his prayers to the formidable god he worshipped, and smeared his chest and arms with ash. He twisted his moustache and, satisfied with their proud tips, bowed to the court officials who had come to witness my death. Then, he turned, unhurried, and addressed me.

"True, I have set free many lives with these steady arms and sharp blade," said the executioner. His eyes were intent, but his voice was soft, almost a whisper. It was unnerving considering his frightful specialty. He said,

"If my acts were just, Sir Kovalan, the gods will spare me, will they not? If there had been an unjust rolling of the head, I will surely answer for it, will I not? For no one, sir, no priest and no king, can vouch for my testimony and plead mercy on my behalf. Such are the deeds of man and attached to him alone—whether a lawmaker intent on expedience at the expense of equity, a judge who upholds an unjust law, a malicious prosecutor protected by his king's favour, or a cursed executioner—if he errs, no law, whether corporeal or ethereal, can exonerate him."

"How do you sleep, executioner, after a day's hideous task?"

"Sleep, Sir Kovalan, and what leads you to conclude I enjoy that simple pleasure? I am the executioner, am I not? It is my fate, as yours has brought you to this grisly place. It is beyond me to dwell on answers when the questions you spout are flawed."

"And what questions, avatar of death, would you have me ask?"

"How will berating your executioner help you? It is fate, Sir Kovalan, come to collect his dues, has he not? Inescapable as are the next steps to follow; would you not rather wish for a quick clean cleave? If my emotions, moved by your admonishments, let slip my fingers, will the outcome be satisfactory for you or well-done of me?"

"You threaten me with torture and slow death?"

"No, Sir Kovalan, for it is not my words you need fear but the strength of my arms and the aim of my eyes. For we are in a tragic situation and it behoves we conduct ourselves in a manner focussed on the inevitable when the fatal moment is upon us."

"You will have me killed and yet why this pretence at civility, this fake concern for my well-being even as you prepare to rob my life?"

"Not rob you, sir, but I am executioner here to deprive you of your life, as a jailor would deprive a man's freedom for lesser crimes."

"Is there a difference whether you call yourself executioner, killer, or murderer?"

"Yes, Sir Kovalan, there is, for even if we all must ultimately travel beyond the veil, how we purchase death is more important than death itself, is it not? You accuse your executioner of showing fake concern. You are angry. But your anger, sir, moves me not for it is not my teacher. I am tasked by royal edict to redeem a debt, am I not? The debt does not include humiliating you, hurling harsh words at you, or ill-treating you with brawny arms. To do so would exact a price higher than that owed."

"It's easy for you, executioner, to speak with such flourish, for in a short time my body will go taut and my limbs kick wild as my head rolls to the dirt."

"And you will embark on a life anew, and lucky are you, for most of us will know not when he will surprise us. Why do you not prepare for the journey, instead of swatting me as if I was a bothersome fly?"

I considered his words and grasped for ropes, ledges, and outcrops, and even a sliver of grass. Anything. A new life, he said. Could this be true? I had always believed in rebirth, as if death was but a continuation to another existence. But now, facing the blade, I was not sure. I was afraid to die, afraid of the unknown, afraid that the blade slicing down would banish me into oblivion to wander forever, lost in eternal nothingness. I had written rhyming verses and sang melancholic ballads, confident in my youth when death was not yet round the bend. I had been smug in the belief of a better life, that I had time enough to live and reap the rewards of correct living. But these last few days' events had wiped my beliefs clean off my slate, as if they were sand particles picked up and blown away.

Now, this exotic executioner, with a whisper for a voice and deep seeing eyes, gave hope. And even if he spun that hope in smoke, I was ready to grasp it. He had taken many lives. Perhaps he was privy to uniques which elude even the wisest of our sages of antiquity.

"New life?" My thoughts scrabbled, my voice hoarse, and it was all I could muster.

"Yes, sir, a new beginning."

A new beginning, promised the man, and I had scant choice but to believe, for the alternative was—nothing! I had accomplished nothing in this life, but brought disappointment to my parents and grief to my dear Kannagi. I wanted to flee my failures. Slink into the dark and hide my shame. I had reconciled myself to disappear without a trace. A coward's wish, a loser's prize. But a new beginning held the promise of redemption. And death, a new beginning, was a choice given the condemned from a pitiful selection of one.

"Thank you, Sir Executioner. Thank you."

I softened my voice and smoothened my tone. The frightening man's overwhelming sincerity and utter care for right conduct impressed me.

The man did not reply but held my gaze, and for a moment, perhaps a blink, I received him. I saw god. I saw purpose.

And I recalled the day, in the company of Anandan and a troop of attendants, we had gone on a hunt. For sport, to gain a trophy to boast.

We spied a tiger that had taken a spotted deer. As the magnificent lord of the jungle clamped down its jaws, the deer's hooves flailed, piercing the air with sharp crooked jabs. Gradually, the panicked kicks ceased. The legs extended, retracted, and stopped. The deer's eyes relaxed as a look of peace, and recognition even, swept over the animal. It had all happened fast, several heart beats perhaps, but my eyes saw and mind registered, and I retained the scene. Now I was that deer, and my executioner, the tiger. He had stolen my terror and rendered me brave, and I was grateful to him.

"Are there any last words you wish to convey to anyone, Sir Kovalan? In penance for what I am tasked to do, I shall gladly do justice to your wishes."

"You are a kind man, Sir Executioner, but I do not wish to wreck my blameless wife, Kannagi, with dying words, for already I am the source of all her suffering."

I studied the court officials, witnesses to my execution, and after a moment, said,

"But I have words for your king, Nedun-Cheliyan, and tell him, if you can muster the courage, that by denying me my day in court he has committed a deadly unjust. His sceptre is bent and his parasol stained. But I thank you also, Sir Executioner, for the gentleness you have this day shown me."

"I shall convey your words, sir, in this you may rest assured."

"Rest, I will soon, Sir Executioner, and I hope to receive a wish from you."

"If it is within my power, Sir Kovalan, consider it fulfilled."

"I do not wish my wife to behold my decapitated body or to see my blood spilt."

"I shall carry out your wishes, sir, and present you in a dignified condition to your wife."

"Thank you, and now untie me please, for I do not wish to die as a beast bound for sacrifice." Seeing the officials hesitate, I said,

"I am a man, my friends, though perhaps not as brave as you. But I do not fear death, though this is an unjust verdict and sentence, and a cruel infliction upon an innocent. I will not flail my arms and wail, or flee around this chamber even as you reach and grab, and make a spectacle of such a solemn event. Neither will I shout myself hoarse, trying to borrow courage where there is none. I will not fight you or seek to vest injury upon you, for you have families and wedded wives awaiting your return.

"Fear not sirs, my lamentations, during these precious few moments remaining. I will go peacefully and show how a true Tamil, who has eaten the rice and salt of Tamilakam, and drank from her sweet rivers, faces death.

"But alas, the thought of my poor dear wife just now continues to plague me. I have not treated that chaste woman as well as a husband should have treated any wife. It wrecks my heart, which yearns for me to live. Not for myself, but only a little longer to shower her with the life she so richly deserves. For this reason, sirs, I beseech you, if you can find it in your hearts to release me for a few days and postpone my release."

My eyes, in desperate entreaty, studied the assembled men, but it was to no avail.

"Please, Sir Executioner, I beg you again, fetch my wife Kannagi and she will bring the second ankle ring and prove my innocence."

"Sir Kovalan, we have travelled this path many times already, and my answer remains steadfast. We are here to carry out royal orders and no more."

"If not the prime minister, please at least request the captain's presence, for I suspect he is an upright man and will lend me his ears."

'Sir Kovalan, it was by the captain's orders relayed directly to me, but handed down to him from the king himself, that has brought us to meet fate."

I sighed with heavy resolve and found renewed vigour as one defeated with back pressed to the wall but imbued with the nervous energy of the defiant.

"If those are your ultimate words to my plea, then tarry not, dear executioner, and be done with it. Delay not the fatal moment, for he grows impatient."

They untied the restraints and a small sting of heat burned my skin as the rope pulled away. I clasped my wrists and rubbed to rid the numbness, and broke into a sardonic smile.

"What humour you find, sir?" It was the executioner, genuine concern in his voice.

"I am a few moments away from losing my head, but continue to tend to minor discomforts. Notice how my wrists have bloated and the bluish bruises beneath my skin."

"If you massaged your hands a little more, sir, you will feel better, will you not?"

"You fell into the same trance, Sir Executioner, worrying about little discomforts. An ironic humour, do you not think?" I smiled and said,

"I know a man, a wonderful man with an easy humour, and the thought of him gives me some lightness."

"A dear friend, Sir Kovalan, from Poom-Puhar, I suppose?" said the executioner.

"No. A rough man; an Arakan of the hills."

He expressed mild surprise, but I said no more, for already the guards had set about their tasks. They held my arms, one on either side, and led me up the three steps to the large stone slab. My heart pounded, wanting to break free of its cage. A terrible chill erupted in my lower back and swept over me in frigid terror, and I feared I might empty my bladders.

The executioner had asked that I relieve myself. He had not offered water. Despite the correct manner in which he had treated me, I had thought of him as cruel. But now I valued his decision. He was right. My bladder did not brim.

A light pressure on my shoulders brought me down to my knees. The curve in the upright stone slab, where my neck was to fit, looked clean. Was I the first?

More gentle pressure and my head went down and the cold stone touched the skin on my throat. I dry licked my lips. After a deep breath, I squeezed my eyes tight and waited in agony. I detected shuffling of feet, followed by the rustle of fabric and clink of metal. I wish I could plug my ears, keep out the sounds. A tight bandage around my ears would have helped. Then, my air lost, I heaved rapid breaths.

There was a sharp intake of air and I recognised it as the executioner. He must have raised his arms high. The blade.

A low, uncontrollable growl emanated from deep within my being. I felt a dull crunch.

My eyes popped open!

My sight went hazy and images blurred. I felt weightless, as if floating. I saw people, or rather, portions of their blurry bodies—arms, legs, faces—and heard vague voices.

"Truly, he was a fearless man," said a court witness.

"Yes, a brave man indeed," said the executioner.

I stood beside the executioner, or so it seemed, and he stepped back as several guards pushed past him, heaving a stretcher made of rough sack material. They descended the short flight of stairs and laid down the stretcher. Morbid curiosity pulled me to the headless body. A man placed something on the chest. My head! My pop opened eyes. I looked ridiculous.

"I will directly carry the news of the execution to the captain," said a court witness. "He demanded a detailed report and will be glad to know the condemned did not suffer."

"Please suggest, in view of the Romapuri delegation, perhaps we should not exhibit the head in the market square," said the executioner. "The captain has the wet heart and the wise head to accept the suggestion."

After the witnesses took their leave, the executioner—what was his name? I had not asked, and he had not granted it—knelt beside my body. He was silent, in contemplation or perhaps in prayer. He pulled the sack material over the corpse and addressed the jailors.

"Bring suture and needle, a bandage, and some fresh clothes for him."

###

22: Late for Salvation, Early for Vengeance

Madurai was in the throes of carnival. Slow-moving rivers of humanity filled the streets. Produce and people overflowed the markets. Games of martial prowess attracted pressing crowds as men chased and subdued raging bulls, and raced horses, camels, and chariots.

I guided my two salt-streaked horses across a crowded field where a tug-of-war, pitting an elephant bedecked with garlands of flowers against a long string of heavy sweaty men, was in progress. The elephant, the crowd favourite, won as expected and a thunderous cheer went up. Everywhere, there was an abundance of brilliant flowers, and tall colourful drapes caught the breeze and waved. There were competitions pitting archers, athletes, and the ever-popular game of *chadukudu*, where two teams of men chanted, breathless, as they raided their opponent's side. In every street, vendors shouted themselves hoarse, pitching their vocals against the blare of trumpets, clash of cymbals, and boom of drums.

As I approached, people gazed in awe. Seeing a young woman ride a horse, and with such unbridled confidence, many passed comments of admiration. Many more expressed outrage that a woman dared ride with legs astride a horse's back, an uncouth spectacle. My horses were nervous and often neighed and bobbed their heads as I guided them through the knotty crowds.

The palace, an impressive structure of gleaming white marble, rose into the blue sky. The wide boulevard leading to the palace was a sea of people, dressed in fine garments and bright, colourful turbans.

Before the massive palace gates, emblazoned with medallions and pennants boasting the many achievements of the Pandyan lineage, stood soldiers wielding javelins and large curved shields. Romans! Light brown skin, red tunics, and intricate breast plates. On both flanks stood equally resplendent Pandyan soldiers, several ranks deep.

Taking the lead were two officers: a young Pandyan and a weathered Roman. Swords sheathed and hands resting on hilts, they stood with legs planted firm on the ground. The impressive contingent had attracted a thick, unmoving crowd.

As I nudged my horses out of the throng and towards the gates, the Pandyan officer, an angry junior captain, stepped forward and two soldiers hurried after him. He gestured; ordered me to dismount.

"I wish to present a petition to the king." My voice rose above the din, but the man, fired with importance and impatience, gestured for me to alight. I repeated my demand. "I wish to enter, to present a petition to the king."

Again, my mare, nervous, stamped and tip-toed. I patted the animal to keep it calm. When the soldiers grasped the reins of my horses, they snorted and crab-walked, and it took all my skills to keep them from backing into the crush of onlookers.

"Get off your saddle!" ordered the Pandyan officer. "Now!"

The soldier's command and my matched defiance quietened the straining crowd. They fell silent and tried to catch the exchange.

"Or what will you do, sir? Will you manhandle me, a woman, even as your Roman guests there stand witness?"

"You cannot barge into the palace grounds, heedless of invitation and decorum."

"I have a petition for the king, sir, and ask you to let me pass, for my wound is wet and my heart parched of pity and thirsts justice."

The young officer threw a sideways glance, conscious of the eyes on him. He scoffed and said,

"Look behind you, woman. Among that lot, many hold up petitions too, all clamouring for justice to seal some slight. The quota for the day was long ago filled, but they wait under the burning sun. Be gone! On your way with your thirst for mischief as I am charged to use force to reclaim the peace if you disturb it."

"I have no wish to disturb your peace purchased by the point of a spear, sir, but will frustrate you if I must, to see the king."

"You can and will have your day in court, woman, but not today. Do not put up a show for our Roman guests. Be gone, I say again, for my patience is not without limits."

"My patience is also not boundless, sir, and do you not recognise these horses, worn as they are from a taxing ride, to be from Prime Minister Sagasana's own stables? Scrutinise the markings on their coats before you attempt to shoo me away as if I were a pigeon come to sully your pompous parade."

The young Pandyan officer, taken aback, recovered and gestured. A soldier, a man of some years, inspected the rumps of the horses, letting his fingers run and pick on the fur. After which, he whispered into the officer's ear.

"And so they are, it would seem," said the Pandyan, and with renewed confidence he continued, "and stolen perhaps. Instead of an audience, an arrest might be in order."

"Are you a fool, sir, or has the sun robbed you of good judgement?" I said, and someone from the crowd behind me laughed. "If I were a thief, how did I enter your stables? Were you sleeping on the guard? And why am I presenting myself here with irrefutable evidence if, as you so hastily concluded, I stole these horses?"

In the silence that now hung over the place, my voice carried and elicited more sniggers from the crowd. I detected empathy from certain segments; but for most of the people, my exchange with the Pandyan was turning out to be quite a show. And they lapped up the unfolding drama.

The older soldier whispered to his officer, who lent weight to the counsel so offered. After several moments, the officer said something under his breath. The older man saluted and hurried away, shouting to the guards to open the wicket gate. The young Pandyan said in softer tones,

"I seek authority from the Captain of the Guard, my lady. Meanwhile, for I notice your ankles quite swollen, would you like to dismount and flex your stiff limbs a little?"

But I did not move. Seated high, my gaze travelled beyond the contingent and the gate, and to the manicured path leading to the sprawling palace complex.

The sound of birds caught my attention, prompting me to look up. All manner of fowls were in flight, high up and heading west; a dark, shifting cloud of fluttering wings in a strange, never-ending procession.

The soldier of years, the one who had hurried off earlier, rushed back as if chased by wild dogs. The Roman officer, the red plume on his helmet dancing in the brisk breeze, followed the man's progress as he ran past to the Pandyan officer. The two conferred in whispers, the older soldier urgent and the young officer expressing surprise.

"Please dismount, my lady, and enter by foot," said the Pandyan officer as he took my mount's bridle in his hand. "My men here will escort you. Fear not for your horses, for we shall water and take good care of them until further news."

Even before he had completed his words, I swung my leg over the horse's lowered neck and landed on the dusty ground. The crowd gasped with admiration. There were whispers of *woman*, some gentle and others less so.

Without a word, I strode past the officer. The horses snorted and blubbered, and this time I felt it. Ever so slightly, the ground shifted under my feet. All along I had supposed the pressing crowd and noise unsettled the animals, but now I suspected another source.

The soldiers, all at attention, betrayed no movement. In this, they behaved as did the people in the village. I turned and the crowd, intent on my actions, had also not sensed the disturbance underfoot. Instead, the people cheered and waved, thinking my intention in turning to look back was to garner their encouragement. Some threw petals, others followed suit, and several strings of flowers snaked into the air and landed around my person.

Remembering the task at hand and anxious of the confrontation awaiting, I summoned my outrage to bolster my courage. I walked fast, almost at a run, with the two soldiers trying to keep ahead of me without themselves looking ridiculous. We headed for a wing of the impressive smooth-walled building and entered a modest door used by lesser officials. I followed the hurrying men down long, narrow corridors and often had to stand aside, hard against the wall, to allow on-coming servants to pass.

After a bewildering number of turns and racing down endless corridors ending at doors, they showed me into a parlour.

It was of modest proportions and sparse in its furnishing. Swords and shields hung on the wall. A soldier's room.

A woman appeared, and from her attire and deference, a maid-servant. She offered water and a tray of fruits.

"Please refresh yourself, my lady. My master will arrive soon."

Before I could detain her to interrogate who her master was, the woman vacated the room, locking the door as she exited. In the cool shaded space, fatigue took over. I felt faint, probably from the morning's relentless activity and an empty stomach intent on grumbling about its discomfort. I swayed and grasped a chair and sat down. It was not hunger or fatigue, but the ground that had moved.

It was a long wait and as impatience was about to froth forth, the door opened with a snick and an impressive man, in a fine silk tunic and a thick black moustache, entered. A scimitar hung from his broad waist belt. He did not have the raw round strength of the Arakan but the sculpted muscles of a man who had toned his physique in regimented training. Behind him came the maid-servant and a guardsman.

"You must be Lady Kannagi."

"You know me, sir, but I know you not."

"I know of the prime minister's horses lost in the Arakan lands and a few other matters which led me to conclude your identity."

"Then you know my husband. How is he, sir?"

"Yes, I have met Sir Kovalan, but please, Lady Kannagi, have a seat." As a mark of respect, he removed his turban.

"My husband, how is he? Tell me, sir, is he safe?"

"Please," repeated the man and extended his arm in invitation. He was distant and confident, did not smile, but there was an ingrained respectfulness about him.

"I will remain standing, sir, and may I ask, who are you?"

"My name, as I am, is unimportant but for now I am Captain of the Royal Household Guard, and I apologise for my young subaltern just now at the gates. He was less than decorous when receiving you. He was under the public's glare and somewhat unsettled. I have since counselled him."

"Thank you, Sir Captain, but please delay no further. What news of my husband? I come with evidence to prove his innocence, and my heart crackles with anxiety."

"Prove his innocence? How so, my lady?" The captain's eyes, till then steady and piercing, flickered.

"My husband had sent for his friend, my brother Anandan, to prove his innocence. Did my husband mention my brother's name?"

"I know this name, Anandan, and the prime minister—."

"Sagasana!"

"Yes, Prime Minister Shree Sagasana sent his personal rider to fetch the witness, Sir Anandan. Unfortunately, we received desperate news by carrier pigeon that Arakans had waylaid and killed him. Even now, we have a search party scouring the kurinji hills. How did you come by the prime minister's horses?"

"The Arakans did not kill my dear brother, Sir Captain. Sagasana's rider on Sagasana's orders murdered him." I paused for a sudden reaction, but there was none. "The news shocks you not?"

"I make no judgement, my lady, but you level a grave accusation on a flawless man. Are your words supported by proof or float on shifting sands of suppositions?"

"Proof from my brother Anandan," I said and, from the folds of my sari, produced the roll of leather, "even as he bled to death from wounds grievous inflicted by Sagasana's rider."

"And where is the rider now?" said the captain as he took the leather scroll.

"Held in the hills to answer for his guilt. I would have drunk the murderer's foul blood, but my Arakan brothers recognised him for many atrocities exacted on that stretch of road. And for now, they hold him until I return with my husband safe."

"There is some dangerous play here, I surmise," said the captain, "an attempt perhaps to force the course of justice. The rider is a trusted confederate of the prime minister and your strange *brothers* will reap a martial response for his kidnap. There have been many raised voices in court because of atrocities already committed in the commons and based on what evidence there is, the perpetrators are Arakans, your declared brothers."

"The play, Sir Captain, is in the halls of this palace and you hold a specimen script."

"Intriguing, for this scroll hints at some treachery, my lady, but it mentions not the prime minister's guilt. The rider, if he is the murderer also, will receive punishment, but by Pandyan laws. I'll send an escort with you to meet your Arakan brothers and you will counsel them to release the man."

"You have galloped ahead, Sir Captain, but do you not see Sagasana's hand in the murder? My Arakan brothers witnessed the attack, and the rider confessed."

"Perhaps it was the Arakans, my lady, who attacked, and the rider made to confess under threat. And even if the rider was the killer, one cannot assume it was a task committed at the behest of Prime Minister Sagasana, who is a man of impeachable integrity."

"How then did I come by Sagasana's horses?"

"The Arakans, whose kinship you claim, gave them to you, did they not? Perhaps the question pregnant for an answer is, how did the Arakans acquire the horses?"

"I can see that my words, Sir Captain, move you in circles."

"I am no judge but a *kaavalan*, a guardsman, my lady, tasked to uphold peace. There are men wiser than me, to counsel the king, who make weighty decisions regarding innocence and guilt. But apprised of the untimely death of your brother, you repaired here waving petition and purported proof, and provoking play and spectacle at the palace gates. Show me your proof and speak only words of promise."

"Though you received and treated me correctly, Sir Captain, I would rather present my proof to the king himself. With the prime minister already a suspect, even if you do not subscribe to my accusation, the only surety for my innocent husband's release is to utter my words of promise, unhindered and unsullied, in open court."

"You trust me not, my lady?"

"I'm not prepared to wager my husband's life."

"I understand your reserve," said the captain. He paused before adding. "There is another matter, one of weighty import."

The captain sucked in a long breath of air and exhaled. He moved to the window and stood looking out, as if gathering his thoughts and words. Turning, he said,

"I do not know, my lady, if there will ever be a correct way to say this but as a commander of men who risk their lives, one of my misfortunes is to carry news of warrior deaths of sons, fathers, brothers and *husbands* to their womenfolk."

It took some moments of stunned silence for his words to soak. Then I grabbed the man's sleeve and shook. I did not utter a word, but tears flowed and wet my garments.

The captain did not restrain my hands, but neither did he offer words of comfort. He stood solid as a grand tree even as the floor trembled again. He knew, from his stated experience, that words were no balm for the terrible tear rendering my heart.

With chest heaving in despair, a fiery red coal in my stomach, and my knees threatening to soften, I said,

"Tell me now and leave no gaps for mystery."

"When we found your husband with an ornament, one similar in rarity to an anklet lately lost from the queen's precious jewellery, we arrested him. The royal jeweller identified the anklet as belonging to the queen. The prime minister—."

"Sagasana!"

"Yes," said the captain, and he paused before continuing to recite, in his dispassionate tone, the rehearsed news. "The prime minister accorded your husband every opportunity to plead his guilt and seek clemency at the king's feet. Your husband declined and persisted his innocence."

"Why must he plead guilty when the crime was not his?"

"Even after we presented him with arguments of sound logic and unassailable sense, your husband declined confession in exchange for clemency. He remained steadfast. The king, his hand thus forced, passed sentence and tasked me to carry out his orders."

"And you murdered my husband!"

"I am servant to king and kingdom, my lady, and yes, I had the king's orders carried out at dawn today. Not by my hands, but it could have been just as well."

My knees bent and I sank to the floor, but the captain held me up. Without thinking, I leaned on the strong arms that took my husband's life. But my growing anger brought me to my senses, and I pushed myself away from his touch and said,

"My husband killed and my brother murdered; now take me to your king, guardsman, where I shall present proof of my husband's innocence. I am cursed for being so late to save my poor husband, but am early enough to wreak vengeance. Revenge will not be reward enough, but I demand it, and what a sorry trade for lives so precious already lost."

"We have Romapuri in court."

"The Cholan allows petitions from his people when court convenes, no matter the occasion, is it not the same here in Pandyan?"

"It is as you say, but petitions aplenty fill the day. There is not time enough to present more claims."

Realising that this man, this self-assured man who had my husband killed but considered himself guiltless, could deny access to the king, I did the unthinkable. I pleaded with him.

"Please, sir, I have lost everything. Take me to court and allow me to redeem my husband's name."

The captain considered my plea. He gestured to the soldier and servant, and said,

"Escort Lady Kannagi to the subterranean cells." He turned to me. "My lady, there you will collect your husband's body and accord him burial for his peace and yours. My people will help transport and see to the funeral arrangements. Meanwhile, I shall make representations and try to secure time for your petition."

"Thank you, upright son of a blessed mother, for believing my words of promise."

"It's not important what I believe, my lady, but only important that all who seek audience in our Pandyan court win an opportunity. If you fail to win today, return tomorrow, and if failure accosts you, return again and again, as many do, until you satisfy your day in court."

###

23: In the Second Hides Truth

As Captain of the Guard, I occupied a loft and, from that vantage point, gained an excellent view of the busy auditorium below.

The Peerless Pandyan King Nedun-Cheliyan and Queen Mother Kopperun-Devi sat on a raised dais at the end of a long hall that had heavy drapes on the walls. Cool air entered the tall windows of the *Rajya Sabha* and wiped away the heat. Huge rectangular kites made from fabric hanged from the crossbeams, built into the high ceiling. Servants, hidden behind curtains, tugged on ropes routed over pulleys, and these swung the kites back and forth and their lazy movements further cooled the congested hall. An abundance of flower arrangements lent a colourful vista and emitted a sweet fragrance. Soothing incense smoke coiled to the ceiling, curved, and caressed the flowing drapes.

Sages and teachers sat in places of honour, as did the Roman delegation and senior Pandyan nobles, first among them the wizened Prime Minister Shree Sagasana, and generals and merchant princes. There were also many of the foremost artisans, including Thiru Pillay the Royal Jeweller, and masters from the performing, visual, and literary arts. And people of all classes and castes—by the king's decree, even the lowliest—filled the standing room behind the line of luminaries.

Accomplished panegyrists recited paeans praising the king's deeds of charity, the queen's works of piety, and the richness and abundance of the Pandyan polity. After each such rendition, royal retainers presented gifts to the bards.

A murmur rippled forward from the far end of the hallway near the entrance. I sensed grave foreboding and hurried from the loft, and down the tight winding stairs, hidden behind the curtains. As I rushed down, the noise grew.

It was the raised voice of a woman—Kannagi!

By the time I reached the ground floor, there was a loud inhuman shout and the great doors pushed open. Kannagi rushed in with several guards at her heels. She ran here and there, avoiding the soldiers' grasping hands. People exclaimed and gesticulated.

A guard had wrapped his arm around Kannagi's waist but, determined, she dragged him behind her. More guards arrived and were about to lift the struggling intruder off her feet when I issued a sharp command. The men stopped, and so did Kannagi.

In a few quick strides, I approached Kannagi and snapped in a low voice.

"Stop this spectacle!"

"You promised an audience!" said Kannagi, and she bristled.

She was a woman possessed. In her raised hand, she grasped an ankle ring. In unyielding black clothes, lush hair hanging loose, and eyes wide and ringed black, she personified an avatar of Kali herself.

"Captain, please bring the good lady forward, so she may enlighten us," said the prime minister. I leaned down and whispered to Kannagi.

"I made no such promise for today, but apparently you already have your day in court. Hear my good advice, Lady Kannagi. Speak your evidence, such as you claim to have, and leave alone conjectures lest these muddy your petition." I escorted her to the front and stepped back.

"The hour is too late for my husband to seek justice," said Kannagi in a sharp voice that carried to the corners of the great hall, "but I am early enough to exact vengeance on his behalf. I am here to reveal the innocence of my poor husband, who lies lifeless, murdered, away from the scrutiny of honest eyes."

"Contain your anger, woman," said the prime minister, 'so we may seek gentle recourse for whatever ails you to have so challenged the peace in our Rajya Sabha."

Kannagi's gaze swept the royal court from left to right, seeking the person who had spoken; but her eyes looked without seeing, perhaps trying to catch everyone's attention and no one in particular.

"Who, who spoke those words? Reveal yourself!" she screamed.

"Why this show," said the prime minister, "and who gave such fierce insult compelling you to barge into these proceedings? But please, good lady, before you speak your petition, pay this court proper acknowledgements."

"Your king is an unjust king!" retorted Kannagi. "It is not meet for me to pay him, or any others, dues. This king's judgement has stained your court's virtue. Let your king, as charged, speak, for I wish to hear his pitiful defence!"

But her outrageous accusations roused the assembly, stunned into silence until then by the unprecedented interruption. The small murmurs travelled round the auditorium and gained strength. The courtiers in the assembly took up the cry and clamour. Garlands and petals, meant for showering praise, turned into snaking javelins and pelted missiles, and the people waved fists and let their displeasure known.

"Your jeers seek to drown my words," shouted Kannagi. "But you will hear the truth in this chamber this day."

The prime minister held up his hand and called for silence. An undertone of discontent remained palpable among the people, and they were ready to explode in anger. Kannagi wheeled on the prime minister and hissed.

"Who are you?"

"I am Sagasana, born of the lowliest classes, but by the grace of our Great Pandyan's father, now a humble servant to king and country and also to you, my lady, and first minister to His Majesty, Maha Rajan, Nedun-Cheliyan." He paused and, not receiving a response from Kannagi, he said,

"A heavy accusation that, *unjust king*, a charge so forceful never heard in this chamber since time started, and you have so readily identified our king as the accused even before we know what trespass has so unsettled you."

"You are Sagasana, are you? You let loose a monstrous scheme and beware, for it has come to feast on your flesh. You spew elegant words, and exude wisdom and justice, but you are quicksand beneath a placid pond. And while the water bears the blame, it is the scheming sand which sucks under the lives of the unwary."

"You speak in riddles, my lady, and even if you do not acknowledge my position, it behoves you to show decorum to my years. Moreover, since you seek redress in this court, you must accept this court's authority. And such acceptance requires you to pay proper respects. Please grant us your name and speak your grievance."

"Keep your peace then, old man, and hear my complaint."

"Let not your voice boom, good lady, for you see, truth needs no thunder to herald its coming."

"But truth needs the herald of a booming voice, Sagasana, to rouse the slumberous indifference under the watch of this king."

"Please, good lady, I ask again, and with some insistence, honour us with your name and circumstances, and even do so with the gentleness found in all true women of Tamilakam."

"Satisfy your curiosity then, Sagasana. I hail from Poom-Puhar, where the Cholan hears whispers too but only from truth and justice."

"You claim to seek justice, good lady, when your own words do no such thing to this august assembly, for you shower rowdy flippancy and disparage the entire Pandyan Court in Romapuri's presence. Do you not see the welcomed and valuable embassy?" The prime minister gave a courtly bow to the Roman delegation.

"Not disparage, Sagasana, but to accuse and curse you and this entire Pandyan Court." And she undid a knot in the folds of her sari, took out a handful of sand and threw it into the air.

"Oh god," said the prime minister. "Oh my dear child." He closed his eyes and held both hands to his ears. After a moment, he said in a heavy and sad voice.

"My child, your hurt is grievous, but we have yet to determine where from the source of this great pain. Even if you consider all present here as vile, I ask again, where are your manners? Why are you so rude even to our wrinkled skin and grey hair? Bereft of all things good as we might be in your estimation, has your culture forgotten deference? Are you not of Tamilakam? Have your parents and teachers failed you in this too?"

The prime minister's words stunned Kannagi, as if some old lesson had revealed its secrets to her. She sobbed loud and said,

"You have taken everything from me, sir, everything. I am reduced to nothing and have lost all that is good and gentle. I am empty and from my utter void only curses well. These I shall shower upon you in great abundance, for I have only curses."

Many in the assembly showed anger; some looked perplexed; and all the while interpreters whispered into the ears of the Roman delegation, who leaned back to lend attention but from the corners of their eyes studied the fascinating woman.

"Let me recount to this sham assembly my complaint. Know also how a Cholan once offered his flesh to appease a hawk forced to free a pigeon. Another king of my motherland gave justice to a grieving cow who had lost her tottering calf to a prince, a royal son who had run over the calf with his chariot. When the cow rang the bell at his gate, the king declared his own son guilty, and in recompense, had the young prince crushed under a chariot wheel. This is the measure of justice from the Cholan kings.

"From their capital city of Kaveri-Poom-Pattinam, where the harbour is so deep that the leviathans of the heaving seas enter without having their heavy loads taken off, came my beloved husband Kovalan; my one true lord, an accomplished merchant, and only son of Sir Masattuvan, himself a respected and honest grain merchant of a long line of peerless philanthropists. To overcome his cruel fate, my lord Kovalan and I came to your city to rebuild our lives. But you put him to death, you unjust people of Madurai. By your word you had my husband Kovalan killed, you unjust king. I seek justice, no, *demand* justice! You ask who I am. I am Kannagi. I am your death!"

"Thank you, good lady, your complaint is clear now," said the prime minister. "And now, allow us to enlighten this eminent assembly on certain matters before we delve into the intricacies of your particular grievance. The Pandyan Court will never diminish the great works of our mighty Cholan compatriots in the east. May the rains shower their lands and yield bountiful harvests, and their herds multiply and escape affliction from diseases. And so, we offer prayers for their well-being. We, Pandyans of the south, have very little deeds and accomplishments to our name, true, and what little success we claim, pales in comparison with your illustrious Cholans."

Great shouts of protests erupted from the aristocrats and some stood up and eulogised Pandyan deeds. The prime minister allowed the interruption. And after enough voices rose and multiple stories of Pandyan exploits recounted, and satisfied that they had assuaged immediate tempers, he continued.

"Yes, outstanding masters of the *aaya-kalaigal*, the sixty-four branches of knowledge, and high nobles of the blood royal, but our praises are best left to others to sing, for we are students and yet to learn from this good lady the songs of self-praise. And though our Pandyan is mighty in arms and even Rome of the western empires seeks congress and has a magnificent cohort stationed on our shores as tribute in trade, we accede perhaps we are younger in the better wisdoms of Tamilakam.

"Our naïve nature compels us to believe in the supremacy of man over beast. We do not feed human flesh to carrion-eating birds nor kill our sons to appease a cow, revered as that gentle creature is in our mores. Though we grieve for the cow having lost her suckling calf, how much greater the grief of the queen who lost her prince, a mother who carried her baby son for ten months in her womb. Only a mother, my lady, will know that pain. In that regards please accept my sympathies, for you have yet to receive the blessings of bearing a child."

Kannagi bristled, but before she could utter a word, the prime minister raised his hand and said,

"That as it might be, did the prince's siblings, manoeuvring for their father's throne, rejoice or shed tears even as the wagon wheel crushed the young royal's head? Was this justice for an animal's grief or statecraft in play? Perhaps there are lessons and truths in your Cholan's actions, good lady, which continue to elude us, old as we are in years but young in wisdom and yet having much to learn."

Kannagi's features twisted with fury and she laughed in a high-pitched voice, a jeering sound which morphed into cackles. The people in the assembly raised their arms and railed. The prime minister again held up his hand to counsel peace.

"Please, good lady, even as we held our peace when you spewed, will you not lend us your ears without further impolite interruptions?"

Hearing the prime minister, Kannagi dropped to the floor and crossed her legs, knees spread wide. Her uncouth posture shocked and disgusted the men of breeding assembled in the sabha. The old prime minister, unfazed, continued in a measured tone.

"You speak of a cruel fate having befallen your husband, Kovalan," said the prime minister. "You tie the deeds of the great Cholan kings to your husband, hoping the liaison will bestow favourable testimony to his righteousness, making his death even more wicked and unjust. But is it not true he consorted with and lost his fortune to a courtesan, a woman of base repute? Is that not why you trekked over desolate lands, even risked the Arakan, to reach the unsullied sanctuary of Madurai, thinking the winds will not carry the stink of human tales? You now seek justice for a philandering husband who robbed you of your honour and happiness. This is the true nature of his wretched fate. Our beautiful Madurai was a mere stage for the last act of his pitiful play. Smear not, my lady, the impressive accomplishments of your impeccable kings by weaving their illustrious deeds to your husband's sordid repute, for this is undeserved association."

In a snatch, Kannagi stood up but before she could utter her outrage, the Pandyan King raised his sceptre and said,

"Thank you, esteemed prime minister, and please settle back, for you have apprised us of the full circumstances of this woman's complaint." King Nedun-Cheliyan turned to Kannagi and said,

"My good lady, it matters not to us the character of the person wronged, but only whether he has suffered any injustice at our hands. We took a while to recall, occupied as we were by many matters of state and each clamouring for our first and undivided attention. Yes, your husband forfeited his life by our orders. Why do you say it is a travesty of justice? Please, speak your evidence without further ado as we sense our court grows impatient with the boiled seeds spilled here this day, for these promise no sprouting roots, let alone a bountiful harvest."

"Do you agree then, Nedun-Cheliya, that you are the accused?"

Upon hearing her disrespectful address, a murmur rippled through the length and breadth of the royal court. The king raised his hand to subdue the discontent.

"Yes, we concede. We are the accused."

"Do you then submit to questions as an accused?"

"We do so submit, yes."

"Did you or did you not pass a verdict of guilt and a judgement to have my husband, Kovalan of Puhar, beheaded?"

"Yes, we so did."

"And what was the charge?"

"We charged him and found him guilty of stealing Queen Kopperun-Devi's anklet. And we shall save you further time, eager as your voice betrays to uncover the truth. We apprehended your husband, trying to raise money with the queen's anklet, an identical twin to the second and there are only two of the kind ever fashioned."

"How would you know there were only two of the kind?"

"Our former royal jeweller and peerless artisan, Guru Nallathamby, known throughout Tamilakam and the Aryan lands even, made the queen's pair. As fate would have it, thereafter, the guru left us and denied posterity the secret of his skills. Dear lady, there were only two of the uniques."

"If my ankle ring was identical to your queen's, then I declare there were not two pieces but two *pairs* made, one of which belongs on my feet."

"That's impossible, good lady, for the guru made only one pair. And he destroyed the mould by royal orders. Our orders. What you hold is, at best, a worthy imitation. But an imitation and no more."

"Were you there, Nedun-Cheliya, when this great Guru Nallathamby of yours broke the mould?"

"No, but—."

"Was anyone else present, anyone now here present? How about you, Sagasana, were you present when the mould shattered?"

"Is that your defence of your husband's innocence?" asked Nedun-Cheliyan. "And you so readily cast aspersions on a man who left this world before his natural time, a man of impeccable dedication to the furtherance of the sciences of gemmology and metallurgy, and long service to Pandyan craftsmanship. We have been generous and indulged you long enough, good lady. Now, speak your proof or forever hold your tongue."

"Then hear me, Nedun-Cheliya, contained within my anklets are rubies, cut and polished from the finest and by the best." Kannagi held up her ankle ring and shook it. Nedun-Cheliyan laughed and said,

"Oh my dear lady, if that is your evidence, it's a matter easily resolved. The queen's ankle rings contain flawless pearls; selected and perfected by Mother Nature herself. Hers are not gems mutilated by the hand of a mere man, no matter what his mastery of skills."

"Then prove it and here is my proof!"

Kannagi smashed her ankle ring on the polished green granite floor. The ornament shattered and out flew rubies, blood red and angry.

"Rubies!" said Kannagi. Queen Kopperun-Devi, anxious, hesitated and said,

"O dear sovereign of my body and soul, please don't accept her challenge, for I fear trickery. See how the woman heaves, her eyes so wild and portent of black magic."

Though I stood far, I read the queen's lips and heard the words in my mind.

"The dice rolls, Maha Devi, and will soon reveal the truth," replied the king with a gentle smile. "Protest not, for how else should we meet this challenge? And who else but for your husband to enjoy the privilege of touching your feet?" The king knelt, and twisted and removed an ankle ring from his queen's feet. "Fret not, my Devi," he said in a soft voice unheard by all but the queen, and those who read lips. "I'll gift a new pair even more exquisite than these."

Rising to his full impressive height, Nedun-Cheliyan raised his hand above his bejewelled turban and threw the ankle ring down.

It smashed against the floor and cracked open, spilling white pearls that bounced and raced to the feet of the seated. The nobles cringed and curled their slippered toes, lest their touch soiled the royal jewels.

"There! Pearls!" The king declared in a triumphant voice. "You have your proof."

"The truth hides in the second, Nedun-Cheliya," replied Kannagi. "Rip it off your queen's feet and break it."

"Redeem our honour, my king," said the queen who had already removed the second anklet, "and reinforce our justice."

"As you command, Maha Devi," said the king with a bow. He took the anklet and, holding it up, addressed the assembly.

"People of our storied Pandyan nation, we welcome Justice to reveal herself."

He threw with force and the anklet flew hard into the ground. As did its twin, the gold ornament cracked and released a shower of—rubies! After a stunned silence, the king gasped.

"Rubies."

"Yes, rubies, Nedun-Cheliya, bearer of the bent royal sceptre. Bright blood rubies screaming my honour and lamenting my husband's innocence!"

Nedun-Cheliyan, clutching his chest, sank into his throne chair. A great clamour erupted from the assembly. Voices rose, arguments broke out. The queen's crying voice drowned in the noise. The royal physician stood up and called for this and that. People shouted.

Seeing the retainers rush forward, I rallied my men to the king and formed a ring of shields around the royal dais.

"Stand back! Give the king air! Stand back," I shouted.

The floor shook, and a tremor rolled under our feet. People screamed. Several swayed, as if debauched by demon drinks, and fell. But my men and I held firm.

"Stand fast! Protect the king. The king!" My voice rose above the clamour.

Another rumble and a third tremor, more powerful and pronounced than the earlier two, shook the auditorium. More screams erupted as panic spread among the people.

I allowed only the prime minister, the royal physician, and trusted retainers to attend to the king and queen.

From the deep corridors, a loud cracking sound erupted, followed by shouts and cries of alarm. The floor rocked, and again my command rang out.

"Hold fast, men. Rally to me."

Throughout the commotion, Kannagi's voice shrilled.

"Do you wish to cling to your pathetic life, you pitiless excuse for a king? Do you hope to prolong your failed life until food tastes bland, eyes grow foggy, and ears hear no melody, and your manhood sags in shame? Do you hope to grow infirm and fall from the heaviness of age? Should you not pluck out your evil heart in payment for the gross injustice vested on my poor husband?"

With shaking hands, the king pushed himself to his feet, his bearing weak and incapacitated. He cast aside his turban of pearls and precious stones. Grabbing his chest, pulling his silk linens tight, he called in a weak voice. The ground shook and, as a man seized by falling sickness, the king wavered on his feet. A shout rang out.

"The roof! The roof!"

Large pieces of stucco broke and fell, and strings of dust descended as if the roof leaked a sand storm.

"You have not shamed me, good lady." The king shouted, but his voice choked; was feeble. "You cannot shame me, for I have purchased the shame by my own words and deeds."

"And yet you continue to draw breath!" Kannagi, now a madwoman, screamed.

"Then see me fall and consider my debt settled."

Nedun-Cheliyan collapsed and rolled down the steps. His attendants, shouting, hurried down after him. The king's arm fell out-stretched, and his mouth gaped wide open in death. Seeing this, Kopperun-Devi screamed, and she, too, collapsed. With great shouts of alarm, the prime minister and servants milled around the royal couple.

"The king has died!" Shouts rang out. "The king has died!"

"The queen has fainted!"

Courtiers converged, but as pieces of plaster fell, they pushed back. Others shoved forward. Shouts and loud protests erupted as the melded body of people surged and receded.

A loud explosive crack echoed, and the stunned people screamed in terror. More commands rang out and attendants tried to guide the mad-stricken people out through the doors to the corridors. Another frightening sound erupted, and the ground separated in a long, jagged crack. More screams and shouts. People fell and others, desperate to escape, stepped on bony limbs and wobbly bodies.

Kannagi, as if a woman possessed with warrior traits, leaped on a plinth and grasped a burning torch. Waving it from side to side, she laughed. Her agility and small crouched frame, swaddled in black, personified a jinn from the netherworld.

Sensing her intent, I broke free from the cordon and closed on Kannagi. But she eluded my grasping hands, proving herself more agile than I had given her credit.

"Stand back!" She screamed and held the torch close to the curtains.

I hesitated. All around me, people scrambled and ran, toppling over chairs and stepping on fallen debris.

"The torch, Lady Kannagi, hand me the torch," I said.

I threw a quick glance at my soldiers. One man tossed a spear. I caught it and swung back; at the ready.

"Stand back, Sir Captain," said Kannagi.

"Hand me the torch, my lady, or I'll spear you."

"Slay me then, for you, a Pandyan, already murdered my husband and this will complete the reason for your bloody birth from a screaming mother."

I did not intend to kill but only to disable; a pierce to the foot or hand. But again, Kannagi was swift, or perhaps it was hesitation on my part that rendered her the advantage. She torched the billowing curtains; the flames caught, raced up, and spread.

Another tremor rattled the ground and, with a loud crack, a second jagged split appeared and raced across the polished floor, throwing up explosive bursts of gravel and spits of sand.

Kannagi, fascinated by the earth cracking a few paces from her feet, stared with wide-open eyes.

Just as a shower of stones fell, I rushed forward and pushed her away, but a stone, about the size of a fist, hit me.

Like a sack, I dropped. If not for my turban, I might have died. My vision blurred, and all around me things moved leisurely, as if time had slowed his run to a stroll. It was many moments before I recovered a measure of faculties and felt warm blood streak down my face.

"Captain, Captain!" A soldier cried. "Look, the ceiling is in danger of collapsing, sir, we must leave!"

I was still recovering from the blow, and through grit encased eyes watched the terrible scene playing out.

"Sir, sir!" said the soldier. But the man's voice might as well have been a distant dream.

A brisk breeze fed the flames and ignited a firestorm. People, their hair and clothes on fire, screamed and scrammed. Others raised their hands against the now constant rain of larger and larger pieces of plaster popping off the ceiling and walls. Thus distracted, they stumbled and fell. Bloodied and dust-covered men picked themselves up, only to collapse under falling debris.

A round man with wobbling flesh, Thiru Pillay, evaded my gaze and hurried away, only to run right under a toppling plinth. His scream died as the stone crashed down and his stomach exploded in a burst of bloody red entrails.

Pushing and wriggling past the people rushing out, Kannagi stood mesmerised by the fierce inferno. Another tremor split the floor and the granite tiles popped one after another in quick succession.

A loud groan and a massive pillar dislodged from its anchor and leaned forward; a shower of debris heralded its impending collapse. My men, the fallen queen, and the prime minister, and the tight crowd of courtiers cowering under the shields were in danger.

"Save yourselves men. Move out, everyone," I shouted. But it was too late.

The boulders rained down and my men died under the deluge, holding up their shields till the end. Explosive bursts of gravel and grit shot past, and I held up an arm to shield my face.

Something dull hit my chest, fell at my feet, and bounced away and rocked to a stop. It was a turbaned head, separated from its torso. I recognised the sad but serene face of Prime Minister Shree Sagasana.

"Captain!" screamed Kannagi.

In an instant, I jumped back and locked eyes with her. A shock of stones smashed the spot I had occupied a moment earlier. The stinging dust burst and engulfed me, and I lost sight of Kannagi.

213

24: The Little Sister Deified

The captain disappeared in the searing dust, and the massive pillar, its girth wider than the oldest tree, crushed the royal dais and all the people gathered under the soldiers' shields. A great ball of fiery dust and smoke boiled and raced towards me.

I covered my face and, after some time, when I looked, the impressive auditorium did not shimmer in gold dust but suffocated in thick opaque soot; curtains did not wave in the breeze but tongues of angry flames licked and revelled in their death dance; and voices did not shout in anger, but screamed in fear and terror. The heat grew intense and the oil in my dishevelled hair smoked.

A sharp burst, similar to the sound of a pregnant water skin exploding, filled the air, followed by tinkling and splintering sounds. A shower of glass shards came crashing down. I drew a sharp breath and looked down, engrossed by the raw wound gouged into my chest. A wedge of glass had sliced off my left breast.

The waves of pulsing pain punched out my breath and in a mindless panic, I dashed out the splintered door.

"Kannagi! Kannagi! The witch comes."

A man, his rich clothes torn and bloody scalp hanging loose over one ear, pointed at me and screamed before dashing away.

And I too ran after him and into a swirling dust storm that had blotted the sun. Like a blind drunkard, I toddled this way and that. People carrying gold figurines and all sorts of loot from the palace pushed and rushed past me. I do not remember how long I wandered, but reached and climbed over the twisted remains of the majestic gates through which I had earlier in the afternoon entered.

The tremors from the palace grounds continued to follow me into the city. Each rattle produced loud cracks in the street and sharp slabs of stones pushed up, destroying roads and blocking the path of fleeing people. Many called for their loved ones; some grabbed pitiful possessions; and others, overwhelmed, stood dazed or aimlessly wandered.

Cows and long horned bulls stampeded and trampled people. Goats leaped over mangled bodies and smoking debris and, landing on the other side, waved their brisk little tails and hurried into the dust. Sheep, their wool on fire, cooked alive as they bleated and dashed. Elephants, crazed with fear, thundered and trumpeted, and humped down the streets, trampling picket fences and felling trees in their path. Everywhere I looked, I saw dead and dying people.

The ever-thickening and thinning crowds knocked me here and there. Crying in anguish and having lost my way, I ran along the dusky, dust-filled streets. The fire had spread from the palace to the servant quarters, and the wind carried fiery embers and set alight trees and the many shanty stalls in the nearby markets. Oil lamps, found in every house, toppled by the earthquake, ignited new fires and devoured dwellings. The firestorm grew in ferocity, and smoke and dust suffocated and blocked out the sun.

Amidst the mayhem, I heard the neighing of horses and shouts.

"There! There goes the witch! Seize her!"

The mounted soldiers thrust their hips and spurred their horses.

With a shriek, and for a moment forgetting the excruciating pain in my chest, I ducked into a house and ran into the occupants, who were dashing out carrying their possessions. A young man stopped, fascinated by my singed and smoking hair; my chest, bloody red; and my bulging eyes, wild and darting. An older man appeared out of the dust and pulled the young man away, and both disappeared into the swirling smoke.

I stumbled through the house, passed the debris-strewn backyard and reached the neighbouring street. The city had turned dark and towering rings of smoke blanketed the cheerless sky. The rumble of earthquake continued unabated, the ground shifted, and I swayed as if on a rocking boat.

"There she is," cried a voice, and again horses neighed and hooves clattered as my pursuers picked up speed.

"Stop! Stop!"

But I ignored the shouts. My head spun as I staggered from corner to crevice and, unable to move any farther, collapsed onto a pile of recent debris. My breath shot ragged and sharp, and with each exhale, dust rose around my nostrils.

The whinnying of horses drew closer and my eyes flickered and squinted through gritty stinging smoke.

Tip-toeing hooves appeared in my arc of vision, followed by a pair of sturdy feet that landed with thuds on the ground and kicked up little puffs of dust. The legs, as thick as tree trunks, approached, and a heavy hand settled on my shoulder.

"Fear not, little sister."

***

I was on my back, my head rocking from side to side; a covering of cloth and hides shivered and shook above. The distinct sound of hooves and squeak of wheels meant I was jolting along in a carriage. Feeling a stiff tearing pain, I lifted the heavy blanket and peered underneath. Wet, bloodied bandages wrapped around my chest.

Memory flooded back—the grinning face of Savaali blocking the sky as he looked down. His face twisted into deep concern as he surveyed my torn body. Placing a roll of hides under my head for a pillow, he gave a reassuring smile and disappeared. But I could hear him moving about and talking in urgent whispers.

The Silent One appeared, as if to assure me further, and I was grateful for the consideration shown by these brutish fellows. Then, he too disappeared from sight. But the brothers remained in the vicinity. Savaali gave voice to soothing words for my comfort. I gathered they were lashing together a stretcher, for I was in no condition to sit on a saddle.

"The soldiers," I whispered, my voice hoarse. "Beware the soldiers."

"Fear not, little sister," said Savaali, who appeared over me again. "We only frightened them away. The earthquake destroyed much of the city. The inferno engulfs the rest. We'll move east by north and reach The Edge before sunrise."

"Brother Savaali, not to The Edge; not to your village." My fingers grasped his thick, sweaty arm. "The soldiers will follow and exact vengeance on your people. Leave me here to die. Save

216

yourself. Go." My energy drained, I again shut my eyes and laboured to breathe.

"Eraivan tasked me to protect your well-being and do your bidding."

"Then I bid you, let me die."

"Death will come when he is ready, little sister. Now, bid me something else or save your energy."

"Then take me west, to the Cheran land."

"To the Western Ghats?" Savaali scratched his chin, and his face lighted. "A good plan, little sister. Better than you suspect."

And he left. But I could hear the two Arakans work in silence.

On several occasions, some dazed wanderer, covered in grey ghostly dust or streaked by lines of blood, staggered forth. But seeing the fierce Arakans, these souls screamed in terror, found renewed energy, and ran away.

Then, a small band of soldiers advanced with drawn swords and levelled spears. When they were about half a bow shot away, Savaali called out to them.

"We're not your foes, Pandyan. And on this terrible day, of cracking earth and raging firestorms released by the earth beast, spend your attention and energy elsewhere. Do your better tasks than to shed more blood." Drawing his broad curved blade that emitted a pronounced shearing sound, he added, "And by blood, I speak of your blood."

The soldiers bent low, ready but hesitant. They looked towards the senior soldier among them, a man of impressive stature.

"We take our little sister, who lays there with grievous wounds, and will soon be on our way," said Savaali. "Stop and listen well, lest you invite death before he is ready for you."

The soldiers halted; perhaps they too did not wish to see more blood spilled, even Arakan blood. But they did not back off.

My Arakan brothers, their incurved tongues bulging through parted lips and eyes popped open and frightening, hunched, ready to pounce.

The senior soldier wore a thin turban and, upon closer scrutiny, it was but a bandage. The man had been bleeding from a head wound. He stared, and I recognised him. His fine tunic was dusty and torn in places; face swollen; and black moustache impressive but streaked with grey dust. He said something and his men, grateful to avoid combat, stepped back and lowered their weapons.

"He is Captain of the Royal Household Guard, loyal to the Pandyan, but an upright man." Dazed as I was, my frail voice whispered, as if on its own volition, rendering me a curious onlooker.

"An upright man, declares my little sister, but is there such a wonderful man in all the Pandyan reach?" Savaali studied the captain from head to toe and said,

"Upright or not, perhaps you're the right man to complete my task. We had as our guest until lately a rider who works for Sagasana, your first minister."

The Silent One stood unmoving and eagle eyed, but Savaali sheathed his sword and took a step forward and said,

"The rider confessed to stealing the life of my little sister's friend and her innocent husband's salvation, Anandan of Puhar, and I wonder whether you know these matters?"

"I know the name Anandan," said the captain, the caution in his voice growing confident, "but the rider's deeds, for now, stand only as accusations, and his guilt is not for me to pronounce."

"You underestimate the situation, *captain*," said Savaali. "Your king perished and took with him all his liveried courtiers of any slim worth. You might be dispensing justice as the new *kovalan*, king, for I see men with strong arms and ready weapons already rallying to you."

"Speak your task, Arakan, that which compels you from seeing to Lady Kannagi already so grave, and also keeps me from my more urgent distractions, as you so succinctly laid bare."

"You speak in plain words, a true task-master it would seem, and so be it," said Savaali. "Hear me then, upright captain. The rider works for Sagasana and, upon further persuasion, confessed to working also for another of a more dangerous kind. A scorpion lurking in the crooked crevices of the palace."

"Does this scorpion have a name?" asked the captain.

"Do you know the one called Thiru Pillay?" said Savaali.

"If by that name you mean the royal jeweller, yes."

"We speak of the same scorpion then, for though the rider stung the innocent Anandan's life, the venom came from the veins of this Pillay," said Savaali.

"You have proof of this?"

Savaali tossed a roll of leather and the captain caught it in mid-air.

"The rider's confessions, written by his own hand. My king, Eraivan, true to his promise, set the slave free. And even now the bird flees north, for he knows death awaits him in Pandyan courts."

"What for are these names listed here?"

"Those are names of lives lost in the commons, topmost of which is the scorpion's own teacher, Guru Nallathamby. The rider robbed those lives on the behest of your villain, and the blame vested on and paid by us, the hill tribes of kurinji. Go now, upright captain, for much doing awaits your keen attention."

The captain continued to study the scroll a little longer. Then, shoving it into his waist belt, he said,

"Thank you, but this alters nothing between us, Arakan, for there is much blood debt owed and, in a time, not distant, I might return to the kurinji hills with many pointed spears and true arrows prepared."

"And we Arakans will prepare ourselves too, but with armour alone and not spears, for you are our brethren, fellow Tamils. Perhaps friend or foe, we will settle another time. Go now, upright captain, dally no more but dwell on all that has today befallen this sad land of ours. And fare you well."

"Lady Kannagi," said the captain, "thank you just now in the sabha; your call alerted and saved my life."

"I am glad for your safety, Sir Captain," I said, and fell back, exhausted.

"Sir," said the captain, a new gentler note in his voice as he addressed Savaali. "Rubble blocks the West Gate; it is impassable. The south burns. Use the East Gate on your left and you will find a less treacherous route."

The captain, betraying no emotion, stepped back and disappeared with his men into the thinning dust.

"You're right, little sister," said Savaali. "He's a rare one. Perhaps our people have hope."

The brothers tethered the two-wheeled stretcher to a horse and placed me on the makeshift bed. And as we set off, Savaali made clear his plan.

"This fragile contraption will not do for any journey of length, but suffice to get us to Puranchery. When they see us approach, the villagers will shriek in terror but will survive their ignorance. After some suitable rest and medicinal herbs, we'll harness a gentle cart to take us to the Cheran lands and the Western Ghats, where safety awaits among the Kuravars, who are kin to the Arakan."

It was about this time that the pain surged and I lost all consciousness. I did not recall the reception upon our arrival at Puranchery. But Savaali and his generous ways must have prevailed and won over the villagers, for I detected the hand of women who had cleaned and dressed my wounds. And the carriage lent further evidence that our visit to the village concluded well, for I spied bundles of herbs and other such unguents meant for the infirm. But the pain returned, and it burned. I did not cry lest it distressed my brave Arakan brothers who continued to risk their lives on my account.

The wagon shook as we drove off the road. It was daytime, this much I could tell from the sharp shafts of light piercing the gaps in the covers. The wagon stopped. And after a while, birdsong, sounds speaking of life and hope, reached my ears. But for me, only death awaited.

The covers parted, and Savaali pushed his head into the carriage. Seeing me awake, he grinned, his face growing broad and filling with large white teeth.

"Are you in pain, little sister? Your wounds look clean, but who is to know how they fever?"

I shook my head from side to side.

"Are you fevered?"

"No," I said in a soft voice. He touched my forehead with the back of a heavy hand and said,

"You need more practice, little sister, for you are a poor liar." He placed a wet cloth on my brow. "These roads are well-travelled." He whispered as he fussed to make me more comfortable. "Many townsfolk seek refuge in the west. The Pandyan has grown lawless and even now another unruly band comes over the hill. We'll hide among the trees until danger decays."

"What news, brother Savaali," I asked in a weak voice. "Is Puranchery safe? Did you see Amah Gayathri and her daughter?"

"No, I did not see mother and daughter. I'll tell you what I know. When we arrived at the village, though not ravaged by the earth beast, there was no chirping of birds or chittering of insects. Even the dogs laid low and ignored the cats. The rats, survivors as their kind are, long departed with the snakes and other wild creatures.

"And upon seeing my brother and myself, as creatures come down to tear away their virginity, the village women shrieked and ran away, beating their chests and heads. The men were not masters of their fear either, though some, forgetting their terror, ran at us with hoes and sticks raised high. But seeing how our eyes, my brother's and mine, blazed with fury and our incurved tongues bulged out of our mouths, the men wet themselves and ran away, even overtaking their women and stepping over one another in their impatience to save their worthless lives.

"But just as well, for with the village thus abandoned, the Silent One and I went about unmolested and helped ourselves to whatever herbs and salves were familiar.

"Brave as I may be in the face of a ferocious tiger, in matters of medicine, one needs courage of a different sort. And so little sister, I sewed. My hands trembled as if I were a feeble old woman. But they had their task. They tugged and stitched to close your gashed wounds, and raced to complete their task before consciousness and her terrible twin, pitiless pain, awoke.

"And while I cleaned and tended thus, the Silent One wandered in search and coming upon this wagon here harnessed our horses. We suspected the village cowards would seek soldiers and bring them down on us, claiming an entire horde of my Arakan brethren had descended upon their village, for how else to justify their soiled clothes and redeem their honour. We therefore could not linger for your rest, but allowed impatience free rein to put distance between us and imminent danger."

"You unclothed me?" The hot pain overwhelmed but did not did hide my blush. The Arakan went quiet and, upon recovering, he said,

"Let no shame hold your head down, little sister, for you witnessed our Arakan women, the raw and the ripe, go about bare-breast, and many even with less."

"What about my modesty, big brother Savaali?"

"There's no shattered modesty, little sister," he said, "more so when life is at stake. What I beheld was a pitiful torn fragility. Your wounds pulsed angry blood and as I plugged the weeping holes, new squirts sprung here and there. Trust me, little sister, I saw no more but mangled flesh and threatening death. I could have fabled that some fairy or feminine, perhaps the villager Gayathri, ministered to your needs. But it would be another lie and enough of that kind of talk has already brought us to this day."

"Even so, big brother dear, my inborn reserve shies and I am unable to meet your eyes."

"Then pluck out and burn my eyes," he said and thrust a carving blade at me, "for my eyes are too large for my black face, and frighten me when they look from the water."

Even in my wretched state, I could not but betray a smile. His lips stretched wide in a grin, but I spied the pain in his eyes and the innocence peeping from within. And that wrecked me.

A bird whistle reached us and Savaali tensed, but for a fleeting moment. He said,

"The Silent One is not so silent." Another bird whistle, this time shriller and more urgent. "I must go now, little sister, for a bird offers its neck for wringing." Again, flashing a wide white grin, he left the confines of the wagon.

The Arakan had not defiled me or acted in immodesty; it was I who judged him wrong—yet again. How many times had I been wrong? When would I learn that chastity and modesty hang not only on clothes and actions but more so in one's harboured thoughts?

Cautiously, I lifted the cover. My left breast was missing. Cleaved! And memory came flooding back: the upright captain injured, his generous blood staining and spreading on his tunic; the sound of splintering glass; and the sharp swish of slicing sheets flying down. I watched as a clump of flesh fell off my chest. Then the agony hit. The thought of that slice sent a chill down the length of my body.

Without warning, for even with his bulk he moved with the stealth of a cat, Savaali pulled aside the curtain, flooding light after him, and said, "The road is clear, little sister, and we resume our escape to the western hills where our cousins will keep you hidden and safe from any jeopardy."

As we got onto the road and trundled along, the covers of the wagon parted and I saw in the distance thick streams of black smoke snaking high into the sky.

Madurai continued to burn.

***

My brother, the Silent One, and I kept to the trees, nursing our little sister the best we could during daylight and travelling at night.

We reached the Cheran lands and the Western Ghats, and our kin, the Kuravars, another maligned race, gave us shelter and succour in their village. Their existence unmolested by the Cherans, the Kuravars lived in luxury, in thatch-roofed huts instead of holes in precarious hillsides.

Seeing our little sister's dire state, they accorded her a hut with a clean floor and a foreyard well shaded by trees. The village medicine man worked wonders and with every sunrise, the little sister's condition improved. I rejoiced and made many sacrificial offerings to the gods.

The little sister preferred to lie outside, with a soft kambali covering the bed. She loved to listen to birdsongs, and dozed off when fatigue overtook her. At other times, she stared at the blue sky. With nightfall, she marvelled at the sky, pin-pricked by stars of white, blue, red and yellow. During such moments, I spied the child in her.

But whatever recovery we noticed, or thought we noticed in her, was false—a candle that flamed up before flaming out, for she deteriorated.

"She's weakened," said the ancient medicine man, himself straddling a foot each in tenuous life and inevitable death. He prodded the flaming logs and teased out red sparks as the embers settled. He said,

"I've no herbs to staunch the ooze of her living juices, for hungrily they seek the freedom of light."

"But she is a strong one." I spoke in anger. "Perhaps your herbs soaked many times and already drained of their vitality, old man. Find fresh ones and I'll pay you with new hunted meat."

The Silent One placed a hand on my shoulder. That touch said much, for ill-temper was a companion I did not entertain. Our Kuravar hosts, seated around the fire, kept their silence and continued to devour their meaty dinner. Their smacking lips and munching sounds reminded me of continuing life.

"The little sister has lost her will to live, Savaali, and in severe self-denial, refusing to even suck air to quench her burning lungs." The ancient relic was himself frustrated by his limited powers. He said,

"She's ready, Savaali, and it's you who need to prepare for the inevitable."

***

It was dark yet, and dawn hesitated over the faraway plains below. The village was in slumber, save for the Silent One, keeping vigil a few paces away.

Kannagi lay warm under the woollen kambali covers and I hunched beside her.

"The sky looks kind, brother Savaali. A good day to die."

Her thoughts were far off, in the vague past where only good dwelled. My little sister spoke in whispers, her words coming slowly, and the effort eating what little life remained.

"Father used to call me gold and diamond," she said, "and ruby and pearl, and more. I never could guess which he would pull out of his chest. How about you, brother Savaali, did your father have special names for you?"

"I had several fathers, little sister, yes, and each had a rude name for me."

"You are funny, do you know?"

"I prefer *male beauty*," I said. She tried to laugh and it must have hurt, but she said,

"Listen, birdsong, trilling and so full of joy."

Closing her eyes, she relished the tune, her new and only indulgence since we arrived. But it was early yet and there were no birds. The ancients say when one is about to depart, one is closer to God. Perhaps she heard things deaf to the rest of us.

"I never learned music," she said. Then, she opened her eyes and spoke fast, as if the last sands were leaking out, emptying the gourd.

"I like your dance," she said with innocent relish; her new energy giving me desperate hope. "Perhaps, one day you can teach me your Arakan dance." She sighed, and my hope deflated.

"Yes, perhaps," I whispered.

"Promise?"

"I promise, little sister," I said, and watched as she shut her eyes and dozed off.

Again, with panicked urgency in her tone, she opened her eyes and said,

"Brother Savaali, will I meet my dear Athan? I miss him so." She grasped my necklace of bones and tugged. "Will I?"

"Yes, little sister, you'll meet your dear Athan."

"I am afraid, brother Savaali, that I will not see him again."

"But you will see him again, little sister. Close your eyes. Will it with all your heart and it'll be so."

"Yes, with all my heart, and when I awake, he will be by my side." She sighed and gave me a curious look, as if seeing something beyond.

"Yes, he will."

"I feel cold; very cold," she whispered. "Cradle me, brother Savaali, like Father used to, and keep me warm while I sleep."

With great gentleness and care, I leaned over my little sister and placed an arm, barely touching, across her. As if startled by a new thought, she opened her eyes.

"You're here. Good. Don't leave me. I've been alone for too long." Her eyelids drooped, and she mumbled. "Don't leave me."

"I'll not leave you, little sister. See, you can feel my hand on your cheek."

Her face, so tiny, snuggled into my large hand and she smiled, as contented as a child going to sleep with the promise of an enjoyable festival come morning. My arm rose and fell with her breaths, and I watched until I looked without seeing.

My arm stopped moving, and my little sister's face turned cold; the chill not of the air or water. I looked skywards. Then, the trees drew my attention.

Here and there, birdsongs came alive. And I hummed a funeral dirge, one I sang when my mother went to her long sleep.

The journey awaiting the soul was a joyous one. The old ones, who knew more than I could ever imagine, told me so. If it was joyous, why did I feel a great wrenching pain? Perhaps, if I willed it enough, with all my heart, I too would become happy. Perhaps. So, I laughed. And laughed. I laughed hard and long until I cried. So did the Silent One. But he looked ugly when he laughed.

And then the birds burst into full choral flourish and in the east, the first rays of a stunning sun promised a good day. My little sister was right—it was a good day to die.

***

Cheran townsfolk, who came across some Kuravars, heard talk of a chaste maiden who, having rendered desolation on the Pandyan, had retired to the western hills, where a big Arakan with gentle hands and a ready laugh had cared for her. There were many stories, often conflicting, regarding the strange couple.

Whatever the realities, the paramount ruler of the western regions, Cheran King Senkuttuvan, heard the exaggerated tales of a fierce woman who burned down the Pandyan with her curse and plucked and threw her raw breast to churn the earth in a terrible quake.

Living with a man, even an adopted brother, troubled the sensitivities of the *civilised* people. They rewrote the story and established the terms of my little sister's last days: the *brother* became a woman; an Arakan woman. But even that was too wild. In time, she became an ascetic. Female ascetic. One of the civilised.

A chaste woman, mourning the death of her husband, embraced one of three prescribed avenues for grieving widows: perish on her husband's funeral pyre; disfigure her beauty; or suffer penance unto release. Strange and brutal practices of the civilised.

Keeping with their cultural norms, a story took life that my little sister chose the last of the three—she starved to death.

Cheran Senkuttuvan elevated Lady Kannagi to a deity of sorts. A statue rose, a poor copy of my little sister, but I was happy for her.

Thus, fate bestowed fame on my little sister; she of the slight frame and deep nature. Her life proved the astrologers right; she found fame in the west country.

For many years, and perhaps even now, wanderers in the windswept western hills sometimes heard, in concert with the birdsong so well-loved by my little sister, the clean tinkling song of ankle rings. Ruby encased in gold.

As for myself, I returned to the fatty folds of my jolly woman and proposed marriage. She demurred, but I persisted and won her over with my charms. The great hunks of fresh meat I laid at her doorstep helped.

We washed our feet in milk and, as prescribed by ancient custom, flung blood-soaked rice balls at all four corners to appease the gods—and the demons. It was difficult to tell them apart.

The fat one, with round hips and papaya breasts, already had five children, boys and girls. I believe one or two of the litter was of my seed. It mattered not, for this was the way of love at first sight, *kalavu*, pre-nuptial marriage, as practised in the kurinji realms. It also mattered not if other hands had fondled the fruit, for it tasted no less sweet.

The townspeople practised *karpu*—consummation after marriage. The civilised valued a woman's virginity. We tribals, we valued the woman.

But my kind, the Arakans of the kurinji hills, were a dying race. So said the wise ones—people such as my father, Eraivan, who would be a god. Perhaps the townspeople knew better about the art of survival. Perhaps. But these matters were beyond my simple mind.

And so, I married and lived a happy life with my bastard children and fat wife. Wives! She was enough to make two.

"Hah-hah-hah-hah-hah-hah-hah-hah!"

END

About the Author

At age 16, Eric Alagan grabbed an entry level job in the aviation industry where he learned the intricacies of cleaning toilets and making lousy coffee for mechanics. He was the youngest labourer in Singapore's fledgling aviation industry, and also the best looking. The former was a fact, and the latter was a hope. In time, he graduated to fixing airplanes and engines.

Twenty years later, he slipped into the corporate suites but kept his tool box behind his desk. It was a conversation piece—grease monkey made good. But his secret—the tool box kept him rooted. After swimming with sharks for a further twenty plus years, he retired to pursue his passion—writing.

Eric has published fiction and non-fiction books.

Married with three adult children, Eric considers himself fortunate—the children take after his wife. His hobbies include road cycling, philately, and reading books. His wife continues to love him. Like Creation, her love remains a mystery for him.

He retains his tool box—true. Continues to brew lousy coffee—also true.

If you like his novels, post a review on your social media and email him the link. His email: alagan.eric@gmail.com Thank you!

###

Books by Eric Alagan

VEL PARI: The Tamilakam War

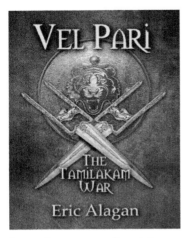

The first novel-length book in English (not a translation) that traces the life and death of Vel Pari, the legendary king of ancient Parambu Nadu, and his friendship with Kapilar, one of the most famous poets of Sangam era South India.

The novel reveals the possible truth behind Pari's gift of his chariot to a Mullai vine; debunks the alleged treachery of the three kings (Cheran, Cholan, and Pandyan); and addresses several legends surrounding his extraordinary life.

Read about the milestones in Kapilar's life: how he came to write his famous book, Song of Kurinji (*Kurinji Paattu*), where he detailed ninety-nine flower varieties of Tamilakam; and what led him to commit suicide by facing north and starving, *vadakirrutal*.

In the novel, Kapilar and his nemesis, Raj Guru Kachagan of the Cholan Empire, relate the events in the first person.

Available from Amazon. Pick up a copy. Hear the voices from the past.

***

Scan the QR code above for Vel Pari: **Amazon Books**.

***

PULI THEVAR

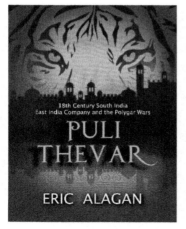

In 18th century India, the English and French vied for supremacy. The Europeans relied on their native allies whose loyalties were transient. Anarchy prevailed.

In the south, Mohammed Ali Wallajah, aided by the English East India Company, fought Chanda Sahib and his French allies in a bloody civil war. Mohammed Ali prevailed and became the Nawab of Arcot, sovereign of the southern countries. But the war was costly, and the Nawab was deep in debt to the English.

Unable to collect taxes from the Polygar kings in the southern countries, the Nawab assigned tax collection to the

English. The Company was brutal; widespread looting and slaughter followed. The Polygars fought the English and the Nawab; and their resistance lasted about fifty long years.

Foremost among the early rebels was Puli Thevar, who defeated the English in several engagements.

This novel also traces the storied encounters between Puli Thevar and an his enigmatic contemporary: Yusuf Khan a.k.a. as Marutha-Nayagam Pillay who served the English and subsequently rebelled against them.

This is the story of Puli Thevar, based on the facts and legends surrounding him.

**

Scan the QR code above for Puli Thevar.
It will take you to: **Amazon Books**.

**

MAHABHARATA

Mahabharata: The Beginning (Book 1 - published)

Mahabharata: Dice Game & Exile (Book 2)
Mahabharata: Kurukshetra (Book 3)
Books 2 and 3 scheduled for release in 2022.

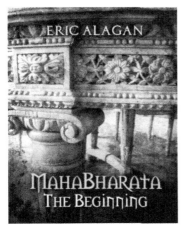

There are several regional versions of Mahabharata and the stories in this series do not adhere to any one version.

The three novels in this trilogy are abridged and adapted for the modern reader.

The author crafts storylines that inject realism to the myths and legends. Readers will not encounter cardboard type good-guys and bad-guys. The heroes and villains in this version struggle to uphold high principles and cope with their shortcomings.

***

Scan the QR Code below for Mahabharata: The Beginning.
It will take you to: **Amazon Books**.

***

One Hundred Very Short Stories

Each micro-fiction takes no more than three minutes to read.

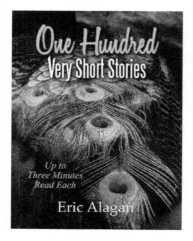

There is something for everybody: history; mystery; mythology; family life and love; horror; humour; uplifting stories; tear-jerkers; business snippets; politics; and thrillers.

***

Scan the QR Code below for One Hundred Very Short Stories. It will take you to: **Amazon Books**.

***

Eric's Non-Fiction Books on Human Resource.

Human Capital Growth Model – Build Best in Class Teams

5 Easy Steps
Scorecard Model

***

Scan the QR Code below for Human Capital Growth Model. It will take you to: **Amazon Books**.

***

Performance Appraisal – A Scorecard Model

Built from the ground up, and incorporates the Ten Goals of an ideal performance appraisal model.

***

Scan the QR Code for Performance Appraisal.
It will take you to **Amazon Books**.

***

Keep in touch with Eric.

Scan the QR Code below and it will take you to his blog:
Written Words Never Die

###

Printed in Great Britain
by Amazon

20064154R00140